Beneath the Oregon Pines

HISTORICAL CHRISTIAN ROMANCE

VIVIAN BELLE

STERLING RIDGE PRESS LLC

Cover designed by Sterling Ridge Press LLC

Published by: Sterling Ridge Press, LLC www.sterlingridgepress.com

ISBN: 978-1-966093-24-4
Printed in the United States of America

First Edition: April 2025

For permissions, contact: support@vivianbelle.com or visit www.vivianbelle.com

Dedication

To dreamers, builders, and believers—
To everyone who dares to plant hope where the wilderness is wildest,
who mends hearts as well as fences,
and who knows that even stubborn pines can bend toward the light.
And to my own circle of family and friends—
Thank you for being my roots and my refuge,
for believing in happy endings,
and for reminding me that love, like wildflowers and grace,
always finds a way to grow.
Vivian Belle

About The Author

Vivian Belle is a talented author known for her sweeping **Historical Christian Romance** novels set against the untamed beauty of the American frontier. With a deep love for history and storytelling, she brings to life **resilient heroines, steadfast heroes, and faith-filled journeys** in the vast, rugged landscapes of the past.

Nestled in the **majestic mountains of northern West Virginia,** Vivian finds endless inspiration in the rolling hills, winding rivers, and boundless sky that mirror the spirit of her stories. When she's not writing, she enjoys **kayaking on tranquil waters, hiking through breathtaking mountain trails, and, of course, getting lost in a good book.**

Vivian's novels capture the heart of **faith, love, and perseverance**—where strong women and honorable men overcome life's trials to find hope, home, and happily-ever-after. Whether she's exploring the great outdoors or crafting her next frontier romance, Vivian's passion for adventure and storytelling shines through in every word she writes.

You can find out more about Vivian and her latest releases at www.vivianbelle.com or follow her on social media for updates and behind-the-scenes glimpses of her writing process. Stay connected—you won't want to miss the heartfelt stories of love and family she has in store!

Also by Vivian Belle

Where the Heart Finds Home
Faith on the Frontier
Love in Hopewell Creek
Abigail's Promise
Beneath Montana Skies
Rocky Mountain Promise
Hearts Unbroken
Beneath the Oregon Pines

Contents

Chapter 1

The scent of rosemary and thyme lingered on Rose Bellamy's fingertips as she carefully wrapped her grandmother's worn mortar and pestle in soft linen. The smooth stone bowl, darkened from years of grinding herbs, felt cool against her palms. Outside her small Pennsylvania cottage, spring rain tapped gently against the windows, as if nature itself were saying farewell.

"Are you certain about this decision, Rose?" Mrs. Whitaker asked from her perch near the door, watching as Rose placed the cherished tool in her traveling trunk. The older woman's brow furrowed with concern beneath her white cap. "Oregon Territory is practically the edge of civilization itself."

Rose tucked a loose strand of golden hair behind her ear and straightened, meeting her neighbor's worried gaze with a smile that reflected both determination and faith.

"I've never been more certain of anything, Mrs. Whitaker. The advertisement specifically requested a teacher willing to establish a school in a logging settlement called Trinity Station." She picked up the weathered letter that had traveled thousands of miles to reach her, the paper now soft from countless readings. "When I prayed about it, I felt such peace. As if God Himself were directing my path westward."

"But after what happened with your parents—" Mrs. Whitaker stopped, pressing her lips together.

Rose's fingers instinctively reached for the small silver cross at her throat. "Perhaps because of what happened with my parents. Their passing showed me how precious life is, how important it is to use whatever gifts God has given us where they're most needed." She traced the edge of her Bible, resting atop a stack of beloved books. "Those children deserve education just as much as any in Philadelphia or Boston."

Mrs. Whitaker sighed in resignation. "You always did have more faith and courage than most young people. I simply worry. What sort of people await you in such a wild place?"

Rose closed the trunk lid, the latch clicking with finality. "People created in God's image, same as here. They may live differently, but they need the same things we all do: knowledge, hope, and kindness."

"And what if there's no suitable gentleman there?" Mrs. Whitaker asked, her tone softening. "At twenty-one, you should be considering a husband, not rushing off to the wilderness."

Rose smiled. "If God intends marriage for me, He will provide at the proper time, whether in Pennsylvania or Oregon. Right now, He's calling me to teach."

As she secured the trunk's brass buckles, Rose thought of the teaching position she was leaving behind at the small schoolhouse in town. Her students had wept at her departure, presenting her with a handkerchief with tiny embroidered pine trees on it. The memory strengthened her resolve.

"The stagecoach arrives at dawn," Rose said, moving to her small writing desk. "I've left instructions for my herbs. The feverfew should be ready for harvesting in a few days, and the valerian root should be tended carefully until your grandson and his family arrive and move in."

Mrs. Whitaker stepped forward and embraced her. "Write to us. Let us know you've arrived safely."

Rose returned the embrace, breathing in the familiar scent of lavender water that the older woman had worn for as long as she could remember. "I promise."

Later, as evening shadows lengthened across her cottage floor, Rose knelt beside her bed, hands clasped in prayer.

"Lord, guide my journey. Grant me wisdom and courage for whatever awaits in Trinity Station. Help me bring Your light to those children, and to that community." Her whispered words fell into the quiet room. "And if it be Your will, help me find where I truly belong."

Chapter 2

The journey west proved more arduous than Rose had expected, despite the warnings she'd received. Six weeks of constant travel. First by rail as far as it reached, then by stagecoach over increasingly rough roads, and finally by wagon along trails that barely deserved the name. Her body ached from the endless jostling, and her once-neat traveling dress now bore the dust of half a continent.

Yet with each passing mile, the landscape transformed in ways that took her breath away. Gone were the familiar rolling hills and neat farms of Pennsylvania, replaced by vast plains, towering mountains, and finally, the seemingly endless forests of the Oregon Territory.

"That there's the Umpqua River, miss," her guide, Mr. Fletcher, said as their wagon crested yet another hill. He was a weathered man of few words who had agreed to transport her from Portland to Trinity Station. "The logging camp is built alongside it. They float the timber downstream."

Rose gripped the wagon seat as they began their descent down a steep, rutted trail. Below, a ribbon of water wound through a valley blanketed in the most magnificent forest she had ever beheld. The trees, Douglas firs, Mr. Fletcher had called them, stretched skyward like cathedral spires, their tops lost in a soft mist that clung to the hillsides.

"It's beautiful," she breathed, momentarily forgetting her discomfort.

Mr. Fletcher made a noncommittal sound. "Pretty enough from up here. It's a different story when you're livin' in it. Oregon ain't for the faint-hearted, especially come winter."

"I've weathered Pennsylvania winters my entire life," Rose said with more confidence than she felt. "I'm sure I'll manage."

"Pennsylvania ain't Oregon," was all he said in response, urging the horses forward.

As they drew closer to the settlement, Rose's anticipation mingled with mounting apprehension. Trinity Station gradually revealed itself not as the small but proper town she had envisioned, but as a rough collection of log structures carved out of the wilderness. The constant ring of axes and shouts of men carried through the trees, growing louder as they approached.

The wagon rolled into what appeared to be the main clearing. Rose's eyes widened at the scene before her. Lumberjacks moved about like ants around a disrupted hill, their powerful bodies dwarfed by the massive logs they manipulated. The air hung heavy with the scents of fresh-cut timber, sweat, and wood smoke.

"This is it," Mr. Fletcher announced, halting the wagon. "Trinity Station Logging Camp."

Rose stared at the rough buildings, their logs still bearing the mark of axes, the spaces between them chinked with mud and moss. A few small cabins stood apart from what appeared to be bunkhouses. No church spire rose above the settlement. No proper schoolhouse caught her eye.

"Where might I find the person in charge?" she asked, her voice steady despite the flutter of uncertainty in her chest.

"That'd be Boone McAlister. Foreman of this operation." Mr. Fletcher pointed toward the river's edge, where several men were guiding logs into the water. "Man with the axe on his shoulder. Dark hair, bout the tallest one there."

Rose squinted in the direction indicated. Even from this distance, she could discern a commanding presence, a broad-shouldered figure directing the work with authoritative gestures.

"Thank you for bringing me safely, Mr. Fletcher." She gathered her reticule and prepared to descend. "Perhaps you might help me with my trunk?"

The guide's weathered face registered something like pity. "Miss Bellamy, you might want to speak with McAlister 'fore we unload. Make sure everything's... as you expected."

The hesitation in his tone sent a chill through her. "Is there something I should know?"

He shrugged, avoiding her gaze. "Just sayin' things out here ain't always what folks from back East might imagine."

Rose straightened her shoulders. "Then I shall speak with Mr. McAlister immediately."

With as much dignity as she could muster in her travel-worn state, Rose climbed down from the wagon. Her boots sank slightly into the muddy earth, and she winced at the immediate soiling of her hem. Conscious of curious glances from nearby workers, she lifted her skirts slightly and picked her way carefully toward the riverbank.

The closer she drew to the activity, the more out of place she felt. Her navy traveling dress, though practical by Eastern standards, now seemed ridiculously formal amid the rough canvas and buckskin attire of the lumberjacks. Men paused in their work to stare openly at her approach, some nudging others and whispering.

"Afternoon, ma'am," one called out, tipping his battered hat with exaggerated politeness that drew chuckles from his companions.

Rose acknowledged him with a slight nod, keeping her expression composed despite her discomfort.

The men were engaged in "river driving"—a term she'd learned during her journey here from Mr. Fletcher. They used long poles to guide newly cut logs into the current, forming what appeared to be a floating highway of timber. The work looked incredibly dangerous, with men balancing on the rolling logs with practiced ease.

"Mr. McAlister?" she called, stopping at what she judged was a safe distance from the water's edge.

Several heads turned, but her attention fixed on the man, who straightened at her voice. He stood ankle-deep in the river, one boot braced against a massive log. As he turned toward her, Rose's breath caught involuntarily.

Boone McAlister's appearance embodied the wild landscape around them. He stood well over six feet tall, his powerful frame honed by physical labor rather than gentlemanly sport. His face, partially obscured by several days' growth of dark beard, was weathered and tanned, with lines etched around eyes the color of storm clouds. Those eyes now narrowed as they took in her presence, his expression shifting from surprise to unmistakable displeasure.

With a sharp command to one of his men to take his position, McAlister strode out of the water, his movements displaying a rough grace that spoke of complete comfort in this rugged environment. He approached her with the wariness one might show a strange and potentially troublesome creature.

"I'm McAlister," he stated, stopping several feet away. His voice was deep and tinged with suspicion.

Rose extended her hand in greeting, struggling to maintain her composure under his scrutiny. "Rose Bellamy, Mr. McAlister. I've come from Pennsylvania to take up the teaching position."

His brow furrowed, and he made no move to accept her outstretched hand. "Teaching position?"

Rose lowered her arm awkwardly. "Yes. I responded to an advertisement seeking a teacher for Trinity Station. I have the correspondence here—" She reached for her reticule.

"No need," he interrupted, his expression darkening further. "I didn't expect anyone would actually come." He ran a hand through his damp hair, leaving it standing in disheveled peaks. "Especially not a woman alone."

The dismissive tone stung, but Rose stood her ground. "The advertisement didn't specify gender, Mr. McAlister, only qualifications. I assure you, I'm fully trained and experienced in education. I've taught for three years and—"

"Miss Bellamy," he cut her off again, his gaze sweeping over her with an assessment that made her feel utterly foreign to this place. "Look around you. This is a logging camp, not a town. Most men here work from dawn till dusk, then fall into their bunks, too exhausted to think about reading or figures."

"And their children?" Rose prompted. "The advertisement mentioned families settling here."

A muscle twitched in McAlister's jaw. "There are a few families, yes. Some with young ones. But not enough to warrant bringing a teacher all the way from Pennsylvania."

"The letter was signed by a Mr. Joshua Campbell, representing Trinity Station's interests."

Recognition, followed by irritation, flashed across McAlister's features. "Campbell. Of course." He shook his head. "He's our connection to the timber company in Portland. Man has grand ideas about turning this camp into a proper settlement. Gets ahead of himself."

Hope stirred in Rose's chest. "Then there are plans for development? For a community beyond just logging?"

"Plans," McAlister emphasized the word with skepticism. "Campbell has plans. Meanwhile, we have trees to fell and contracts to meet." He gestured toward the river, where work had noticeably slowed as men strained to overhear their conversation. "This camp exists for one purpose, Miss Bellamy. Everything else is secondary."

Rose drew herself up to her full height, which still left her looking up at him considerably. "Education is never secondary, Mr. McAlister. It's the foundation upon which communities are built."

"Reading and writing won't fell trees or fight off a bear, Miss," he replied, his voice holding a trace of grim humor. "Out here, practical skills mean survival."

"And is survival all that matters?" she challenged. "What of the spirit? The mind? Are the children of Trinity Station less deserving of education than those in Boston or Philadelphia?"

Something flickered in his eyes. Respect, perhaps, though quickly masked by impatience. "The children here learn what they need to know. How to work, and how to survive in the wilderness."

"And how to read the Bible? To calculate figures? To understand the world beyond these trees?" Rose pressed, her passion for teaching overcoming her initial intimidation. "Sir, I've traveled over two thousand miles based on good faith and correspondence. I've left behind everything familiar to answer what I believe is God's calling to serve here."

At the mention of God, McAlister's expression hardened. "God doesn't concern Himself much with places like Trinity Station, Miss Bellamy. You'd do well to recognize that early on."

The statement, delivered with such finality, revealed more about the man before her than perhaps he intended. Not just skepticism, but pain lay beneath his words.

"God concerns Himself with all His creation, Mr. McAlister. Especially the places that feel furthest from His hand."

Indifference flashed in his stormy blue-gray eyes. "Well, that's a matter of opinion." He glanced back toward the river, clearly eager to end their conversation. "Campbell shouldn't have brought you here."

Rose felt the ground shifting beneath her plans, but refused to be deterred. "Where might I find Mr. Campbell?"

"Portland. He won't be back here for at least two weeks." He finally seemed to notice her travel-worn appearance, and something like a reluctant conscience crossed his features. "Look, I can't turn you around and send you back today. Fletcher won't be near Portland for over a week. You can stay at Ethel's cookhouse until then. She has a small room for guests."

The thought of returning after coming so far never entered Rose's mind. "I have no intention of leaving, Mr. McAlister. If there's been a misunderstanding about formal arrangements, then I'll simply have to create my own opportunity."

His eyebrows rose. "Meaning?"

"Meaning, I'll establish the school myself. Find a space, gather students, and prove the value of education to Trinity Station."

McAlister stared at her with frank disbelief. "You're more stubborn than a mule stuck in river mud." He shook his head slightly. "And more naïve than a spring fawn if you think Eastern determination is enough to survive here."

"Perhaps. But I would rather try and fail following God's calling than turn back at the first sign of difficulty." Rose met his gaze steadily. "Now, might you direct me to this Mrs. Ethel's cookhouse? I've had a long journey."

For the briefest moment, admiration flickered across his features. Then he sighed heavily and pointed toward a log building larger than the others, with smoke rising steadily from its stone chimney.

"Cookhouse is there. Ethel Hayes runs it. Tell her I sent you." His tone made it clear the conversation was over. "We eat at sundown."

"Thank you, Mr. McAlister." Rose turned to go, then paused. "I look forward to showing you what education can bring to Trinity Station."

"Miss Bellamy," he called as she began walking away. She turned back questioningly. His expression was inscrutable, his broad shoulders silhouetted against the forest behind him. "Trinity Station isn't like anywhere you've known before. It has its own rules and its own hardships. I suggest you remember that before you start building castles in the air."

With that warning, he turned back to the river, barking orders that sent men scrambling back to work. Rose watched him for a moment, struck by the natural authority he commanded and the weight of responsibility that seemed to press upon his powerful frame.

As she made her way toward the cookhouse, Rose felt the enormity of her decision settling on her shoulders. Trinity Station was indeed unlike anything she had imagined—rougher, wilder, and more primitive. And its foreman was a man clearly hardened by life in this untamed place, a man seemingly closed to both faith and the gentler aspects of civilization she represented.

"Lord," she whispered as she walked, "I didn't anticipate this particular challenge. But I trust You haven't brought me all this way without purpose."

Chapter 3

The strong aroma of cooking food grew stronger as Rose approached the cookhouse. The building was larger than most in the camp, with a covered porch stretching across its front. Through open windows, Rose could hear the clatter of cookware and a woman's voice singing a hymn that brought unexpected tears to her eyes, a familiar sound in this strange new world.

"Well, who might you be, dear?" The singing stopped as Rose stepped onto the porch. A stout woman with grey-streaked brown hair appeared in the doorway, wiping her hands on a flour-dusted apron. Her face was weathered but kind, lively eyes quickly taking in Rose's appearance with undisguised curiosity.

"Rose Bellamy, ma'am. I've just arrived from Pennsylvania to teach. Mr. McAlister directed me to you for lodging."

The woman's eyebrows shot up. "Did he now? Well, I'll be." She extended a flour-dusted hand. "Ethel Hayes. Cook for this sorry lot of tree-fellers and the closest thing to civilization they see most days."

Rose accepted the handshake gratefully, warmed by the woman's friendly manner after McAlister's cold reception.

"Come in, come in. You look about ready to drop." Ethel ushered her inside, where the smell of baking bread and simmering stew filled the air. The cookhouse consisted of one large room, dominated by a massive stone fireplace with cooking hooks and a large iron stove. Long tables with benches stretched across most of the space. "You said teaching? We ain't got a school here."

"So Mr. McAlister informed me, rather directly." Rose couldn't help a small smile. "There seems to have been some miscommunication about my position."

Ethel clucked her tongue. "That'd be Joshua Campbell's doing. Always getting ahead of himself, that one. Heart's in the right place, mind you. Wants to see Trinity Station grow into something more than just trees and sweat."

She led Rose through the main room toward a door at the back. "I've got a small room I use for storage that has a proper bed. Not much, but it's clean and private. You can stay there until things sort themselves out."

"You're very kind, Mrs. Hayes."

"Ethel, please. Nobody stands on ceremony in the wilderness." She pushed open the door to reveal a modest room, simply furnished with a narrow bed, a small table and chair, and a chest for storage. A tiny window looked out toward the forest edge. "It ain't much compared to what you're likely used to."

"It's perfect," Rose said sincerely. The prospect of a real bed after weeks of travel seemed like a luxury. "Truly, I'm grateful."

Ethel studied her with shrewd eyes. "So you came all this way to teach. Must be quite the calling."

"I believe it is." Rose set her reticule on the small table. "Though Mr. McAlister seems to think education has little place in a logging camp."

"Ah." Ethel's expression softened with understanding. "Don't take Boone's gruffness too personally. He's... well, he's had his share of hardships. Sees his duty as keeping this camp running and his men alive, and doesn't have much patience for anything that doesn't directly serve that goal."

"He strikes me as a man carrying a heavy burden."

Ethel paused, seeming to consider how much to say. "He's a good man, Rose. One of the best I've known. Life just hasn't been kind to him." She sighed. "But that's a story for another time. You must be exhausted and starving after your journey."

As if on cue, Rose's stomach rumbled audibly, causing them both to laugh.

"I'll fetch you some stew and bread while you settle in," Ethel said. "Your trunk's still with Fletcher?"

"Yes."

"I'll send one of the younger boys to bring it. Don't you worry." Ethel patted her arm. "Rest a bit. Wash up if you like. There's a basin and pitcher on the chest there. We serve dinner when the men finish work, but I'll bring you something now."

Left alone, Rose sank onto the edge of the bed, the reality of her situation finally settling fully upon her. The journey, the alien environment, the unexpected reception, it all crashed over her in a wave of exhaustion. For the first time since leaving Pennsylvania, doubt crept in, whispering that perhaps she had made a terrible mistake.

"No," she said aloud, pushing the thought away firmly. "This is where You've led me, Lord. I trust there's purpose in it, even if I can't see it clearly yet."

She moved to the small window, looking out at the towering pines that surrounded Trinity Station like ancient sentinels. Their majesty reminded her of verses from Psalms about the cedars of Lebanon that proclaimed God's glory. Perhaps there was something sacred, even in this rough place.

Rose's gaze drifted back toward the river, where she could just make out Boone McAlister's tall figure directing the log drive. Even from this distance, she could sense the authority and competence with which he moved. A complex man, clearly. One whose dismissive words belied a deeper character that intrigued her.

Turning from the window, Rose unpinned her travel hat and began to freshen up, using the water from the pitcher to wash the dust of her journey from her face and hands. As she did, she mentally began formulating plans. If Trinity Station had no schoolhouse, she would need to find an alternative space. If there was no established position, she would create one, proving her worth through results.

By the time Ethel returned with a tray of steaming stew, fresh bread, and a pot of coffee, Rose had renewed her determination.

"You're looking brighter already," Ethel observed, setting the tray on the small table.

"I feel better for washing away some of the trail dust." Rose sat gratefully before the meal. "Mrs. Hayes—Ethel—might I ask you about the families here? Mr. McAlister mentioned there are children."

"Oh yes, a fair number now." Ethel pulled a chair closer to the table and sat down. "When the operation first started three years back, it was just men. But as things got more established, some brought their wives and little ones. The Abernathy's have three children, the Rileys have two little boys, the Wilsons a girl and a boy... I'd guess there's about fifteen children altogether of schooling age."

Hope sparked in Rose's chest. "Fifteen! That's certainly enough to justify a school."

"The mothers would welcome it, that's certain." Ethel's eyes twinkled. "Many of them trying to teach their young'uns themselves, but after keeping house in these conditions and often helping with camp work too, there's precious little time or energy left."

"And is there any building that might serve as a temporary schoolhouse? Even part of one?"

Ethel considered. "Well, there's the old storage shed near the edge of camp. It's sound enough. Campbell had it built for storing winter supplies. Winters can be mighty tough around here at times."

Rose's mind raced with possibilities. "Would Mr. McAlister object if I were to repurpose this smaller storage shed?"

"Object? Probably." Ethel chuckled. "But that doesn't mean you shouldn't try. Sometimes Boone needs pushing to see beyond the immediate needs of getting logs downriver." Her expression grew serious. "In my opinion, Trinity Station needs to be more than just a logging operation if it's to last. Campbell sees that too, even if Boone's too focused on his responsibilities to admit it."

Rose took a spoonful of the rich stew, savoring the hearty flavors after weeks of travel food. "Ethel, might I ask... Mr. McAlister mentioned God doesn't concern Himself with places like Trinity Station. Has there been hardship here? Something that would cause such bitterness?"

Ethel was quiet for a long moment, her weathered hands folded in her lap. "Trinity Station's had its share of sorrows, like anywhere on the frontier. Accidents, illness... life is harsh here." She paused, seeming to choose her words carefully. "But Boone's words come from a more personal place. He lost his wife about a year ago. Mary was...

well, she was the light of this place in many ways. Her passing hit everyone hard, but none harder than Boone."

"I'm so sorry," Rose said, understanding dawning. The man's gruff exterior, his resistance to anything beyond practical survival, it suddenly made more sense.

"Mary died in a logging accident. Rare for a woman to be caught up in such..." Ethel trailed off, shaking her head. "Boone blames himself, though there was nothing he could have done. Since then, he's thrown himself into work, keeps the camp running with an iron hand, but the joy's gone out of him. And his faith along with it, I fear."

Rose's heart ached at the tale. She knew too well the hollow feeling of losing loved ones, the questions that haunted even the faithful in times of grief.

"Thank you for telling me," she said. "It helps me understand him better."

"Just don't go mentioning it to him," Ethel warned. "He rarely speaks of Mary, not to anyone. Just buries himself in work from dawn till dusk." She stood, smoothing her apron. "Now eat up before that gets cold. Once you're settled, I can introduce you to some of the families. Best way to start gathering your students is through the mothers."

"I'd appreciate that greatly." Rose smiled warmly at the older woman. "And thank you, Ethel. Your kindness means more than I can express."

After Ethel left, Rose savored each bite of the satisfying meal, her mind working through all she had learned. Trinity Station was not the settled community she had envisioned, and its foreman was a man wrapped in grief and cynicism. Yet, there were children who needed education, and there was a man who needed reminding that life held more than just survival.

"One step at a time," she whispered to herself, echoing her grandmother's favorite saying. "First the children, then perhaps their parents... and maybe, in God's time, even the reluctant foreman."

Chapter 4

By early evening, with Ethel's help, Rose had settled into her small room. Her trunk had been delivered by a gangly young boy of about twelve, who had stared at her with undisguised curiosity before dashing off to his chores.

"That's Timmy Wilson, the blacksmith's boy," Ethel had explained. "Bright as a new penny, but hasn't had much chance at learning his letters."

Now, refreshed and wearing a clean, simple blue dress from her trunk, Rose stood beside Ethel outside the cookhouse on the porch, watching as the workday came to an end. Men streamed in from various parts of the camp, their bodies bearing the evidence of hard physical labor. Most glanced curiously in her direction, a few nodding respectfully, others whispering among themselves.

"Word travels fast in a small camp," Ethel said under her breath. "Everyone knows we've got an Eastern lady teacher now."

"I hope they're not too disappointed when they see how ordinary I am," Rose replied with a small laugh.

"Ordinary ain't the word that comes to mind, dear. Most women wouldn't have the courage to travel alone to a place like this." Ethel nodded toward a group approaching from one of the smaller cabins. "Here comes one of the families now."

A sturdy man with kind eyes led a woman and three children toward the cookhouse. The youngest, a girl of perhaps three or four, rode on his shoulders, while two older children, a boy and a girl, walked beside their mother.

"Tom and Beth Abernathy," Ethel murmured to Rose. "Good people. Their eldest, Eliza, is eight, perfect age for schooling."

As the family drew closer, Rose noted the shy curiosity in the children's eyes.

"Evening, Ethel," Tom greeted, then his gaze shifted to Rose. "And you must be the teacher Fletcher was talking about."

"Rose Bellamy," she confirmed, extending her hand. "It's a pleasure to meet you, Mr. Abernathy."

He shook her hand firmly, his calloused palm dwarfing hers. "Tom, please. This is my wife Beth, and our children—Eliza, Samuel, and little Hannah."

Beth Abernathy, a woman whose pretty features showed the strain of frontier life, offered a warm smile. "We're so glad to meet you, Miss Bellamy. When we heard a teacher had arrived, I could scarcely believe it."

"I understand there was some confusion about my position," Rose said, "but I'm determined to establish a school here, even if it begins modestly."

Beth's eyes lit up. "That would be a blessing beyond words. I try to teach them myself, but..."

"Mama says you're gonna teach us readin' and numbers," the oldest girl, Eliza, spoke up, her eyes wide with excitement.

Rose knelt at the child's level, smiling. "That's right, Eliza. Would you like to learn those things?"

The girl nodded enthusiastically. "Pa says I'm smart as a whip. I already know my letters, some of 'em anyway."

"That's wonderful! You'll be able to help the younger children in no time."

Tom rested a hand on his daughter's shoulder, pride evident in his expression. "She takes after her mother and has a quick mind." He glanced at Rose. "Though I have to ask, Miss Bellamy, what does Boone think of all this? He's not a man who welcomes change easily."

Before Rose could answer, a hush fell over the gathering crowd. She turned to see Boone McAlister himself approaching the cookhouse, his powerful frame moving with that same confident grace she had noticed earlier. The crowd parted slightly to let him pass, a subtle but clear indication of his authority in the camp.

His eyes found Rose immediately, narrowing slightly at her changed appearance and her position among the families. For a moment, something unreadable flickered across his features. Then his gaze shifted to Tom.

"Riverbank secured?" he asked without preamble.

"Yes, sir. Logs are chained for the night. We'll resume driving at first light."

Boone nodded curtly, then turned to Ethel. "We're down a few supplies after that last run. Need to talk to you about rationing until Campbell returns."

"After dinner," Ethel replied firmly. "These men need a good meal in them, and we have a new addition to welcome." She gestured toward Rose with unmistakable protectiveness.

Boone's jaw tightened almost imperceptibly.

Rose stepped forward, determined to establish a civil relationship despite their earlier friction. "Earlier, I was discussing the possibility of using the old storage shed as a temporary schoolhouse. Mrs. Hayes thought it might be suitable."

Several nearby lumberjacks exchanged glances, clearly waiting for their foreman's response. Boone's expression remained impassive, but Rose noted how his shoulders tensed slightly.

"The storage shed," he repeated flatly.

"Yes. Since it's currently unused, I thought—"

"It's needed for winter supplies," he interrupted. "We'll be stocking up as fall approaches."

Tom cleared his throat hesitantly. "Begging your pardon, Boone, but we won't start needing that smaller storage shed for a few months. The bigger storage shed holds three times as much. We might be able to arrange things better in the larger shed to store needed items for winter."

A muscle worked in Boone's jaw. He clearly disliked being challenged, especially in front of the camp. "The matter can wait until after we've eaten," he said finally, his tone brooking no further discussion.

"Of course," Rose agreed, though her determination hadn't diminished. "I wouldn't want to delay dinner after everyone's worked so hard today."

Ethel clapped her hands, breaking the tension. "That's right! Inside, all of you. The stew's hot and the bread's fresh."

As the crowd began moving into the cookhouse, Rose stood with Boone on the porch.

"Mr. McAlister," she said, "I realize my arrival is unexpected and perhaps unwelcome to you, but I assure you I have no intention of disrupting your operation. I simply wish to offer what I can to the children here."

He regarded her for a long moment, his blue-gray eyes searching her face as if trying to solve a puzzle. "Miss Bellamy," he finally said, his deep voice low enough that only she could hear, "Trinity Station isn't some Eastern town with white picket fences and Sunday socials. It's a place where one mistake, one distraction, can mean death."

"I understand the dangers—"

"No," he cut her off, "you don't. Not yet." Something haunted flickered behind his eyes. "Teaching children to read won't protect them from falling trees or river accidents. Practical skills keep people alive here."

"And what of their minds? Their spirits?" Rose countered gently. "Surely survival isn't the only measure of a life well-lived."

For the briefest moment, his stern expression faltered, revealing a glimpse of the pain Ethel had described. A man who had known loss and who perhaps once valued more than mere survival.

"You speak of things you haven't earned the right to judge," he said finally, his voice rough. "Live through an Oregon winter. Watch a man die because a rope snapped, or a tree fell wrong. Then tell me about what matters."

Without waiting for her response, he turned and entered the cookhouse, leaving Rose standing alone.

She took a deep breath, steadying herself against the wave of uncertainty his words had stirred. The challenge before her was greater than she had imagined, but so too, she suspected, was the need. This wasn't just about teaching children their letters. Something deeper was at stake in Trinity Station. Something in the wounded spirit of its leader, in the hunger for community she sensed in the Abernathy's and others.

"Give me wisdom, Lord," she whispered. "And patience. Especially patience."

With that prayer on her lips, Rose straightened her shoulders and walked back into the cookhouse, stepping fully into her new life beneath the Oregon pines.

Chapter 5

The cookhouse buzzed with conversation as the lumberjacks and their families finished their hearty meal. Rose sat between Beth Abernathy and Ethel, occasionally nodding and smiling at the curious glances cast her way.

"How long have you been teaching, Miss Bellamy?" Beth asked, helping her youngest daughter manage a spoonful of stew.

"Three years now," Rose replied, breaking off a piece of crusty bread. "I taught at a small school in Pennsylvania after completing my education."

"And what made you travel all this way?" Tom asked from across the table. "Oregon Territory isn't exactly known for its educational opportunities."

Rose considered her answer carefully, aware that several nearby lumberjacks had quieted to listen. "I believe education should be available to all children, regardless of where they live. When I saw the advertisement for Trinity Station, I felt... called to come." She glanced toward the end of the table, where Boone sat in discussion with a white-bearded man. "Though I'm beginning to understand that my arrival was somewhat unexpected."

"That's putting it mildly," a voice chimed in. A towering lumberjack with a friendly face leaned forward. "Name's Simon Blackwood, miss. Been with Boone since this camp started. Never seen him quite so ruffled as when you walked up today." His eyes crinkled with good humor.

"I don't intend to ruffle anyone," Rose said. "I simply want to offer what skills I have to benefit the children here."

"And we're grateful for it," Beth said firmly, casting a meaningful glance at her husband.

Tom nodded. "Our Eliza's been begging to learn more than just her letters. She's quick with numbers, too."

"I can count to fifty!" The girl piped up from her seat, face shining with pride.

Rose smiled warmly at the child. "That's excellent, Eliza. Perhaps you could help me with the younger children after we start our lessons."

The girl's eyes widened. "Could I really?"

"Certainly. Every good teacher needs an assistant."

As conversations continued around her, Rose took the opportunity to observe the cookhouse more carefully. Despite the rough-hewn logs and simple furnishings, Ethel had created a space of warmth and community. Dried herbs hung from the rafters, adding color and fragrance. Handmade curtains framed the windows, and several crude but cheerful drawings—clearly the work of children—were tacked to one wall.

Rose's gaze inevitably returned to Boone McAlister. Unlike most of the men who had relaxed as they ate, the foreman remained alert, his posture suggesting a man always on duty. He ate efficiently, pausing occasionally to answer questions or give brief instructions to men who approached him. Even here, surrounded by his community, he held himself apart.

As the meal progressed, more of the camp residents introduced themselves to Rose. Martha Riley, mother of two boys aged six and nine, expressed enthusiastic support for a school. William Wilson, the blacksmith and widower raising a daughter and son alone, asked detailed questions about what subjects she intended to teach. Each conversation strengthened Rose's conviction that despite Boone's resistance, education was indeed needed and wanted in Trinity Station.

When dinner concluded, men began to file out, some heading to evening chores, others to their bunks after the long workday. Several families lingered, seeming reluctant to end this social gathering. Rose noticed Boone rising from his seat, heading toward the door, and knew she needed to act quickly.

"Mr. McAlister," she called, rising from her bench. "Might I have a word about the storage shed before you leave?"

The surrounding conversations quieted. Boone paused, his broad shoulders tensing visibly before he turned to face her.

"Miss Bellamy, I believe I made my position clear."

"You mentioned winter supplies," Rose acknowledged, approaching him with steady steps. "The children could use that space now, while the weather permits, until the time comes to start stocking up on supplies for the winter months."

Boone's eyes narrowed. "And where would you propose we store those supplies when the time comes if you're occupying the building?"

"By then, perhaps a more permanent solution could be arranged for the school," Rose suggested. "Or we might share the space, if necessary. I require little room for basic education."

Tom stepped forward. "Boone, we've got plenty of strong backs to build something new before winter. Campbell's been talking about expanding anyway, you know that."

"Campbell talks about many things," Boone replied dryly. "Meanwhile, I deal with realities."

"The education of our children is a reality," Beth said. "One that we've neglected too long."

Ethel moved to stand beside Rose. "The shed's just sitting empty, collecting spiders. What harm could it do to let Rose use it for a spell? Give the young ones something beyond chores to fill their days."

Rose watched as Boone's jaw tightened, the muscle there flexing with tension. He clearly disliked being challenged publicly, yet seemed equally reluctant to dismiss the evident desire of the families.

"The shed needs repairs," he said finally. "The roof leaks. The floor's uneven. Hardly suitable."

Rose recognized the shift in his argument, from outright refusal to practical concerns. It was an opening, however small.

"I don't require luxury, Mr. McAlister," she replied. "Just four walls and space for the children to gather. As for repairs, I'm willing to help however I can."

"I can fix that roof," Simon offered. "Been meaning to, anyway."

"And we can level the floor," Tom added. "Wouldn't take more than an afternoon with enough hands."

Boone looked from face to face, his expression growing increasingly trapped. Rose felt a twinge of sympathy despite their disagreement. He was a man accustomed to command, now cornered by the united wishes of his people.

"There's another consideration," Rose added more gently. "I noticed Trinity Station has no church. The shed could serve for Sunday worship as well. A small place for the community to gather in faith."

At the mention of faith, pain flashed in Boone's eyes. For a moment, she feared she'd overstepped.

"Most of us were raised God-fearing," William Wilson spoke up. "My Sarah, before she passed, always said children need both learning and the Lord. It's been too long since many of us have enjoyed a proper church service."

Beth nodded. "I read the Bible to my little ones, but it's not the same as gathering together."

The room had grown completely still, the remaining families and workers watching the exchange with undisguised interest. Rose held her breath, sensing they stood at a pivotal moment that went beyond just the use of a building.

Boone broke the silence with a heavy sigh. "The shed needs a new door as well. And windows—it's too dark in there as it is."

Relief washed through Rose as she realized he was yielding, however grudgingly. "Then we shall have windows and a new door," she said simply.

"I've got some saved glass," Simon volunteered. "From that abandoned homestead we found last year."

"And I can make a proper door," Tom added.

Boone ran a hand through his dark hair, a gesture Rose was beginning to recognize as a sign of resignation. "Very well. The shed is yours, Miss Bellamy... temporarily. But I expect it cleared when winter supplies begin to arrive, unless a suitable alternative is provided before then."

A ripple of approval moved through the room. Children grinned while their parents exchanged satisfied glances.

"When can we start school, Miss Bellamy?" Eliza asked, bouncing slightly with excitement.

Rose smiled at the child. "As soon as the building is ready, which depends on how quickly your father and the others can make the repairs."

"We'll start tomorrow," Tom promised. "After the morning cutting."

"And I expect those repairs won't interfere with regular duties," Boone added firmly. "Logging comes first. We have contracts to fulfill."

"Of course," Rose assured him. "I understand your priorities, Mr. McAlister."

Their gazes met, and for the first time, Rose sensed something beyond resistance in his eyes, perhaps a grudging respect, though carefully guarded.

"Then if that's settled, I'll bid you all goodnight," he said, turning toward the door. "First light comes early."

As he left, conversation erupted around Rose. Excited chatter about the school, offers of help with preparations, and questions about what supplies might be needed. Tom and Simon immediately began planning how they could fashion simple benches and tables from available materials. William promised to contribute lumber he'd been saving for his own cabin expansion.

Ethel squeezed Rose's arm gently. "Well done," she murmured. "I haven't seen them this animated in months."

"I just hope Mr. McAlister doesn't regret his decision," Rose replied.

"Boone may grumble, but he cares about these people more than he lets on," Ethel said. "He just focuses so hard on keeping them alive that he sometimes forgets about living." She patted Rose's hand. "Now, let's see what we can scrounge up for school supplies."

For the next hour, Rose found herself at the center of Trinity Station's first community project. Families volunteered what they could—a slate board from the Riley's, a small bookshelf William had crafted for his daughter, and chalk that Martha Riley had brought west but rarely used. Each offering, however modest, represented a shared hope for something beyond mere survival.

As the evening deepened and families finally began to depart, Rose felt a profound sense of purpose settling in her heart. Despite the day's challenges and uncertainties, she knew with growing conviction that she was precisely where she needed to be.

"May I help you tomorrow with the shed?" Beth asked as she gathered her sleepy children.

"I'd appreciate the company," Rose replied warmly. "Perhaps anytime after eight o'clock?"

After the last families had gone and Ethel had begun cleaning up the dinner remains, Rose stepped outside onto the cookhouse porch. The night air carried the scent of pine and the distant murmur of the Umpqua River. Stars blazed overhead with a brilliance she had never witnessed in Pennsylvania, their light undimmed by city glow or coal smoke.

"Thank You," she whispered, her prayer rising with her breath into the clear night. "For bringing me here, for opening this door."

"Talking to yourself already? That's usually a sign someone's been in the wilderness too long."

Rose startled at Boone's deep voice. He emerged from the shadows at the edge of the porch, a tall silhouette against the night sky. She hadn't realized he was still nearby.

"Not to myself," she said. "To God. Expressing gratitude for how things turned out this evening."

He moved closer, his features becoming visible in the lamplight spilling from the cookhouse windows. "You got what you wanted tonight, Miss Bellamy. Don't mistake it for divine intervention."

"I believe God works through people, Mr. McAlister. Through their hearts and desires. The families here want education for their children and a place to worship. That desire didn't originate with me."

He leaned against a porch post, regarding her thoughtfully. "You managed to win over half my camp in one dinner. That's no small feat."

"I didn't come here to win anyone over," Rose said honestly. "Only to serve where I'm needed."

"And you believe you're needed here? In this rough place?"

"I do. Perhaps more than I initially realized."

Boone studied her face for a long moment.

"The shed won't be comfortable," he said abruptly. "Even with repairs."

"Comfort isn't necessary for learning. Enthusiasm is."

"And you have plenty of that." It wasn't quite a compliment, but his tone lacked the earlier dismissiveness.

"When it comes to education, yes." Rose gathered her courage, deciding to address what troubled her. "Mr. McAlister, I hope you don't feel I undermined your authority tonight. That wasn't my intention."

He gave a short, humorless laugh. "You did exactly that, Miss Bellamy. Quite effectively, too. But perhaps it needed doing. The children here deserve more than what we've given them."

His admission surprised her. "Then you do value education?"

"I value preparation for the real world. If reading and figures help with that, so be it." He straightened from his casual stance. "But don't mistake this for complete surrender. Trinity Station is still primarily a logging operation, and that must remain our focus for survival."

"I understand. The two needn't be at odds."

"We'll see." He glanced toward the dark forest edge. "I came back to tell you something practical. Don't wander beyond the camp clearing alone, especially near dusk or dawn. We've spotted bear tracks recently."

The warning reminded Rose of how truly foreign this environment was compared to her eastern home. "I appreciate the caution."

"It's not caution, Miss Bellamy. It's survival. This isn't a place for carelessness."

"I'm not careless," she said. "Just determined."

"So I've noticed." For the briefest moment, amusement flickered in his eyes. "Get some rest. Tomorrow will be busy if you're to transform a storage shed into a schoolhouse."

"Goodnight, Mr. McAlister. And thank you for reconsidering about the shed."

He nodded once, then turned to leave, his long strides carrying him toward the foreman's cabin at the camp's edge. Rose watched him go, struck by the contradictions in the man—his gruff exterior masking moments of unexpected thoughtfulness, his resistance to change counterbalanced by an evident care for his people.

She returned inside to find Ethel wiping down the last table, humming softly.

"You've had quite a day," the older woman observed. "How are you holding up?"

Rose sank onto a bench, very aware of her exhaustion. "It's been... overwhelming. But in the best possible way."

"You've already brought something back to Trinity Station that's been missing for a long while," Ethel said, her eyes warm with approval. "Hope."

"I've done very little yet," Rose demurred.

"Sometimes all it takes is showing up with faith and determination." Ethel hung her dishcloth to dry. "I noticed Boone talking to you outside. Everything all right?"

"Yes. He was actually warning me about bears and not wandering off alone."

Ethel's eyebrows rose. "Was he now? Well, that's interesting."

"How so?"

"Boone doesn't waste words on those he considers lost causes." Ethel smiled knowingly. "He may fight you every step of the way, Rose Bellamy, but that man already respects you more than he'll admit."

Rose felt a curious warmth at the thought. "He's not what I expected after our initial meeting."

"Few things are in the wilderness," Ethel replied. "But that's what makes life interesting, isn't it?"

After bidding Ethel goodnight, Rose returned to her small room. As she prepared for bed, she reflected on the day's events, from the uncertainty of her arrival to the unexpected victory of securing a schoolhouse. Through it all, she kept returning to the image of Boone McAlister, not the resistant foreman of their first meeting, but the man acknowledging that the children deserved more.

"Lord," she prayed as she climbed beneath the simple quilt, "thank You for opening hearts today. Guide my hands and words as I build this school. And please, if it be Your will, help me understand the man You've placed in authority here. There's pain behind his strength, and perhaps that's where healing must begin."

Outside, somewhere in the distant forest, an owl called into the night. Rose drifted to sleep with the sound of the Umpqua's gentle flow beneath the ancient pines. No longer a stranger, but a woman finding her place in this rugged new world.

***

From the shadows near his cabin, Boone watched as the lights in the cookhouse gradually dimmed. The last window to go dark was the small one he knew belonged to Rose Bellamy's room. He hadn't intended to linger, certainly hadn't planned to speak with her again tonight, but something had drawn him back toward the cookhouse after his evening rounds.

The woman was trouble. The disrupting kind that brought change and complication. Yet, he couldn't deny the genuine joy he'd seen in the children's faces tonight, or the sense of community that had briefly flourished as they all planned the schoolhouse renovations.

"Mary would have liked her," he whispered to the night, then immediately regretted giving voice to the thought.

He turned away sharply, striding toward his empty cabin. Rose Bellamy, with her unwavering faith and gentle determination, had managed to accomplish more in one day than Campbell had in months of grand planning. It was irritating and inconvenient.

And somehow, despite himself, just faintly admirable

Chapter 6

Rose's arms ached as she hauled the last of the cobweb-filled crates from the storage shed. A splinter dug into her palm, but she pushed through the discomfort, determined to clear the space. Dust clung to her simple brown work dress, and perspiration dampened her hairline despite the morning's cool air.

"Goodness gracious," she muttered, setting down the crate alongside the others she'd stacked outside. She straightened, pressing a hand to her lower back, and surveyed what would soon become Trinity Station's first schoolhouse.

The structure was humbler than she'd anticipated. Rough-hewn logs formed walls that didn't quite meet at the corners, allowing drafts to whistle through. The roof, as Boone had warned, showed signs of leaks in several places. The dirt floor was indeed uneven, with a noticeable slope toward one corner. The only window was a square opening covered with oiled paper that had torn in places, admitting thin beams of light that did little to dispel the interior gloom.

But it had four walls and a roof. It would do.

Rose pushed a loose strand of hair behind her ear and stepped back inside, breathing in the musty scent of abandoned space. With determined optimism, she began mentally arranging the future classroom. Benches along this wall, perhaps a small table here for her own use, and the slate board the Riley family had offered could hang there...

"Miss Bellamy?"

Rose turned to find Beth Abernathy at the doorway, her three children clustered behind her. Beth's eyes widened as she took in the shed's condition.

"Good morning!" Rose greeted cheerfully. "I've just finished clearing out the old crates. What do you think of our future school?"

Beth hesitated, her expression shifting between dismay and politeness. "It's... certainly a project."

"Mama, it's dirty," little Hannah declared, wrinkling her nose.

Eliza, ever enthusiastic, pushed past her mother into the shed. "We can clean it! Pa says I'm the best sweeper in the family."

Samuel, the middle child, remained skeptical. "Where will we sit? The ground's all bumpy."

Rose laughed. "You've identified our first challenges perfectly. Yes, it needs a thorough cleaning, and yes, the floor needs leveling. But I believe, with enough willing hands, we can transform this space."

Beth stepped inside, her practical gaze assessing the task before them. "The men promised to help with repairs, but they've got logging duties first. We women can at least get started on the cleaning."

"Exactly my thought," Rose agreed. "I brought what supplies I could find. There's a broom just outside, and some rags Ethel contributed."

"I brought another broom and some lye soap," Beth added. "And Martha Riley is coming with her boys once they finish their morning chores."

A warm sense of community washed over Rose. These people, strangers just a day ago, were rallying around her vision despite their already demanding lives.

"Miss Bellamy, what will you teach us first?" Eliza asked, excitement brightening her face.

Rose smiled at the child's eagerness. "Well, we'll need to assess where everyone stands with their letters and numbers. Some children might need to start with the basics, while others like yourself might be ready for more advanced lessons."

"I want to learn about faraway places," Samuel piped up. "Pa says there's oceans bigger than the biggest river."

"Indeed, there are," Rose confirmed. "Geography will definitely be part of our studies."

Beth set down her basket of supplies. "Children, if you are eager to learn in this schoolhouse, you'd best help make it suitable. Hannah, you can pick up the smaller sticks and debris. Eliza and Samuel, help me sweep out these cobwebs."

As they began working, more families arrived. Martha Riley with her two energetic boys, William Wilson's solemn-faced son, Timmy, and his bright-eyed daughter Abby. Three other families Rose hadn't formally met yet introduced themselves, bringing the potential student count to fifteen children ranging from age four to twelve.

The mothers fell naturally into the work, scrubbing walls, sweeping out years of dust, and discussing how best to arrange the limited space. The children soon turned cleaning into a game, competing to find the largest spiders or the oddest bits of debris.

"I'm thinking benches in rows grouped by age," Rose explained to the gathered mothers. "The children can use slates on their laps for writing practice until proper desks might be constructed."

"My John is handy with tools," Martha Riley offered. "He made all of our furniture. I'm sure he could fashion some simple benches, given the lumber."

"And what of heat come winter?" asked a woman who'd introduced herself as Silvia Cooper, mother to twin eight-year-old boys. "This place will be bitter cold with those gaps in the walls."

"We'll need to chink the logs better," Beth agreed. "And some form of stove or fireplace."

Rose nodded, mentally adding these concerns to her growing list. "Mr. McAlister mentioned the building would only be available until winter supplies arrive, but perhaps by then, we'll have a more permanent solution."

The women exchanged glances that Rose couldn't quite interpret. "What is it?" she asked.

Martha sighed. "It's just that Boone tends to be... inflexible once he's made up his mind. If he says temporary, he likely means it."

"Especially since Mary died," Silvia added quietly. "He's been even more set in his ways."

Beth shot the other women a warning look. "Rose doesn't need to be burdened with camp gossip."

"It's not gossip if it's the truth," Martha countered. "And she ought to know what she's up against."

Rose paused in her sweeping. "I appreciate your concern, truly. But I believe Mr. McAlister is a reasonable man beneath his gruff exterior. He clearly cares deeply about this camp and its people."

"Too deeply, sometimes," Silvia muttered. "Forgets there's more to life than just surviving from one day to the next."

The conversation halted abruptly as a shadow fell across the doorway. Simon Blackwood, the tall lumberjack who'd spoken up at dinner the previous night, ducked his head to enter the low door frame.

"Ladies," he greeted, his weathered face breaking into a friendly smile. "Thought I'd assess this roof."

"Shouldn't you be at the cutting already?" Martha asked, hands on her hips despite her welcoming tone.

Simon shrugged his massive shoulders. "Boone sent me. Said if we're determined to have a schoolhouse, it might as well not leak on the first rainfall." His eyes twinkled as he glanced at Rose.

Rose felt a surge of hope. "He sent you?"

"Yes, miss," Simon chuckled, moving to examine the ceiling. He poked at a sagging section of the roof. "This'll need new shingles altogether. Got a good bit of rot here."

"Is it dangerous?" Rose asked.

"Not about to collapse on your heads, if that's what you're asking. But it won't keep out the rain, and that's a fact." He moved from corner to corner, examining the structure with experienced eyes. "The floor needs more than leveling, too. Should put in proper boards, raise it off the ground a few inches. Otherwise, the first heavy rain will turn this place into mud."

The practical challenges were mounting, but Rose refused to be discouraged. "What materials would we need for these repairs?"

"Lumber, we've got plenty of," Simon said. "Nails are precious out here, but I reckon we could spare enough for the floorboards and roof repairs. Window glass is a problem. Can't make that from trees."

"You mentioned you have a piece of glass saved," Rose reminded him.

"Might be enough for one small window. You'll want more light than that for teaching." Simon stroked his beard thoughtfully. "There's an abandoned settlement about ten miles upriver. A couple of families tried settling there two years back, gave up after the first winter. There might be some usable windows there, if someone's willing to make the journey."

"Could you—" Rose began.

"I'd offer, miss, but we're behind on our cutting quota after the time lost to broken equipment last week. Boone's not likely to spare men for a salvage mission just now."

Martha frowned. "Surely, the children's education is worth a day's journey?"

"To you mothers, certainly. To a logging operation with contracts to fulfill?" Simon shrugged again. "Boone sees things from a different angle. His responsibility is keeping this camp profitable and his men employed. Can't fault him for that."

Rose absorbed this practical reality check. "Then we'll make do with what we have for now. Oiled paper can serve for windows until glass becomes available. The important thing is to begin teaching as soon as possible."

"That's the spirit," Simon approved. "I'll see about those roof repairs after today's cutting. Tom and a few others volunteered to help with the floor."

"We're grateful for any assistance," Rose said sincerely.

After Simon departed, the women resumed their cleaning with renewed determination. By mid-morning, the shed had been swept clean of cobwebs and debris, the walls scrubbed as best possible, and the dirt floor smoothed somewhat with rakes. Though still crude by any standard, the space already looked more promising.

"It's remarkable what willing hands can accomplish," Rose observed, surveying their progress.

"Many hands make light work," Beth agreed, wiping perspiration from her brow. "That's how we survive out here. Everyone contributing what they can."

As they worked, the children peppered Rose with questions about what they would learn, revealing both their eagerness and the gaps in their education. Timmy, the blacksmith's boy, proudly demonstrated his ability to write his name, but admitted he knew little beyond that. Martha's boys could recite basic arithmetic, but had never owned a proper book. Eliza, though bright, had only the barest familiarity with letters from her mother's teachings.

Their enthusiasm both inspired and sobered Rose. These children hungered for knowledge, yet had so few opportunities to obtain it. Her determination to succeed grew stronger with each innocent question, and each eager face looking at her with hope.

Near midday, Ethel appeared at the doorway, carrying a large basket covered with a checkered cloth.

"Thought you all might be ready for some sustenance," she announced, setting down the basket. "Can't prepare a schoolhouse on empty stomachs."

The children gathered eagerly as Ethel unveiled bread, cheese, and apples—simple fare, but welcome after the hard work they'd all put in.

"Children, thank Ethel properly, then take your food outside to eat," Rose instructed, seizing a teachable moment. "We don't want crumbs attracting mice to our new schoolhouse."

"Yes, Miss Bellamy," they chorused, accepting their portions with varying degrees of politeness before scampering outside.

"You've got them listening already," Ethel observed with approval. "That's half the battle."

The mothers followed their children outside, leaving Rose briefly alone with Ethel.

"How's it coming along?" Ethel asked, handing Rose a piece of bread and cheese.

"Better than I initially hoped," Rose admitted, accepting the food gratefully. "The building needs significant work, but the community's support is heartening."

Ethel nodded, her sharp eyes taking in the transformed space. "Trinity Station's folk are good people at heart. They want better for their children than what they've had."

"Even Mr. McAlister, it seems," Rose said. "Simon mentioned he sent him to examine the roof."

"Did he now?" Ethel's eyebrows rose. "Well, that's Boone for you. Man fights what he can't accept until he can't fight it anymore, then he makes sure it's done properly."

Rose took a bite of the crusty bread, considering this insight. "I don't wish to be at odds with him, Ethel. His approval would make everything easier."

"Boone McAlister's approval isn't easily won, but his respect can be earned, and that's worth more." She paused, seeming to choose her next words carefully. "You should know something about this shed, Rose."

"What's that?"

"Before Mary died, she'd been talking about starting a school for the children. Nothing formal like what you're planning, but teaching them their letters at least. This shed was where she planned to do it."

Rose felt her breath catch. "No wonder Mr. McAlister was so resistant."

"It's not just a storage shed to him. It's another reminder of what was lost." Ethel straightened, adjusting her apron. "I'm not telling you this to discourage you. Just so you understand what you're really up against. It's not education Boone resists, it's the pain of seeing someone else fulfill what Mary dreamed of doing."

This revelation cast Boone's opposition in a new and poignant light. His resistance wasn't merely stubbornness or practical concerns, it was grief protecting a painful memory.

"I had no idea," Rose murmured. "Should I... perhaps find another building?"

"Absolutely not," Ethel said firmly. "Mary would want this building to be used for teaching, no matter who was doing it." She touched Rose's arm gently. "The best way to honor her memory isn't to abandon her dream, but to fulfill it."

Rose nodded slowly, understanding the delicate balance she needed to navigate. "I'll proceed with compassion, then. And prayer."

"That's all any of us can do," Ethel agreed. She glanced outside, where the children were playing after finishing their meal. "Speaking of proceeding, I should get back to the cookhouse. Dinner won't prepare itself."

"Thank you, Ethel. Not just for the food, but for... helping me understand."

After Ethel departed, Rose sat alone for a moment in the partially transformed shed, seeing it with new eyes. This wasn't just a building; it was a legacy interrupted by tragedy. By taking it over, she wasn't merely establishing a school. She was, in some small way, continuing something precious that had been lost.

"Lord," she whispered, "guide my steps. Help me honor Mary's memory while serving these children who need education so desperately. And if it is Your will, heal Mr. McAlister's heart enough that he can see this not as replacing what was lost, but as fulfilling it."

Chapter 7

The afternoon brought fresh challenges and unexpected allies to the storage shed. Two more families appeared, having heard about the school through the camp's efficient grapevine. They brought additional children, raising the potential enrollment to eighteen, and offered more hands for the work.

By late afternoon, the interior and exterior were as clean as possible, given the constraints. The mothers had lined up stones to create divisions within the room, designating areas for different age groups. William Wilson arrived with the promised slate board, which Simon mounted on the wall before returning to his logging duties again. Another lumberjack, passing by after his shift, noticed them working and offered a tiny pot of green paint he'd been saving "for no particular purpose." The women used it sparingly to add a touch of cheerful color to the otherwise drab interior.

Rose unpackaged some of her precious books from back east, arranging them carefully on a crude shelf that one of the fathers constructed from scrap wood. The small collection, a Bible, McGuffey's

Readers, a basic arithmetic text, a slim volume of American history, and a beautifully illustrated natural science primer, represented the core of what she could offer these eager young minds.

"When can lessons begin, Miss Bellamy?" asked one of the loggers passing by.

"That depends on how quickly the essential repairs can be completed," Rose replied. "At minimum, we need the roof fixed and the floor leveled. Benches would be helpful, though not strictly necessary to start."

"The men are planning to work on it tomorrow after logging duties," Beth informed her.

"Then perhaps in a few days, we might hold our first class," Rose suggested, hope rising in her chest.

The children, overhearing this, erupted in excited chatter.

"Will we get our own slates to write on?" one asked.

"Do we need to bring our own pencils?" wondered another.

"Will there be punishment if we don't learn our letters fast enough?" This last question came from a wide-eyed young boy of about eight, whose twin brother immediately elbowed him into silence.

Rose knelt to meet the concerned child at eye level. "What's your name, young man?"

"Peter Cooper, ma'am," he whispered, looking at his worn boots.

"Well, Peter, in my classroom, we learn at our own pace. Some minds absorb reading quickly, others excel at numbers, and still others have special talents for art or storytelling. God gives each of us different gifts." She smiled reassuringly. "There will be rules, of course, and expectations for behavior and effort. But no one will be punished for learning slowly if they're truly trying their best."

The boy's shoulders relaxed visibly, and several other children seemed to breathe easier as well. Rose realized they had likely heard tales of strict schoolmasters with their switches and dunce caps.

"Our school will be a place of encouragement and discovery," she continued, addressing all the children now. "Yes, there will be discipline and structure because those things help us learn. But above all, it will be a place where we grow together in knowledge and character."

As Rose spoke these words, she became aware of a tall figure lingering. Boone stood watching, his broad shoulders nearly filling the entrance, his expression unreadable. He'd clearly been there long enough to hear her educational philosophy.

"Mr. McAlister," she acknowledged, rising to her feet. "Have you come to inspect our progress?"

The children and adults alike fell silent, aware of the tension between the schoolteacher and the camp foreman.

"Passing by after checking the eastern cutting site," he said, his deep voice neutral. "Quite a transformation already."

"The community has been wonderfully supportive," Rose replied. "Your men as well. Simon provided valuable advice about the repairs needed."

Boone nodded, his eyes scanning the room with a thoroughness that missed nothing. The cleaned walls, the arranged stones, the modest bookshelf, and the children's eager faces.

"Floor needs proper boarding," he said.

"Yes, Simon mentioned that. He said lumber wouldn't be a problem, but nails might be precious."

"I'll allocate what's needed from the camp stores," Boone said, surprising her. "Can't have children sitting in mud when the rains come."

A ripple of relief went through the gathered parents.

"That's most generous," Rose said sincerely. "The children and their parents appreciate your support."

Boone's gaze shifted to the small collection of books, lingering on them with an expression Rose couldn't quite decipher, not quite interest, not quite dismissal, but something more complex.

"You plan to begin teaching soon?" he asked.

"As soon as the essential repairs are complete. Day after tomorrow, perhaps, if all goes well with tomorrow's work."

He considered this, then addressed the parents directly. "Work on the schoolhouse comes after regular duties. We still have logging quotas to meet."

He turned to leave, but Rose called after him.

"Mr. McAlister?"

He paused, looking back at her questioningly.

"Would you be willing to speak to the children sometime after we begin classes? About the practical aspects of logging and running a camp? It would be educational for them to understand the work that sustains their community."

The request clearly caught him off guard. For a brief moment, Rose glimpsed something almost like vulnerability cross his features, quickly masked by his usual reserve.

"We'll see," he said gruffly.

After he departed, the atmosphere in the small building lightened perceptibly.

"Well done," Beth said. "Involving him directly is clever."

"It wasn't a strategy, per se. The children should understand logging if they're to grow up in a logging community."

"Still," Beth said with a small smile, "you've just ensured he can't simply ignore the school once it's operating. Quite diplomatic."

Rose felt her cheeks warm at the praise she hadn't been seeking. "I simply believe education should connect to the children's lives and future prospects."

As the afternoon waned, the families gradually departed to tend to evening chores and prepare for the next day's work. Rose remained behind, wanting a quiet moment to think.

She walked slowly around the building, her mind filled with possibilities. Along that wall, perhaps a map of the United States could eventually be hung. In that corner, a nature table for interesting specimens the children might bring—pine cones, unusual stones, and pressed wildflowers. By the door, hooks for coats during the rainy season...

"Making plans already?" Ethel's voice interrupted her thoughts. The cook stood in the doorway, a shawl wrapped around her shoulders against the cooling evening air.

"There's so much potential here," Rose replied. "Despite the humble beginnings."

"That's true of most worthwhile things," Ethel observed, stepping inside. "Trinity Station itself wasn't much more than a clearing and some tents three years ago." She surveyed the transformed space with approval. "You've accomplished more in the two days you've been here than most would manage in a week."

"Not me—all of us together," Rose corrected. "The community truly came together."

"That's been the most remarkable thing to witness," Ethel agreed. "I haven't seen such a cooperative spirit since..." She hesitated.

"Since Mary was alive?" Rose asked gently.

Ethel nodded. "She had a gift for bringing people together. After she died, something vital seemed to go out of the camp. Folks retreated into their own concerns, focused on getting through each day." She touched one of the stones marking classroom divisions. "This is the first time I've seen them truly working toward something beyond mere survival."

Rose absorbed this, feeling the weight of responsibility that came with stepping into such a void, however unintentionally. "Ethel, you told me earlier this was Mary's project originally. I want to be respectful of her memory as we move forward."

"The most respectful thing is to create something beautiful and lasting where she would have," Ethel said firmly. "Mary wasn't one for monuments. She believed in living well and doing good with the time you're given." She smiled softly. "In that way, you remind me of her. Different in many ways, but similar in spirit."

The comparison was humbling. "I wish I could have known her."

"She would have been your strongest ally in this endeavor, that's certain," Ethel sighed. "Well, I came to fetch you for dinner. You must be exhausted after today's work."

"I am rather tired," Rose admitted, suddenly aware of the ache in her muscles and the grit of dust on her skin. "But it's a satisfying kind of tiredness."

As they walked toward the cookhouse, the camp was settling into evening routines. Men returned from cutting sites, tools over their shoulders, exchanging jokes and commenting on the day's work. Women called children in from play, and smoke rose from cabin chimneys.

"Mr. McAlister surprised me today," Rose commented. "Offering nails from the camp stores."

"Don't look so shocked," Ethel chuckled. "Despite his gruff manner, Boone's a fair man. Once he accepts something is happening, he doesn't do it halfway."

"You sound like you know him well."

"Been cooking for him for three years, watched him build this camp from nothing. He's like one of those old oaks. He doesn't bend easily, but provides shelter for many." Ethel glanced sideways at Rose. "I heard you asked him to speak to the children."

"Yes. Was that inappropriate?"

"No, just unexpected. Most folks are too intimidated to ask Boone for personal involvement in anything outside logging operations."

"I imagine he knows a lot about the practical aspects of survival here," Rose reasoned. "The children should learn from his expertise."

"True enough. But there's something else to consider." Ethel lowered her voice, though no one was near enough to overhear. "Boone hasn't spent much time around the camp children since Mary died. He keeps his distance, probably because it pains him to see what they might have had together."

Rose hadn't considered this angle. "They had no children of their own?"

"No, though Mary dearly wanted them." Ethel sighed. "That's part of why she was so determined to start teaching the camp children. She had such love to give."

They arrived at the cookhouse, and Rose offered to help with the evening meal, but Ethel shooed her toward the washbasin.

"Go clean up. You'll want to look presentable. Word of the school's progress has spread through the entire camp. Expect plenty of questions tonight."

Grateful for the warning, Rose retired to her small room to wash away the day's dust and change into a fresh dress. As she brushed the tangles from her hair, she reflected on all she had learned about Trinity Station, its people, and its complex foreman.

Boone McAlister remained an enigma—gruff and resistant one moment, practically supportive the next. His grief for Mary was clearly a still-open wound, yet he functioned with remarkable competence despite it. The camp relied on his strength and leadership, even as some questioned his narrow focus on survival and production.

And now, through circumstances neither of them had planned, Rose had become entangled with one of his most private sorrows, taking over the very project his wife had dreamed of implementing. No wonder he had initially resisted so strongly. It wasn't just about practicalities or disruption to camp operations; it was about painful memories and dreams unfulfilled.

"Lord," she prayed as she pinned her hair, "give me wisdom in my interactions with Mr. McAlister. Help me honor Mary's memory while establishing this school for the children who need it so desperately. And if possible, Lord, use this endeavor to bring some measure of healing to those who still grieve her loss."

***

The dinner hour brought the expected flurry of questions and comments about the emerging schoolhouse. Men who hadn't been directly involved wanted to know what repairs were needed and offered additional help. Mothers discussed what supplies their children would need. Even some of the unmarried lumberjacks showed interest, with a few admitting they'd never properly learned to read and wondering if evening lessons might eventually be possible for adults.

"One step at a time," Rose responded to this unexpected request. "Let me establish the children's school first, but I certainly won't rule out adult education in the future."

Boone sat at the head table, engaged in conversation with Simon and another senior lumberjack. Though he didn't participate in the school discussions, Rose noticed him listening attentively, his expression thoughtful rather than dismissive.

After the meal, as people began to disperse, Tom and several other men approached Rose.

"We've been talking about tomorrow's repairs," he said. "We'll start on the roof and floor first thing after the morning cutting. Simon thinks we can have the essential work done in one day if enough hands help."

"That's wonderful news," Rose responded warmly. "The children are so eager to begin lessons."

"We've also been discussing benches," added a stocky, red-haired man who introduced himself as John Riley, Martha's husband. "I've got some designs in mind—simple but sturdy."

"And Simon's glass will be enough for one proper window," Tom continued. "We'll place it where it catches the most light throughout the day."

Rose was moved by their thoughtful planning. "You've all clearly put considerable thought into this. I'm genuinely grateful."

"Our children deserve a proper education," John said simply. "Something more than we had."

As the men discussed technical details of the repairs, Rose became aware of Boone approaching their group. The men fell silent, respectfully waiting for their foreman to speak.

"Simon tells me the roof needs complete re-shingling," he said without preamble. "I've authorized the use of the cedar shingles we'd been saving for another building. Better to do it right the first time."

"Thank you, Mr. McAlister," Rose said, genuinely surprised by this generosity. "That's most thoughtful."

"It's practical," he corrected, though without his usual gruffness. "Oregon rains would turn patched shingles into a leaking mess within weeks. No sense wasting time and materials on temporary solutions."

The men nodded in understanding, clearly appreciating their foreman's practical wisdom, even if his motivations remained strictly utilitarian.

"We'll make good use of those shingles," Tom assured him. "Should have the roof weather-tight by tomorrow evening."

"See that you do," Boone replied. His gaze shifted to Rose. "Miss Bellamy, a word?"

The men exchanged curious glances as Boone led Rose slightly apart from the group. His expression remained unreadable, but there was a tension in his powerful frame that suggested internal conflict.

"I understand you learned today that Mary had planned to use that shed for teaching," he said without preamble.

Rose nodded. "Yes. I hope you know I had no intention of disturbing painful memories."

"What's done is done," he replied, his tone not unkind but carefully controlled. "But there's something you should have." He reached into his pocket and produced a small, worn key. "This opens a chest that is stored in the back corner of the large storage building down by the river. It contains some books and teaching materials Mary had collected. They should be put to their intended use rather than gathering dust."

Rose accepted the key with a sense of reverence, understanding the significance of this gesture. "Mr. McAlister, are you certain? These must be precious memories for you."

"They're tools," he said, his voice rougher now. "Mary would want them used for their purpose, not preserved like... like relics." He seemed to struggle with his next words. "She believed strongly in education, especially for girls. Said it was the only way they'd have choices beyond what their circumstances dictated."

This glimpse into Mary's beliefs and Boone's memories of her felt like a rare gift. "She sounds like a remarkable woman."

"She was." Three simple syllables, heavy with loss. Boone took a step back, his moment of openness clearly over. "The chest is heavy. Have one of the men bring it to the schoolhouse."

"Thank you for trusting me with this," Rose said sincerely.

He nodded once, then turned and walked away.

Rose watched him go, the key cool and weighty in her palm. This small metal object represented more than access to educational materials. It was another step toward Boone accepting her presence and purpose in Trinity Station.

When she returned to the group of men, they regarded her curiously but had the tact not to ask about her conversation with Boone.

"We'll start work at midday tomorrow," Tom said simply. "Should have good progress to show by evening."

"I've no doubt of that," Rose replied. "Trinity Station clearly doesn't lack for skilled hands or willing hearts."

Chapter 8

The rhythmic pounding of hammers filled the air as Simon Blackwood and William Wilson worked on the schoolhouse roof. Sweat glistened on their foreheads despite the cool summer breeze as they carefully positioned cedar shingles in overlapping rows. Below them, three other men labored to install the new plank flooring, their measured movements transforming the dirt-packed ground into a solid wooden surface.

Rose stood nearby, observing the remarkable transformation unfolding before her. Just yesterday, this had been an abandoned storage shed filled with cobwebs and memories. Now it buzzed with purposeful activity.

"Miss Bellamy! Look what I found for your school!" Eliza said as she ran toward her, clutching something in her small hands. The girl skidded to a stop, proudly presenting a bundle of feathers tied with a piece of twine. "Goose feathers! Ma says they make the best quills for writing. I've been saving them special."

"What thoughtful consideration, Eliza. These will be perfect for teaching penmanship."

"Pa says the school might be ready by soon!" The girl bounced on her toes, barely containing her excitement.

"Your father and the others are certainly working very hard to make that possible," Rose agreed, smiling at the child's enthusiasm.

A grunt from inside the building drew Rose's attention. John was measuring the window opening, his massive frame hunched to avoid the low ceiling beams.

"This'll do nicely for the piece of glass Simon has," he said. "Catch the morning light just right for reading."

"I appreciate your careful attention to such details," Rose said, stepping inside.

John straightened, wiping sawdust from his hands. "Ain't just me, miss. Every man here's putting extra care into his work." He lowered his voice. "Truth be told, we're all a bit surprised Boone gave us the rest of the day for it."

Rose looked up sharply. "The rest of the day? I thought you'd only have part of the afternoon."

"That's what we expected, too." John adjusted his worn cap. "But Boone came to the cutting site this morning, checked the progress, then told five of us to put down our axes and get this schoolhouse properly finished." He shook his head in wonderment. "Can't recall the last time he pulled men off cutting before the quota was met."

"Did he give any reason?"

"Just said it needed doing right, not piecemeal." John shrugged his massive shoulders. "Never known Boone to do anything halfway once he's decided on a course."

"Mind your gossip, John," Simon called down from the roof. "Miss Bellamy doesn't need to hear camp talk."

"It's not gossip if it's plain fact," John countered good-naturedly. "The whole camp's talking about Boone's change of heart regarding this schoolhouse."

Rose considered this development. Perhaps Boone's offer of Mary's teaching materials last night had indicated a deeper shift in his thinking than she'd realized.

"Speaking of Boone's offerings," she said, remembering the key that still sat in her pocket, "did anyone retrieve Mary's chest from the river storehouse?"

The men exchanged glances, their expressions suddenly guarded.

"Not yet, miss," Simon replied.

"Perhaps later we can go and retrieve the trunk," she decided. "I'd like to see what materials Mary collected."

The work continued steadily. The roof progressed shingle by shingle; the floor took shape board by board, and the new window frame was carefully prepared for the precious glass. Rose consulted the workers about where benches might best be positioned and how to maximize the limited area.

Near midday, Ethel appeared with a basket of food for the workers. "Can't build on empty stomachs," she announced, setting down her burden on a newly installed portion of floor. "Best come eat."

The men gratefully paused their labor, gathering around as Ethel distributed thick sandwiches wrapped in cloth and passed a jug of water. Rose accepted her portion with thanks, taking a seat on one of the crates that would serve as temporary seating until proper benches could be constructed.

"The transformation is remarkable," Rose commented, looking around at the progress.

"Amazing what can be accomplished when folks work together," Ethel agreed, her shrewd eyes taking in the improvements. "This place has potential I never noticed before."

As they ate, several mothers arrived with their children, eager to see the emerging schoolhouse. The young ones darted about excitedly, asking questions about where they would sit and what they would learn. Rose answered patiently, her heart warming at their enthusiasm.

"When can school start, Miss Bellamy?" asked Samuel Abernathy, his face serious beneath his mop of brown hair.

"Very soon," Rose promised. "If the repairs continue at this pace."

A sudden hush fell over the group. Rose looked up to see Boone standing in the doorway of the shed, his tall frame nearly filling the entrance. His expression was unreadable as he surveyed the work, eyes moving methodically from the new floor.

"Mr. McAlister," Rose greeted him, rising from her seat. "Your generosity in allowing these men more time for repairs is greatly appreciated."

He stepped inside.

"The floor's coming along well," he observed, testing a board with the toe of his boot. His voice was neutral, but Rose detected a tightness in his jaw as she stepped inside.

"Yes, it's a tremendous improvement," she agreed. "The children will be much more comfortable with proper flooring."

Boone nodded, his gaze moving to the small table someone had donated, where Rose had arranged a few books and teaching supplies. Something flickered across his features when he spotted a McGuffey's Reader and the small Bible among them.

"Progress on the river drive?" Simon asked as he stepped inside the building, breaking the awkward silence.

"On schedule," Boone replied shortly. "Cooper's crew should have the logs to the bend by evening."

His attention shifted to the children outside, who watched him with wide-eyed fascination. To Rose's surprise, his stern expression softened fractionally as he looked at them.

"You'll have your schoolhouse soon enough," he told them as he walked back outside, his deep voice gentler than Rose had yet heard it.

Hannah Abernathy, too young to be intimidated, toddled forward. "Will you come to school too, Mr. McAlister?" she asked innocently.

A pained expression crossed Boone's face. So quickly, Rose almost thought she'd imagined it. He took a step back, as if the child's innocent question had physically struck him.

"No, Hannah," he said quietly. "School is for children."

Beth quickly swept up her daughter, murmuring an apology. Boone waved it away, but the moment of connection had shattered. His expression closed once more, becoming the stern foreman rather than the man who had briefly emerged.

"The key, Miss Bellamy," he said abruptly. "For Mary's chest."

Rose felt the collective tension rise at the mention of Mary's name. "Of course," she said, reaching into her pocket. "I was planning to retrieve it after our meal."

"Change of plans. I should be the one to bring the chest."

His insistence surprised her. Last night, he had suggested one of the men could fetch it, but now he seemed determined to handle it personally. Rose extended the small iron key, watching as he took it carefully, avoiding contact with her fingers.

"It's something I need to do myself," he added, his voice low enough that only she could hear.

Rose nodded her understanding. "Of course, Mr. McAlister."

He pocketed the key and turned to the workers. "You have until sundown to complete the essential repairs here. Tomorrow's cutting can't be delayed."

"We'll have it weather-tight by evening," Tom assured him.

Boone acknowledged this with a nod, then without another word, turned and walked away.

Conversation resumed as the men returned to their work and the mothers discussed the school arrangements. But Rose stood still, troubled by what she'd witnessed. The man who had offered Mary's teaching materials last night was at odds with himself, she sensed.

"Something's eating at him today," Ethel murmured, coming to stand beside Rose. "More than usual, I mean."

"He seemed... different," Rose agreed. "Almost pained."

Ethel's weathered face grew solemn. "There are dates that hit harder than others when you're grieving. Anniversaries, birthdays..." she trailed off, then added softly, "Today would have been Mary's birthday."

The revelation struck Rose with unexpected force. "Oh."

Ethel gathered the remains of their simple meal. "That explains his wanting to fetch the chest himself. Some grief you have to walk through alone."

Rose watched as Boone's tall figure strode purposefully toward the river storehouse. She understood grief and its unpredictable waves, how certain days could reopen wounds that seemed to be healing. Her heart ached for him, for the private pain he carried beneath his rugged exterior.

"Ethel, would you mind watching over things here for a little while?" she asked suddenly.

The older woman raised an eyebrow. "Planning to follow him?"

"Not to intrude," Rose clarified quickly. "Just to... be available if needed."

Ethel studied her for a long moment, then nodded. "Sometimes the strongest shoulders need someone to notice when they're trembling. Go on, I'll keep things moving here."

Chapter 9

Rose adjusted her shawl against the cool breeze that had picked up. The path to the river storehouse was clear from here, a well-worn track leading down toward the Umpqua river, where the larger storage building stood near the water's edge. She could see Boone's figure in the distance, moving with a purposeful stride.

She followed at a discreet distance, uncertain of her intentions. What could she possibly offer this man who so clearly guarded his grief privately? Yet something compelled her forward, a conviction that no one should face their darkest moments entirely alone, not even someone as fiercely independent as Boone.

The river storehouse was a substantial building, considerably larger than the shed being converted into the schoolhouse. Built of heavy logs and positioned to receive supplies that came upriver by boat, it stood apart from the main camp, its solitude offering privacy. Rose paused at the edge of the clearing surrounding it, watching as Boone unlocked the heavy door and disappeared inside.

She approached slowly, giving him time. The rush of the Umpqua provided a constant backdrop of sound, its waters flowing ceaselessly past. When she reached the building, she hesitated, uncertain whether to announce her presence or simply wait.

The decision was made for her when a crash sounded from inside, followed by a muffled exclamation. Concern overrode hesitation, and Rose entered, stepping into the dimness of the storehouse.

It took a moment for her eyes to adjust to the shadowed interior. Shelves lined the walls, stacked with supplies of all kinds—tools, rope, barrels of nails, preserved foods, and medical necessities. Boone stood at the far end, next to an overturned barrel, several metal items scattered across the plank floor around him.

"Mr. McAlister? Are you all right?" she asked.

He whirled around, clearly startled by her presence. "Miss Bellamy." His voice was rough. "What are you doing here?"

"I thought you might need assistance with the chest," she offered, stepping carefully over the scattered items. Now closer, she could see it was a collection of metal hooks that had spilled.

"I don't need help," he said tersely, kneeling to gather the fallen items.

Rose knelt as well, helping to collect the hooks despite his protest. "I understand today holds special significance," she said gently.

His hands stilled. In the dim light filtering through the small windows, his face was shadowed, but she could see the tension in his jaw, the rigid set of his shoulders.

"Ethel told you," he stated flatly.

"She mentioned it was Mary's birthday," Rose confirmed, placing the hooks she'd gathered back into the barrel. "I'm sorry if my following you here was intrusive."

Boone straightened, returning the barrel to its upright position with more force than necessary. He moved deeper into the storehouse, clearly expecting her to leave.

Rose remained where she was, watching as he navigated through the neatly organized supplies. His movements were controlled, but held an underlying agitation. When he reached a stack of crates in the corner, he paused, his broad back to her, shoulders rigid with tension.

"I lost my parents and grandparents to diphtheria when I was eighteen," she said quietly into the silence. "I still struggle when their birthdays arrive each year. I still mark the anniversary of their passing each year. Grief changes shape over time, but it never truly leaves us."

He didn't respond immediately, his hands resting on the crates before him. When he finally spoke, his voice held a rawness that caught at her heart.

"Time doesn't heal all wounds, Miss Bellamy, despite what well-meaning people say." He turned partially toward her, his profile stark in the dim light. "Some days I wake with Mary's name on my lips, forgetting for just a moment that she's gone. Those moments of forgetting are almost worse than remembering."

The admission, so personal and unguarded, stunned Rose. She remained very still, afraid any movement might break this fragile moment of honesty.

"I understand," she said. "After my family died, I kept turning to tell one of them something for months afterward. Each time I remembered they were gone was like losing them anew."

Boone lifted a wooden chest from among the crates, holding it with a reverence that spoke volumes. It was a simple pine box, well-crafted but unadorned except for the initials "M.M." burned into the lid.

"Mary collected these books and supplies," he said, his voice steadier now. "Said every child deserved the chance to find a world beyond trees and rivers. I thought it a foolish luxury at first, but her enthusiasm..." He trailed off.

Rose ventured a few steps closer, drawn by the rare glimpse into both Mary's dreams and Boone's memories. "She sounds like a woman of vision."

"She saw possibilities where I saw only obstacles." A ghost of a smile touched his lips before fading. "This camp was little more than a collection of tents when we arrived. While I worried about timber yields and contracts, Mary planted flowers by our cabin door and talked of building a community, not just a logging operation."

The tenderness in his voice revealed a depth of love that transcended death. Rose felt privileged to witness this side of him, so different from the stern foreman who ruled Trinity Station with practical efficiency.

"Her vision is becoming a reality. Trinity Station is growing into a true community. The schoolhouse is part of that."

Boone's expression tightened again. "A community without its heart. You should return to the schoolhouse, Miss Bellamy. I need a moment alone before bringing this."

Rose recognized the dismissal, but felt compelled to offer one last thought. "Mr. McAlister, grief is a burden we all carry differently. But sharing memories of those we've lost can sometimes lighten that burden, not increase it."

His gaze met hers directly. The pain in his blue-gray eyes was raw and unmasked, striking her with its intensity.

"Some burdens aren't meant to be shared, Miss Bellamy. Some guilt can't be absolved through pleasant memories or comforting words. Mary died because of choices I made. I chose to move here. I took this job. If I hadn't brought her here, she wouldn't have died. That responsibility is mine alone to bear."

The starkness of his self-blame shocked her. "Surely, you can't hold yourself responsible for an accident? From what I understand, such tragedies are, sadly, not uncommon in this dangerous work."

He moved past her toward the door; the chest held securely in his arms. "I'll bring this to the schoolhouse shortly."

"Mr. McAlister," she began, following him, "whatever happened that day, blaming yourself, won't bring Mary back. Faith teaches us that—"

He stopped abruptly, turning to face her with an expression that halted her words. "Faith?" The word came out harshly, almost like a physical rejection. "Was it faith that watched Mary die? Was it faith that left this camp without her light? Don't speak to me of faith, Miss Bellamy. I've seen where blind trust leads."

The vehemence of his response revealed the depth of his spiritual wounds. Rose felt her heart ache for him, for the man who had lost not only his wife but also his belief in anything beyond harsh reality.

"Faith doesn't promise the absence of pain," she said quietly. "It offers hope that pain isn't the end of the story. That even in our darkest moments, we're not alone."

"I watched Mary take her last breath while praying for God to save her," Boone said, each word precise and cutting. "There was no divine comfort there, Miss Bellamy. Just silence and the sound of her struggling to breathe." His grip tightened on the chest. "I respect your belief, but don't expect me to share it. I've seen too clearly how hollow those promises can be."

The raw honesty of his grief and anger left Rose momentarily speechless. This wasn't mere cynicism or pragmatism, but profound spiritual wounding that no simple platitude could address.

"I won't pretend to understand the depth of your loss," she finally said. "Or why God allows such suffering. But I do know that rejecting faith doesn't ease pain; it only leaves us facing it without hope."

"Hope is a luxury in the wilderness," Boone replied, his voice quieter but no less resolute. "Practical skills and clear thinking keep people alive, not hopeful prayers."

Rose recognized the impasse they had reached. His wounds were too deep, his defenses too solid for any meaningful connection on this fundamental issue. Whatever bridge might eventually span the gulf between their worldviews would require far more than one conversation.

"I'll return to the schoolhouse," she conceded, stepping back. "Thank you for retrieving Mary's chest. I promise her materials will be used with respect and care."

He nodded once. "As they should be."

Rose walked back along the river path, her mind troubled by their exchange. The gulf between them seemed wider than ever—not just their different approaches to the school or camp life, but their fundamental understanding of faith, hope, and meaning in the face of tragedy. For the first time, she wondered if there was any possibility of truly reaching Boone McAlister, of helping him find healing from the wounds that clearly still bled beneath his controlled exterior.

A man who had watched his beloved wife die while praying desperately for divine intervention, who now shouldered crushing guilt for her death, and who had lost faith in anything beyond harsh reality. How could such a man ever find common ground with someone whose life was built on the very faith he had rejected?

"Lord," she whispered as she walked, "I don't know how to reach him. His pain runs deeper than I imagined."

The impossibility of connecting with Boone struck her with sudden clarity. He was not merely resistant to change or skeptical of education's place in a logging camp. He was actively walled off from anything that threatened to touch his carefully contained grief, including the faith and hope that Rose held dear. The distance between them felt insurmountable in that moment, a chasm no bridge could span.

Chapter 10

By the time Rose reached the schoolhouse, she had composed herself, pushing aside the troubling conversation with Boone to focus on the practical tasks at hand. The men had made remarkable progress in her absence. The floor was nearly complete, and Simon was applying the final shingles to the roof while Tom worked on creating a proper door.

"There you are!" Ethel called from where she sat with several children, showing them how to fashion simple rag dolls. Her keen eyes studied Rose's face. "Everything all right?"

"Fine," Rose assured her with more confidence than she felt. "Mr. McAlister will be bringing Mary's chest shortly."

Ethel nodded, accepting the limited explanation, though her expression suggested she understood more than Rose had said.

For the next hour, Rose threw herself into the preparation work, bringing a few more of the supplies she had brought with her into the schoolhouse and discussing lessons with the mothers who had gathered. She was directing the placement of another crude bookshelf when a hush fell over the bustling activity.

Boone stood in the doorway, Mary's chest in his arms. His expression was composed now, all traces of their emotional conversation hidden behind his usual reserved demeanor. Without a word, he entered and placed the chest carefully on a table Rose had designated as her desk.

"The key," he said simply, holding it out to her.

Rose accepted it, aware of the curious and somewhat awed gazes of the others present.

"Thank you," she said.

A shadow passed across his features. "Use these things well, Miss Bellamy." He turned to survey the work that had been completed in his absence. "The improvements are substantial. You should be able to begin classes tomorrow."

"The children are certainly eager to begin."

Boone addressed the workers directly. "See to it, the window and door are completed by evening. I'll see all of you back at regular duties tomorrow at first light."

"We'll be ready," Simon assured him.

With a nod of acknowledgment, Boone departed as abruptly as he had arrived, leaving behind an atmosphere of curiosity and speculation.

The moment he was gone, the children gravitated toward the chest, their eyes wide with wonder.

"Are you going to open it now, Miss Bellamy?" Eliza asked, barely containing her excitement.

Rose looked at the chest, aware of its significance both as a teaching resource and as a precious link to Mary's memory. "Yes," she decided.

The gathered women and children formed a respectful circle as Rose carefully inserted the key and turned it in the lock. The simple mechanism clicked, and she gently lifted the lid.

Inside was a collection of educational treasures, clearly chosen with care and purpose. Several slim volumes on basic arithmetic and grammar. A beautifully illustrated primer with colored plates of plants and animals. Numerous small slates and pieces of chalk wrapped in cloth. A collection of simple wooden letter blocks, hand-carved and painted. And nestled beneath these practical items, a journal bound in faded blue cloth.

Rose lifted each item and showed them to the eager children. "These will help us learn our letters and numbers," she explained.

Beth examined the wooden blocks with appreciation. "These must have taken hours to make. Each letter so carefully formed."

"Mary always did have clever hands," one of the other women commented, a note of sadness in her voice.

Rose reached for the journal last, uncertain whether it belonged with the teaching materials or was a private record never meant for other eyes. She opened it cautiously to the first page and found not personal entries, but lesson plans and educational ideas written in a neat, flowing hand.

"She'd planned it all so carefully," Rose said, turning pages filled with thoughtful notes about teaching multiple age groups with limited resources, ideas for nature studies using the surrounding forest, and even simple songs to help children remember their alphabet.

Ethel peered over her shoulder. "That's Mary for you. Just like Boone, she never did anything halfway."

Rose felt a profound connection to this woman she'd never met, whose dreams she was now continuing. Mary's vision for education at

Trinity Station hadn't died with her; it had simply waited for the right moment to blossom.

"We'll use her plans," Rose decided, turning to the mothers and children. "Starting tomorrow, Trinity Station will have the school Mary envisioned."

The announcement was met with enthusiastic approval. The women began discussing what their children would need to bring, while the younger ones chattered excitedly about which letter blocks they wanted to use first.

As the afternoon progressed, the schoolhouse continued its transformation. Simon returned with the precious glass for the window, which was carefully installed in the prepared frame. The door Tom had made was hung and fitted with a simple latch. Inside, John and William had constructed benches and 2 more small tables that had been donated to the school by community members were arranged according to Rose's direction.

When a John drove the last nail into a bench and stepped back to admire their collective work, the entire building stood transformed. What had been an abandoned storage shed just days ago was now a schoolhouse, humble but functional, and ready to serve a purpose.

"It's perfect," Rose said, standing in the center of the room as evening shadows began to lengthen. "I don't know how to properly thank all of you."

"Teach our children well," Tom replied. "That's thanks enough."

The workers, mothers, and children departed. Rose remained behind with Ethel, arranging Mary's books on the shelves and organizing the teaching materials.

"So, you followed him to the storehouse," Ethel said without preamble as they worked. It wasn't a question.

"Yes," Rose admitted. "It was presumptuous of me."

Ethel shook her head. "It was kind. Even if he couldn't receive it as such." She placed the wooden letter blocks in a neat row on a shelf. "Boone doesn't let many people see his pain."

"He blames himself for Mary's death," Rose said quietly. "Not just in the general way people often do after losing someone, but specifically. He believes his choices caused her death."

Ethel's hands stilled momentarily. "That doesn't surprise me, though I've never heard him say it outright." She sighed heavily. "The accident happened during a difficult time. We'd had sickness in camp, supplies were low, and Boone was pushing to meet an important contract deadline. Mary went to bring him food by the cutting site, something she often did."

The older woman's voice grew softer. "A large tree branch fell on her. Boone carried her back to camp himself, but her injuries were too severe."

Rose's heart ached at the image of Boone carrying his dying wife, powerless to save her. "What a terrible burden to carry."

"He's carried it alone," Ethel observed. "Threw himself into work, avoided anything that might force him to confront his grief directly. Until now."

Rose understood the implication. Her arrival and the school project had unavoidably disrupted Boone's carefully maintained emotional distance.

"I worry I'm causing him additional pain," Rose confessed.

"Pain that needs facing, perhaps," Ethel suggested. "Mary wouldn't want her memory to keep this camp, or Boone, frozen in grief." She gestured around the transformed schoolhouse. "This is life continuing and growing. It's what she would have wanted."

Rose nodded, drawing strength from the older woman's practical wisdom. "Then we'll honor her vision by making this school everything she hoped it would be."

As they prepared to depart for the evening, Rose took a final look around the schoolhouse. Tomorrow, children would fill these benches, eager young minds ready to absorb knowledge. The thought filled her with both excitement and a deep sense of responsibility.

Her gaze fell on Mary's journal, now placed carefully on her teaching desk where she could reference the thoughtful plans. Despite the distance that seemed to separate her and Boone, their different worldviews, his rejection of faith, and the wall of grief he maintained—they shared this connection to Mary's vision. Perhaps, in time, that shared purpose might form the beginning of a bridge across the chasm between them.

The cool evening air greeted them as they stepped outside. Rose paused to look toward the river, where Boone's cabin stood apart from the main camp. A single lamp glowed in the window, a solitary light in the gathering dusk.

"He'll come around, in his own time and way," Ethel said, following her gaze. "Boone isn't a man who changes course easily, but once he does, he's steadfast."

Rose wasn't so certain. The man she'd encountered at the storehouse seemed locked in grief too profound for simple healing.

How could she ever truly connect with a man who had rejected the very faith that formed the center of her life? A man who saw hope as a dangerous luxury rather than essential strength?

"Perhaps," she said noncommittally. "For now, I'll focus on teaching the children. That's why I came to Trinity Station, after all."

As they walked toward the cookhouse, Rose tucked away her troubled thoughts about Boone McAlister. Tomorrow would bring its own challenges—eighteen eager students ranging from four to twelve years old, a makeshift schoolhouse, and limited supplies. She needed to focus on that practical reality, not on the enigmatic, grief-stricken foreman whose pain ran deeper than she had imagined possible.

Yet even as she prepared for her first day of teaching, a quiet voice in her heart whispered that perhaps God had led her to Trinity Station for more than just educating children. Perhaps there was healing work to be done here that went beyond reading and arithmetic, and wounds that needed tending as surely as young minds needed knowledge.

Whether Boone would ever allow such tending remained to be seen. For now, the gulf between them seemed too wide to bridge, a wilderness of pain and lost faith that no compass could easily navigate.

Chapter 11

"P is for pine tree!" Rose announced, holding up one of Mary's hand-carved letter blocks. Eighteen eager faces stared back at her, some nodding in recognition, others scrunching their brows in concentration.

"Pine trees are what your fathers cut each day to provide for your families," she continued, turning to the window where Trinity Station's surrounding forest was visible. "Can anyone tell me something special about pine trees?"

Hannah's hand shot up so enthusiastically that her whole body bounced on the bench.

"Yes, Hannah?"

"They're really, really tall!" she declared proudly.

Rose smiled. "Indeed, they are. What else?"

"They give us timber for houses and furniture," offered Timmy.

"Excellent observation."

"And they smell nice!" added Samuel. "Especially when Pa brings home fresh-cut wood."

Peter Cooper, still shy despite three days of classes, raised his hand hesitantly. When Rose nodded encouragingly, he said, "They have needles instead of leaves."

"Perfect, Peter! Pine trees have needles rather than broad leaves like maple or oak trees." Rose walked around the small classroom, showing each child the carved letter. "Now, who can think of other words that begin with the letter P?"

The children called out answers with varying degrees of confidence.

"Papa!"

"Porridge!"

"Puppy!"

Each correct answer earned a beaming smile from Rose, who wrote their contributions on the slate board with careful strokes of chalk.

Sunlight streamed through the glass window that Simon had donated, illuminating the wooden floor now swept clean each morning. Benches were lined up, grouped by age—the youngest children the nearest to Rose's desk, the oldest at the back where they could work more independently. Mary's books and teaching materials were arranged neatly on shelves, and children's first attempts at alphabet letters were proudly displayed on the walls.

Rose consulted Mary's journal frequently, incorporating her thoughtful plans while adapting them to the children's specific needs. The students, initially shy and uncertain, had blossomed under her attentive guidance, their natural curiosity overtaking any hesitation.

"Now we'll practice writing the letter P," Rose announced, distributing small slates and chalk to the older children. "Those of you who are just learning your letters, come sit in a circle around me."

As the older students practiced their penmanship, Rose gathered the youngest children around her on a braided rug that Beth had contributed. She laid out the wooden letter blocks, guiding tiny hands to recognize shapes and sounds.

"The letter P looks like a stick with a bubble on top," she explained, tracing the shape with her finger for them to follow.

"Like this, Miss Bellamy?" asked six-year-old Michael Riley, holding up his block.

"That's an excellent P, Michael!"

The morning progressed with the methodical practice of letters and numbers. Rose moved between groups, offering guidance where needed, praise where earned, and gentle correction when necessary. She noticed Peter Cooper struggling with his slate work, his twin brother Paul already finished and fidgeting impatiently.

"Paul, would you please help Eliza collect the chalk?" Rose asked, giving him a task to channel his energy. Then she knelt beside Peter, whose frustration was evident in his tense shoulders.

"These letters don't want to come right," he muttered, refusing to meet her eyes.

"Learning to write takes practice," Rose said gently. "Even I had to practice many times when I was your age." She guided his hand. "Try holding the chalk like this."

Peter's next attempt improved slightly, earning a tentative smile that warmed Rose's heart. These small victories were what made teaching worthwhile. Watching comprehension dawn, confidence build, and minds engage with new ideas.

After an hour of focused work, Rose noticed the children growing restless. The younger ones squirmed on their benches, and even the older students' attention had begun to wander. Outside, the late July day was pleasantly warm, with a gentle breeze stirring the treetops.

"I think we've earned a brief respite," she announced. "Let's all step outside for some fresh air before we begin our arithmetic lesson."

The children needed no further encouragement. They rushed outside with whoops of delight, suddenly transformed from studious pupils to energetic youngsters. Rose followed at a more measured pace, smiling at their enthusiasm.

Standing outside the schoolhouse, she watched as they organized an impromptu game of tag, darting between the nearby buildings with peals of laughter. These moments of carefree joy were precious in the often-harsh frontier environment, where children typically shouldered responsibilities beyond their years.

The camp bustled with activity around them. Women tended gardens or carried washing to the river's edge. Nearby, Simon directed a crew loading supplies onto a wagon bound for another cutting site. The familiar sounds of Trinity Station, axes striking wood in the distance, the creak of wagon wheels, and the calls between workers, created a reassuring backdrop of industry and community.

Rose breathed deeply, grateful for how smoothly the school's first days had progressed. The children were eager to learn, the parents supportive, and even Boone had kept his distance, neither interfering nor showing further interest since delivering Mary's chest. She felt the keen absence of his approval, but had decided to focus on her teaching rather than worrying about their philosophical differences.

A sudden commotion by the river interrupted her reflections. Shouts erupted, urgent and alarmed rather than the usual work calls. Men began running toward the water, their movements sharp with urgency.

"Something's happened," Rose murmured, immediately alert.

"Children!" she called sharply. "Stay here at the schoolhouse! Eliza and Timmy, you're both in charge until I return."

Without waiting for a response, Rose gathered her skirts and hurried toward the river, her heart pounding with concern. As she drew closer, the shouts clarified into calls for help. A group of lumberjacks had gathered near the timber slide, a wooden structure built to channel logs into the river for the journey downstream.

"Get him away from the logs!" someone shouted.

"Careful with his leg!"

Rose pushed through the gathering crowd, her healer's instincts overriding any hesitation. In the clearing at the center, two men supported a third between them, Jed Dawson, a young lumberjack she recognized from the dinner gatherings. His face was ashen beneath his beard, his teeth clenched against obvious pain. Blood soaked his right trouser leg from knee to ankle.

"What happened?" Rose asked, moving forward with calm authority.

"Log rolled," answered Tom grimly. "Caught his leg between another downed tree. Nearly crushed it completely."

"Bring him to level ground," Rose directed, quickly assessing the situation.

The men complied, carefully maneuvering their injured companion to a flatter area where they could lower him to the ground. A growing crowd of concerned workers, women, and children gathered around them, murmuring anxiously.

Rose knelt beside Jed, who groaned through clenched teeth. "Jed, I need to look at your leg. May I cut away the trouser fabric?"

He nodded jerkily, sweat beading on his forehead despite the cool air.

"I need a sharp knife," Rose called, glancing up at the gathered men.

Simon immediately offered his hunting knife, handle first. "Here."

Rose took it with a nod of thanks and carefully began cutting through the blood-soaked fabric. As she pulled the material away, she revealed a deep, jagged gash that ran from just below Jed's knee, almost to his ankle. The wound gaped open, exposing muscle and the white gleam of bone.

Gasps and muttered oaths rose from the onlookers. Rose maintained her composure, though her stomach clenched at the severity of the injury.

"I need to stop the bleeding," she said. "Someone bring clean clothes. And water... both for drinking and cleaning."

"Will he lose the leg?" someone asked bluntly.

Jed's eyes went wide with fear, and Rose shot the speaker a quelling look.

"Not if I can help it," she said with a confidence she didn't entirely feel. "But I must act quickly."

She turned her attention back to Jed. "This will hurt," she warned him gently, "but I need to see how deep the damage goes."

He nodded, his jaw tight. "Do what you must."

With careful fingers, Rose examined the wound, assessing the torn muscle and damaged tissue. The bone appeared to have been scraped but not broken, a small mercy. The major concern was the blood loss and the risk of infection.

"I need my herbs," she yelled. "John Riley, would you please run to my room at the cookhouse? There's a leather satchel under my bed with dried herbs and bandages. Bring it to me, quickly."

John departed at a run, leaving the assembled workers watching Rose with varying expressions of doubt and hope.

"Shouldn't we fetch the doctor from Roseburg?" Simon suggested. "This looks bad, miss."

"Roseburg is two days' travel, at best," Tom pointed out. "Not counting the time to find the doctor once there."

"By then, infection could take hold," Rose said grimly. She placed firm pressure on the wound with a clean cloth someone had provided.

"My mother and grandmother taught me how to treat injuries like this. I've helped with accidents before."

She had assisted with farm injuries back east, but nothing quite this severe. Still, the principles of wound treatment remained the same, and her knowledge of herbal remedies was extensive.

A deep voice cut through the murmured conversation. "What's happened?"

The crowd parted to reveal Boone striding toward them, his expression darkening as he took in the scene. His eyes moved from Jed's bloody leg to Rose's hands, applying pressure to the wound, then back to the injured man's face.

"Log rolled unexpectedly," Simon explained quickly. "Caught him before he could jump clear."

Boone knelt on Jed's other side, his experienced gaze assessing the damage. "Bad gash."

"Yes," Rose agreed, not looking up from her task. "But if I can stop the bleeding and prevent infection, he should heal. The bone isn't broken."

Boone's eyebrows rose slightly at her clinical assessment. Before he could respond, John returned breathless from running, carrying Rose's satchel.

"Thank you," she said, accepting it with blood-stained hands. "Mitchell Cooper, would you bring that bucket of water closer, please?"

As Mitchell complied, Rose quickly washed her hands in the cold water, then opened her satchel. Inside were neatly labeled pouches of dried herbs, small bottles of tinctures, clean bandages, and a selection of implements, including a bone needle and catgut for stitching.

The assembled men watched with a mixture of curiosity, and skepticism as Rose worked with practiced efficiency. She selected several herbs, yarrow for bleeding, calendula for cleaning the wound, comfrey for healing, and willow bark for pain. She quickly prepared them according to need.

"This will sting," she warned Jed as she cleaned the wound with a calendula wash. His only response was a sharp intake of breath and a tightened grip on Boone's offered hand.

Rose worked methodically, cleaning the wound thoroughly before applying a poultice of crushed yarrow to slow the bleeding. As she worked, she maintained a calm, reassuring manner, speaking quietly to Jed to distract him from the pain.

"The yarrow stops bleeding by helping the blood clot," she explained. "My grandmother used it on my cousin when he cut his foot with an axe. The bone was visible then, too, but he walked without a limp within two months."

Jed managed a weak smile. "Hope I'm as lucky."

"It's not luck," Rose replied, carefully applying the herb mixture. "It's proper care and God's healing wisdom in these plants."

She felt Boone shift but didn't look up to see his reaction to her mention of God. Instead, she continued her treatment, packing the wound with herbs known for their antiseptic properties.

"This needs stitching," she announced, after the bleeding had slowed sufficiently. "The muscle layer first, then the skin." She glanced up at Jed's pale face. "I can give you willow bark tea for the pain, but it will still be uncomfortable."

"I've had stitches before," Jed said, though his voice trembled.

"Perhaps some whiskey would help," Simon suggested, looking toward Boone for approval.

Boone nodded. "Fetch the medicinal bottle from my cabin. Bottom drawer of my desk."

While they waited for the whiskey, Rose prepared her needle and catgut, soaking both in alcohol to clean them. The crowd watched as Rose prepared to perform a procedure most had only seen done by grizzled camp doctors or army medics.

When the whiskey arrived, Jed took several deep swallows, grimacing at the burn but welcoming the numbing effect that would soon follow.

"Ready?" Rose asked after allowing the whiskey a few minutes to take effect.

Jed nodded grimly. "As I'll ever be."

With steady hands that belied her inner nervousness, Rose began stitching the deeper layer of muscle tissue, using the techniques her grandmother had taught her. Her stitches were small and even, drawing the damaged tissue together with minimal trauma.

Jed hissed and groaned but remained admirably still throughout the procedure. Boone stayed close, occasionally murmuring words of encouragement to the injured man. The unspoken tension between Rose and the foreman was temporarily set aside in their shared focus on Jed's welfare.

As Rose tied off the final stitch and cut the catgut, a collective sigh of relief passed through the crowd. She sat back on her heels, wiping perspiration from her forehead with her sleeve.

"The worst is done," she told Jed with an encouraging smile. "Now we need to keep it clean and watch for infection."

"How long before he can walk?" Boone asked.

"He shouldn't put weight on it for at least two weeks," Rose replied. "Even then, only gentle movement. Real work won't be possible for a month, perhaps longer."

Boone merely nodded, his expression unreadable. "We can assign him to whittling axe handles and repair work once he's mobile."

Rose began bandaging the leg with clean cloth, wrapping it firmly but not too tightly. "He'll need the dressing changed at least twice daily, and fresh herb poultices applied to prevent infection. Regular willow bark tea will help manage the pain."

"You'll see to this?" Boone asked, though it sounded more like a statement than a question.

"Of course," Rose replied. "Though I'll need to arrange care around school hours."

"School can wait a day or two if necessary," Boone said, surprising her. "This takes priority."

Their eyes met briefly, and Rose saw something unexpected in his gaze—not warmth, certainly, but a grudging acknowledgment of her skills that hadn't been there before.

"We need to move him somewhere comfortable," she said, breaking the momentary connection. "Preferably close to my room so I can check on him throughout the night."

"The other storage room off the cookhouse," Boone decided. "It's warm from the kitchen fires and has a cot already, same as your room."

Simon and Tom carefully lifted Jed, who groaned despite their gentle handling. As they carried him toward the cookhouse, Rose quickly gathered her supplies, aware of Boone's continued presence beside her.

"You didn't mention you had medical knowledge," he said as she closed her satchel.

"You didn't ask," Rose replied simply, rising to her feet. Blood stained her dress and hands, and she knew she must look a frightful mess.

"Where did you learn such skills? That was no amateur doctoring."

"My mother and grandmother were known for their healing throughout our county in Pennsylvania. They both taught me from childhood," Rose explained, falling into step beside him as they followed the men carrying Jed.

Boone nodded thoughtfully. "A practical education."

"Yes," Rose agreed, sensing an opening. "Knowledge passed from one generation to the next, just as I hope to pass along reading and arithmetic to the children here."

A ghost of a smile touched Boone's lips. There and gone so quickly, Rose almost thought she'd imagined it. "Cleverly argued, Miss Bellamy."

Before she could respond, Ethel appeared at the cookhouse door, alerted by the commotion. Her eyes widened at the sight of Jed being carried toward her.

"Lord have mercy! What's happened?"

"Logging accident," Boone answered tersely. "Jed needs the use of the other storage room to recover, so he'll be near Miss Bellamy and the warmth of the fire."

Ethel immediately took charge, directing the men to the small room adjacent to the kitchen. "Bring fresh water," she instructed one of the kitchen helpers. "And clean linens and blankets."

Jed was carefully settled onto a narrow cot. His face was gray with pain and exhaustion. The whiskey had provided only minimal relief.

"I'll prepare willow bark tea," Rose told him, patting his hand. "And a sleeping draught to help you rest."

"Thank you," Jed managed weakly. "Never seen a schoolteacher who could stitch a man up like that."

"I'm more than just a schoolteacher, Jed," Rose replied with a smile.

As she turned to go prepare the promised remedies, she found Boone watching her with an inscrutable expression.

"The children," she suddenly remembered. "I left them at the schoolhouse."

"I sent William to watch them," Boone assured her. "But they should be dismissed for the day. You have other duties now."

Rose nodded gratefully. "I'll go speak with them after I prepare Jed's teas."

In the kitchen, Rose washed her hands thoroughly before beginning work on the herbal teas.

"That was quite a display of skill you performed, I was told," Ethel commented, her voice pitched low, so only Rose could hear. "Never seen these men so impressed by anything a woman's done, excepting maybe Mary's rifle shooting."

Rose measured dried willow bark into a small pot. "I only hope it's enough. The wound is serious."

"Word's already spreading through camp about how you took charge," Ethel continued, her shrewd eyes assessing Rose. "Tom's telling anyone who'll listen how you stitched muscle with hands steady as any surgeon's."

"I only did what needed doing," Rose demurred.

"And that's precisely what they respect," Ethel pointed out. "Not words or intentions, but practical action when it counts." She glanced toward the doorway, where Boone stood deep in conversation with Simon. "Including him, whether he admits it or not."

Rose followed her gaze. Boone's powerful figure dominated the doorway, his expression serious as he discussed work arrangements to accommodate Jed's absence. He seemed unaware of their observation, focused entirely on the practical considerations before him.

"I doubt Mr. McAlister is easily impressed," Rose said quietly. "Especially by skills he probably considers commonplace in frontier life."

"Don't be too sure," Ethel replied. "Good healers are rare and valuable out here, nearly as precious as good teachers. You've just proven yourself to be both."

The willow bark began to steep, releasing its medicinal aroma. Rose added a small amount of honey to mask the bitter taste, then prepared a separate sleeping draught using valerian root and chamomile.

As she worked, she became aware of Boone approaching, his footsteps measured on the wooden floor.

"How soon can you return to the schoolhouse?" he asked without preamble.

"I need to administer these teas and check Jed's bandages again," Rose replied. "Then I can dismiss the children properly."

Boone nodded. "I'll have someone sit with Jed while you're gone."

His matter-of-fact acceptance of her authority in this situation was a noticeable shift from his earlier dismissiveness, and Rose found herself studying his face, searching for clues to his thoughts. His expression remained guarded, but the outright antagonism of their previous encounters had given way to something more neutral, professional respect, perhaps.

"Thank you," she said, pouring the willow bark tea into a cup. "I won't be long."

When she returned to the small storage room, Jed was lying with his eyes closed, his breathing rapid and shallow from pain. He roused at her approach, attempting a smile that came out as more of a grimace.

"This will help with the pain," Rose said, helping him sit up slightly to drink the tea. "And this," she held up the second cup, "will help you sleep."

"Never thought I'd be grateful for bitter tree bark," Jed commented weakly after draining the first cup. His gaze darted nervously to Rose, then away again. "Miss Bellamy, I want to thank you properly. If not for your quick action..." He trailed off, the unspoken possibility hanging in the air.

"You're welcome, Jed," Rose replied gently. "Now drink this and rest. Your body needs sleep to begin healing."

After Jed had taken the sleeping draught and settled back onto the cot, Rose checked his bandages one more time. Satisfied that the bleeding remained controlled, she left him in the care of Ethel, who had volunteered to sit with him while she tended to her school duties.

Outside, Rose was surprised to find Boone waiting for her, arms crossed over his chest as he leaned against the cookhouse wall.

"I'll walk with you to the schoolhouse," he said, straightening as she approached.

Rose blinked in surprise, but nodded her acceptance. They set off side by side, an unusual companionship that drew curious glances from those they passed.

"Jed should recover well with proper care," Rose said, breaking the silence between them.

"Thanks to your intervention," Boone acknowledged. "Most camp injuries are treated with whiskey and prayer until a doctor can be found, usually too late for proper healing."

Rose glanced at him, wondering if his mention of prayer was deliberately ironic given their previous conversation about faith. His expression revealed nothing.

"Proper treatment makes all the difference," she agreed neutrally. "Especially in the first hours after injury."

They walked a few more steps in silence before Boone spoke again, his voice more measured. "Your skills are an unexpected asset to Trinity Station. I admit, I didn't anticipate medical knowledge along with teaching."

Coming from Boone, this was tantamount to effusive praise. Rose felt a small bloom of warmth at the grudging respect in his tone.

"Thank you," she replied simply, deciding not to risk the moment with too many words.

As they approached the schoolhouse, they could see the children playing in the yard under William's watchful eye. They were engaged in some sort of circle game, their voices carrying clear in the afternoon air.

At the sight of Rose and Boone approaching together, the children faltered in their game, their expressions curious and slightly wary. Several of the older ones, Rose noticed, looked between her and Boone with particular interest.

"Children," Rose called, summoning her teacher's voice despite her exhaustion, "please gather your things. School is dismissed early today due to an emergency in camp."

The younger ones rushed inside immediately. The older children moved more slowly, casting questioning glances at Boone.

"Is everything all right, Miss Bellamy?" Eliza asked, noting Rose's bloodstained dress with wide eyes.

"Mr. Dawson was injured while working," Rose explained carefully, mindful of the youngest children's sensibilities. "I've been helping tend to him."

"Is he going to die?" Samuel asked bluntly, causing Hannah to gasp.

"No, Samuel, I don't believe so," Rose assured them firmly. "Mr. Dawson will recover with proper care, but I'll need to check on him regularly over the next few days."

"Does that mean no school tomorrow?" Paul asked hopefully.

Rose glanced at Boone, who had remained silent during this exchange. To her surprise, he answered before she could.

"School will continue," he said, his deep voice commanding immediate attention from the children. "But your lessons may be adjusted to accommodate Miss Bellamy's duties caring for Mr. Dawson."

The children absorbed this information with varying reactions. Rose noticed several of the older boys looking at Boone with undisguised admiration, clearly awed by the camp foreman despite his stern demeanor.

"For tomorrow," Rose added, "I'll prepare lessons that can be practiced independently during those times I need to check on Mr. Dawson. The older children will help the younger ones with their letters and numbers."

This announcement pleased the older students, who straightened with pride at being entrusted with teaching responsibilities.

As the children gathered their slates and other belongings, Rose noticed Timmy lingering near Boone, gathering courage to speak to him.

"Mr. McAlister," the boy finally ventured, "how did the accident happen? Was it a widow-maker?"

Rose expected Boone to dismiss the question, but instead, he considered it seriously. "No, Timmy. It was a rolling log on uneven ground... carelessness and bad luck together. A reminder of why we have safety rules in camp."

Timmy nodded soberly. "Pa says logging's the most dangerous work there is."

"Your father's right," Boone agreed. "That's why we need to pay attention and follow proper procedures at all times." He surveyed the children, who had all paused to listen. "Remember that when you're old enough to join the cutting crews. Caution keeps a man alive in the forest."

Rose was struck by this unexpected moment of teaching. Boone was not merely answering Timmy's question; he was imparting valuable wisdom to the next generation of Trinity Station's residents. Perhaps, she realized, there was more common ground between them than she had initially believed.

As the students filed out, calling goodbyes and hurrying home with news of the day's excitement, Rose stepped into the schoolhouse to gather her things. Boone followed, his tall frame seeming too large for the modest building.

"You've organized this space well," he observed, looking around at the neat arrangement of benches and learning materials.

"Thank you," Rose replied, surprised by the compliment. "Mary's plans were very helpful. She had a wonderful vision for teaching children of different ages together."

At the mention of Mary's name, Rose immediately regretted her words, fearing she had shattered their fragile rapport. But Boone's expression, while solemn, didn't close off entirely as it had in previous conversations.

"Yes," he said, "she did."

A brief silence fell between them. Rose busied herself gathering her teaching materials, acutely aware of Boone's presence as he studied Mary's letter blocks arranged on a shelf.

"Honestly, between you and me, how long will Jed's recovery take?" he asked, turning back to face her.

"If infection doesn't set in, and he follows instructions about rest, at least four weeks before he can return to light duties," Rose answered. "Two months or more before full-strength returns to that leg."

Boone nodded, absorbing this information with the calculating mind of a camp leader who needed to reallocate work and adjust expectations. "We'll arrange suitable tasks for him once he's mobile. Perhaps he can help with school lessons if you're shorthanded."

The suggestion caught Rose by surprise. "That's... a thoughtful consideration."

"Purely practical," Boone replied. "Idle hands lead to discontent, even among the injured."

Rose gathered her courage and ventured a more personal question. "Mr. McAlister, may I ask why you came to the schoolhouse with me?"

Boone considered her for a long moment, his gray-blue eyes inscrutable. "I wanted to see for myself how you've organized things here," he finally said. "After witnessing your competence with Jed's injury, I thought perhaps I'd underestimated your capabilities."

Rose accepted his answer with a simple nod.

"The children could truly benefit from your knowledge of logging and survival skills," she said. "When you have time, of course."

Boone's jaw tightened. "Perhaps. When the current cutting quota is met."

Even this non-committal response felt like progress. Rose smiled slightly, gathering her shawl around her shoulders. "I should return to check on Jed."

Boone nodded and stepped aside to let her pass. As they left the schoolhouse together, Rose paused to lock the door with the key Boone had provided days earlier.

Walking back toward the cookhouse, Rose was acutely aware of the unusual picture they presented side by side, the schoolteacher in her bloodstained dress, and the stern foreman whose approval she had sought since her arrival. The events of the day had shifted something between them, creating, if not friendship, then at least a grudging professional respect.

"Your mother and grandmother taught you well," Boone said unexpectedly as they neared the cookhouse. "Trinity Station is fortunate to have you here."

Rose glanced at him in surprise, warmed by the straightforward acknowledgment. "Thank you, Mr. McAlister. That means a great deal coming from you."

He nodded once, his expression unreadable again. "I'll check on Jed this evening after the day's accounts are settled."

With that, he turned toward the river, leaving Rose to watch his retreating figure with mixed emotions. The wall between them remained substantially intact, their fundamental differences unresolved. Yet today had revealed a possibility she hadn't fully considered before, that respect could develop even where philosophical agreement was absent.

As she returned to Jed's bedside to check his bandages, Rose reflected on the strange path that had led her to this moment. She had come to Trinity Station to teach children, yet today she had demonstrated healing skills she hadn't even mentioned upon her arrival. Perhaps, she thought, this was part of God's greater plan as well, to show that her value extended beyond the schoolhouse.

Jed slept peacefully, the herbs doing their work to ease his pain. His face, relaxed in slumber, revealed his youth, he couldn't be much more than twenty-three or twenty-four. As Rose checked his bandages and found them clean with no signs of increased bleeding, Ethel appeared.

"How is he?" she asked softly, entering the room with a bowl of broth.

"Resting comfortably," Rose replied.

Ethel placed the broth on a small table. "For when he wakes. And I've brought clean water for you to wash."

Only then did Rose fully register her own disheveled state. The dried blood on her hands and dress, and the loose strands of hair that had escaped her pins during the emergency.

"Thank you," she said gratefully. "I must look a fright."

"You look like someone who saved a man's leg today," Ethel corrected. "But a wash will certainly help." She paused, her keen eyes studying Rose's face. "I hear you and Boone had quite the conversation. Half the camp's talking about seeing you walk together."

Rose sighed, dipping her hands into the clean water and watching the dried blood dissolve away. "People here must be desperate for topics of conversation, if a simple walk warrants such interest."

"It's not the walk that interests them," Ethel pointed out. "It's the change it represents. Boone's opening up. He escorted you to the schoolhouse?"

"He merely wanted to see how I'd organized things," Rose explained, though she understood Ethel's point. Any change in Boone's behavior was notable to those who knew him well.

"Mmm-hmm," Ethel murmured noncommittally. "And did he like what he saw?"

Rose thought about Boone's careful inspection of the schoolhouse, his brief acknowledgment of Mary's vision. "I believe he found it... acceptable."

"High praise indeed." Ethel handed Rose a towel. "Don't underestimate what you accomplished today, Rose. Not just with Jed's injury, but with Boone. The fact that he's reassessing his opinion of you is significant."

"Perhaps. But our fundamental differences remain. He still rejects faith and still sees hope as weakness. One successful medical intervention won't change that."

"Perhaps not," Ethel agreed. "But it's a start. A crack in the ice, so to speak." She glanced at Jed's sleeping form. "Sometimes healing happens from the most unexpected beginnings."

Chapter 12

The schoolhouse buzzed with the energy of children taking on adult responsibilities. Eliza carefully arranged wooden letter blocks on the table while Timmy wiped the slate board clean, his movements precise and methodical for a twelve-year-old. Four other older students moved between benches, laying out slates and chalk for their younger classmates.

"Remember, the youngest children will practice writing their letters here," Rose instructed, pointing to the front benches. "Eliza, you'll help them form the shapes correctly. Be patient if they struggle."

Eliza nodded solemnly. "Like you are with us, Miss Bellamy."

"Exactly," Rose smiled, adjusting a crooked row of letter blocks. "Timmy, you and James will supervise the arithmetic practice for the middle group. They need to complete these addition problems while I'm checking on Mr. Dawson."

"Yes, ma'am," Timmy replied, straightening his shoulders with pride. "How long will you be gone?"

"Not more than twenty minutes at a time," Rose assured him. "I'll check on Mr. Dawson before school begins, again at mid-morning, and once during the noon meal. In the afternoon, I'll also take two more twenty-minute breaks to check on Mr. Dawson." She tucked a stray lock of hair behind her ear, surveying the classroom with critical eyes. The preparations had begun well before dawn, when she'd risen early to organize independent work for each age group.

"What if someone misbehaves?" asked James, his red hair standing out vividly in the morning light.

"I trust you all to behave responsibly," Rose replied firmly. "But if there's any trouble, step outside and ring the small bell I've placed by the door. I'll hear it at the cookhouse."

The children nodded, absorbing their instructions with surprising seriousness. Rose felt a swell of pride at their willingness to help. Just days ago, they'd been strangers; now they were her eager assistants, stepping up when needed.

A movement outside the window caught her attention. Boone stood nearby, watching the activity inside the schoolhouse. His expression was unreadable at this distance, but the fact that he'd stopped to observe instead of continuing about his business struck Rose as significant.

"Miss Bellamy?" Eliza tugged at her sleeve. "Will Mr. Dawson lose his leg? Peter Cooper says infections make doctors saw off legs."

Rose crouched down to meet the girl's worried eyes. "No, Eliza. Mr. Dawson's leg is healing well, and I'm watching carefully for any signs of infection. That's precisely why I need to check on him regularly."

"My pa says you saved Jed's leg with your plant medicine," Timmy added, pride evident in his voice. "Said he's never seen stitching so neat, even from the doctor in Roseburg."

Rose felt her cheeks warm at the praise. "Your father is very kind. Now, I believe the others will be arriving soon. Timmy, please ring the bell in five minutes to signal the start of school. I'll return shortly after checking on our patient."

As the children returned to their preparations, Rose glanced out the window again. Boone had moved closer, now standing near the schoolhouse door. Their eyes met briefly, and he gave a short nod of acknowledgment before stepping back.

Rather than entering, he waited outsides. Rose gathered her shawl, curious about his presence but not wanting to keep him waiting.

"I'll return shortly," she reminded the children before stepping outside.

Boone stood with his hands clasped behind his back, his posture military-straight as always. The morning light emphasized the strong lines of his face.

"Mr. McAlister," Rose greeted him. "Is there something you needed?"

"Just observing," he replied, gesturing toward the schoolhouse. "You've organized the older children well to help out during Jed's time of need."

The compliment warmed her. "Necessity often brings out unexpected capabilities in people. The older children are quite capable when given responsibility."

Boone nodded, his gaze moving from the schoolhouse to her face. "You're going to check on Jed now?"

"Yes. I want to change his bandages before the school day begins."

"I'll walk with you," he said, falling into step beside her as she moved toward the cookhouse. "There are some arrangements we should discuss regarding your dual duties."

As they walked, Rose was acutely aware of the curious glances directed their way. Twice in two days, the camp foreman and the schoolteacher were walking together in seemingly amiable conversation, a notable development in Trinity Station's social dynamics.

"How did Jed fare through the night?" Boone asked, his voice pitched low enough that only she could hear.

"Relatively well. His pain was manageable with the willow bark tea, and he slept through most of the night. I checked his bandages often, and there was no excessive bleeding or unusual warmth around the wound."

"Good news. The camp can't afford to lose him, he's a good worker."

"Morning, you two," Ethel called as they stepped into the cookhouse. "Jed's awake and asking for his breakfast. Says he's hungry enough to eat a bear."

"A good sign," Rose replied, smiling at the cook. "I'll change his bandages first, then he can eat."

"I'll join you," Boone said, following Rose toward the small room where Jed recuperated.

Rose knocked lightly on the door before entering. Jed was propped up on several pillows, his injured leg elevated on a folded blanket. His face brightened when he saw Rose, then registered surprise at Boone's presence behind her.

"Miss Bellamy! Mr. McAlister," he said, attempting to sit up straighter.

"Stay still, Jed," Rose admonished gently, setting down her satchel of supplies. "How is your pain this morning?"

"Bearable," Jed replied, though the tightness around his eyes suggested otherwise. "That tea of yours works wonders."

Rose nodded, carefully folding back the blanket to expose his bandaged leg. "I'm going to change your dressing now. It will be uncomfortable."

"I've brought something that might help," Boone spoke up, reaching into his pocket. He pulled out a handful of fresh yarrow, its feathery leaves and white flower clusters unmistakable. "Found this growing by the river this morning. Thought it might be useful for your medicines."

Rose accepted the herbs with barely concealed surprise. "Thank you, Mr. McAlister. Fresh yarrow is indeed excellent for wounds." She looked at him curiously. "How did you know to look for it?"

A shadow passed across Boone's features. "Mary used similar remedies," he said after a brief hesitation. "She kept a small herb garden near our cabin."

"This is very thoughtful of you," she replied. She turned her attention back to Jed, unwrapping the bandages with gentle movements.

The wound looked better than she had dared hope. The stitches held firmly, with only minimal redness around the edges. There was no discharge or unusual swelling, the first promising signs that infection might be kept at bay.

"Looking good," she told Jed, who had been watching her examination with nervous eyes. "The edges are beginning to knit together nicely."

"Thanks to your handiwork," Jed replied earnestly. "Never seen stitching so neat, not even from old Doc Turner in the logging camp up north."

Rose cleaned the wound carefully, then prepared a fresh poultice using some of Boone's yarrow combined with the dried herbs from her satchel. As she worked, she was aware of Boone watching with quiet intensity, missing nothing of her methodical process.

"You work with remarkable efficiency," he observed as she began re-wrapping the leg with clean bandages.

"My grandmother taught me to be thorough but swift," Rose explained. "She said a patient's comfort depended as much on a healer's speed as her skill."

When she had finished securing the bandage, Rose prepared a fresh cup of willow bark tea, adding honey to mask the bitterness. "Drink this now, Jed. I'll have Ethel bring your breakfast once you're done."

Jed accepted the cup, his eyes moving between Rose and Boone with undisguised curiosity. "Never thought I'd have the boss and the schoolteacher tending me together," he commented with a hint of a smile. "Makes a man feel important."

"Don't get used to it," Boone replied, though his tone held no real severity. "Miss Bellamy has a school to run, and I have a camp to manage."

"Speaking of which," Rose said, gathering her supplies, "I should return to the schoolhouse."

"I'll walk with you," Boone repeated his earlier offer. "There are still matters to discuss."

As they left the cookhouse, Rose noticed Ethel watching them with knowing eyes as she prepared a tray for Jed. The older woman gave Rose an encouraging nod before turning back to her kitchen duties.

The morning air had warmed slightly, though a brisk breeze still rustled through the nearby pines. Rose held her shawl close as they walked toward the schoolhouse.

"I've been thinking about arrangements that might make your dual responsibilities more manageable," Boone began without preamble. "Simon suggested that his wife, Clara, could sit with Jed during school hours, allowing you to check on him only when necessary rather than several times throughout the day."

"That's very thoughtful, and I'm sure Ethel will appreciate it, she's offered to help as well," Rose responded, genuinely touched by the consideration. "Does Mrs. Blackwood have nursing experience?"

"Some. She helped care for injured men during the last river drive. She's practical and level-headed."

"That would be a tremendous help. I was concerned about disrupting the children's lessons too frequently."

"The children's education shouldn't suffer because of Jed's accident," Boone stated matter-of-factly. "Both responsibilities are important to the camp."

They walked a few more paces in companionable step before Rose ventured, "You said 'both responsibilities are important.' That's a change from your initial assessment of education's place in Trinity Station."

Boone shot her a sidelong glance, his expression guarded but not hostile. "I'm practical enough to recognize value when I see it. The children are... engaged in a way I hadn't anticipated."

"Learning awakens something in children," Rose agreed warmly. "Knowledge gives them possibilities beyond what they can immediately see around them."

"Though practical skills will always be essential for survival," Boone countered.

"Of course. But education doesn't replace practical skills, it enhances them." Rose grew more animated as they walked, her hands gesturing to emphasize her points. "A lumberjack who can read logging contracts is less likely to be cheated. A mother who understands basic mathematics can manage household supplies more efficiently."

"You make a persuasive case for practical education, Miss Bellamy."

"All education is practical in its own way, Mr. McAlister. Even poetry teaches the precision of language and the power of well-chosen words."

A ghost of a smile touched Boone's lips. "I'm not sure if I'd consider poetry essential to survival in the Oregon wilderness."

"Perhaps not for physical survival," Rose conceded, "but for nourishing the spirit? It's absolutely essential."

As soon as the words left her mouth, Rose regretted mentioning anything related to spiritual matters. Boone's expression immediately became more guarded.

"The children could really benefit from practical knowledge about logging safety," he said after a brief pause, changing the subject. "After witnessing Jed's accident, they should understand the dangers and precautions."

Rose seized this opening gratefully. "Would you consider speaking to them? Perhaps next week when you have time? They'd be fascinated to learn directly from you."

Boone hesitated, his reluctance evident in the tightening of his jaw. "I suppose that would be... appropriate."

This concession, small as it might seem to others, represented a significant shift in Boone's stance regarding the school. Rose felt a quiet triumph at this evidence of progress in their relationship.

"Ah, Boone! Miss Bellamy!" Simon called, approaching from the direction of the cutting site. The big lumberjack tipped his hat respectfully to Rose. "How's our patient this morning?"

"Improving," Rose replied. "Your wife's assistance would be most welcome in monitoring him during school hours."

"Clara would be happy to help," Simon assured her. His gaze moved between Rose and Boone with poorly concealed interest. "The children seem to be taking to their lessons remarkably well. Clara says our Andy actually asked for a story last night instead of falling straight to sleep." He chuckled warmly. "You've got Mary's way with the children, Miss Bellamy. She always knew how to capture their interest, too."

The casual comparison landed like a physical blow. Rose watched Boone's expression shutter immediately, the openness of their previous conversation vanishing behind a wall of reserve.

"I should check on the eastern cutting crew," he said, his voice returning to its customary gruffness. "Good day, Miss Bellamy."

He strode away, his long legs carrying him quickly toward the path that led to the cutting site. Simon watched him go with a puzzled expression.

"Did I say something amiss?" he asked Rose.

"The comparison to Mary was perhaps... difficult for him to hear," Rose explained gently.

Simon's weathered face fell. "Fool that I am. Wasn't thinking." He shook his head regretfully. "Just meant it as a compliment to you both."

"I understand," Rose assured him. "And in time, perhaps Mr. McAlister will as well." She glanced toward the schoolhouse. "I should begin the day's lessons. Please thank your wife for her willingness to help with Jed."

As Simon took his leave, Rose watched Boone's retreating figure for a moment longer, noting the rigid set of his shoulders as he disappeared among the trees. The fragile bridge of understanding they had been building now seemed unstable again, weakened by an innocent comparison that had struck too close to unhealed wounds.

With a small sigh, Rose turned toward the schoolhouse, pushing aside her disappointment to focus on the eager young faces awaiting her attention. Whatever progress had been made with Boone would have to develop at its own pace; she couldn't force healing, any more than she could force a wound to close before its time.

Chapter 13

The afternoon sunshine slanted through the schoolhouse window, casting a long rectangle of light across the wooden floor where the youngest children sat in a circle, carefully practicing their letters with chalk on small slates. Rose moved among them, offering guidance and encouragement as needed.

"Very good, Hannah," she praised as the youngest Abernathy child proudly displayed a wobbly letter H. "That's the first letter of your name."

Hannah beamed, her small face alight with accomplishment. "Can I show Pa when he comes home?"

"Certainly," Rose smiled, gently correcting Michael Riley's reversed letter E. "Your parents will be very proud of your progress."

Rose glanced toward the window, checking the position of the shadows. It was nearly time for her mid-afternoon visit to check on Jed.

A small commotion at the door drew Rose's attention. William Wilson stood there, clutching an envelope and looking somewhat uncomfortable.

"Begging your pardon, Miss Bellamy," he said, removing his hat. "A letter's arrived for you from Portland. Mr. Fletcher brought the mail pouch this morning, but I only just got around to sorting it."

Rose crossed the room to accept the envelope, immediately recognizing the neat handwriting of Joshua Campbell, the company agent who had arranged her position at Trinity Station.

"Thank you, Mr. Wilson," she said, curious about the letter's contents.

"There's news for the camp as well," William added, glancing at the attentive children. "Mr. Campbell writes that he'll be returning to Trinity Station within the week, and he's bringing a minister with him. A Reverend Noah Parker from Portland. Says it's time Trinity Station had proper church services."

A murmur of excitement spread through the classroom. Several of the older children exchanged enthusiastic glances, while others looked merely curious.

"A real minister?" Eliza asked excitedly. "Will we have a church building like in the stories?"

Rose smiled at the girl's enthusiasm. "Perhaps not a dedicated building right away, Eliza. But we could certainly hold services here in the schoolhouse or even the cookhouse until a proper church might be built."

"Will we sing hymns?" Samuel asked eagerly. "Ma sings them at home."

"I expect we will," Rose answered, her own excitement growing at the prospect of formal worship services.

"My uncle used to say preachers just want your money," Paul announced with the blunt confidence of an eight-year-old repeating adult conversations.

"Paul!" his twin brother Peter hissed, embarrassed.

Rose maintained her composure. "Ministers serve God by tending to people's spiritual needs, just as your fathers serve the camp by cutting timber, or as I serve by teaching you. We all have different roles in a community."

A shadow fell across the doorway as Boone appeared, his large frame filling the entrance. From his expression, Rose knew immediately that he had heard at least part of the conversation about the minister's impending arrival.

"Mr. McAlister," she greeted him, forcing a calmness into her voice that she didn't entirely feel. "Mr. Wilson was just sharing news from Portland."

"So I heard," Boone replied, his tone carefully neutral. His eyes scanned the classroom, noting the children's excited faces. "I received a letter from Campbell as well."

"Isn't it wonderful news?" Rose ventured. "Trinity Station will finally have proper religious services."

A muscle tightened in Boone's jaw. "Campbell can bring whoever he wishes. The company owns the camp."

"Will you attend the services, Mr. McAlister?" Timmy asked innocently.

The directness of the child's question seemed to catch Boone off guard.

"I have camp responsibilities," he replied stiffly. "Mr. Campbell and his minister are welcome, but I won't be attending."

The finality in his tone created an awkward silence. Rose quickly turned the children's attention back to their lessons.

"Let's continue with our practice, children. Older students, please help the younger ones with their letter formations while I speak with Mr. McAlister."

She stepped outside, closing the door gently behind her. Boone had moved several paces away, staring toward the river with tense shoulders.

"Mr. McAlister," she began carefully, "I understand this news might be... difficult for you."

He turned to face her, his expression closed. "It's not difficult, Miss Bellamy. It's simply irrelevant to me. Trinity Station needs lumber contracts and safe working conditions. Whether it needs sermons and hymn-singing is another matter entirely."

"Spiritual guidance is important to many in the camp," Rose countered gently. "I've heard several mothers express a desire for proper religious instruction for their children."

"And they'll have it," Boone replied, his voice tight. "The schoolhouse can be used for services, if you agree. What more do you want from me?"

The question hung between them, layered with meanings beyond its surface simplicity. What indeed did she want from this complicated man who had lost not only his wife but also his faith?

"Nothing you're not willing to give," Rose finally answered. "I only hope you might reconsider joining the community in worship. It can bring comfort and—"

"I don't need comfort," Boone cut her off, his tone final. "And I don't need a minister to tell me about God's plan. I've seen enough of that plan firsthand." Without another word, he turned and walked away.

Through the window, she could see the children watching with curious eyes. Taking a deep breath, Rose composed herself and returned to the classroom, forcing a smile she didn't entirely feel.

"Now, where were we? Ah yes, letter practice for the youngest, and the older students were working on multiplication tables." She clapped her hands briskly. "Let's continue, shall we?"

Despite her outward focus on the lessons, Rose's thoughts kept returning to Boone's reaction. Just when they had begun to establish a professional understanding, the mention of religious matters had rebuilt the wall between them higher than before.

Chapter 14

The cookhouse hummed with conversation, most of it centered on the news from Portland. The long tables were filled with families and single men alike, all sharing the excitement of the upcoming visit from both the company agent and the minister.

"We could form a proper choir," Martha Riley was saying enthusiastically to the women gathered at her table. "I sang in our church back east, before we came to Oregon."

"My Tom has a fine bass voice, though you'd never know it to hear him speak," Beth Abernathy added with a fond smile toward her husband. "He's been missing proper worship services."

"The children could present a Bible recitation," Silvia Cooper suggested. "My twins learned the Twenty-Third Psalm from their grandmother before we left Missouri."

Rose listened to the conversations around her as she ate, touched by the community's evident hunger for spiritual connection. Trinity Station was evolving before her eyes from a rough logging camp into a more cohesive settlement, one where education and faith had a place alongside the practical business of timber.

Her gaze drifted to the head of the table, where Boone sat with Simon and two other senior lumberjacks, discussing work matters with focused intensity. His plate was half-empty, his attention clearly on logging rather than the enthusiastic chatter about church services.

"Rose," William Wilson addressed her from across the table, "do you think the schoolhouse could be arranged properly for Sunday services? We'd need some way to make it feel more... churchlike."

All eyes turned to her expectantly. Rose considered the question, aware that somewhere in the room, Boone was likely listening.

"I believe so," she replied. "Perhaps fashion a simple lectern for Reverend Parker. Fresh pine boughs might add a pleasant scent and appropriate decoration."

"What about those who don't fit?" John Riley asked practically. "The schoolhouse isn't large enough for the entire camp."

"We could hold services outside instead of in the schoolhouse while the weather is decent," Ethel suggested from where she supervised the serving table.

The logistics discussion continued, growing more animated as everyone contributed ideas. Rose noticed that the conversation at Boone's table had ceased, the men now listening to the church planning despite their foreman's evident disinterest.

"We should ask Mr. McAlister if it's acceptable to use the schoolhouse this way," one of the mothers said, glancing nervously toward Boone's table.

A brief awkward silence fell as attention shifted to Boone. He looked up from his plate, aware of the many eyes upon him.

"The schoolhouse can be used for services, though it might make more sense to hold services here in the cookhouse where there is plenty of room," he stated flatly. "Campbell will make the final arrangements when he arrives."

"Thank you, Mr. McAlister," William said, relief evident in his voice. "It will mean a great deal to many of us."

Boone acknowledged this with a curt nod before abruptly rising from his seat. "If you'll excuse me, I have work to do." Without another word, he strode from the cookhouse, the door closing firmly behind him.

Conversation resumed after a moment, though somewhat subdued by Boone's departure. Rose caught Ethel's eye across the room, and the older woman made her way over, refilling coffee cups as she came.

"Don't take it personally," Ethel murmured when she reached Rose's side.

"Has he always been so opposed to religious matters?" Rose asked.

Ethel shook her head, leaning closer under the pretense of wiping the table. "Before Mary died, they attended services whenever a traveling preacher came through. The last service he attended was Mary's funeral. He hasn't set foot in anything resembling a church service since."

This revelation deepened Rose's understanding of Boone's resistance. It wasn't just abstract theological disagreement; church services were inextricably linked in his mind with the most painful day of his life.

"I should have been more sensitive to that connection," Rose said, regret coloring her voice.

"You couldn't have known," Ethel reassured her. "The camp needs spiritual leadership, whether Boone recognizes it or not."

Through the window, Rose could see Boone's tall figure walking toward his cabin, shoulders hunched slightly against the evening chill or perhaps against memories he couldn't escape. The lantern in his hand cast elongated shadows across the muddy path, emphasizing his solitary figure against the darkening camp.

"Yes," Rose agreed softly, still watching him. "They do."

***

The small room Rose occupied at the cookhouse was quiet save for the scratching of her pen across paper. By the light of a single oil lamp, she recorded the day's events in her journal, a habit she had maintained since her parents' and grandparents' deaths. Writing helped her process her thoughts, especially on days as complicated as this one had been.

I find myself in an unusual position, she wrote, having gained Mr. McAlister's professional respect through my medical treatment of Jed, while simultaneously widening the spiritual gulf between us with the news of Reverend Parker's impending arrival. We seem destined to take one step forward and two steps back in our attempts at understanding one another.

She paused, tapping the pencil thoughtfully against her chin before continuing.

I cannot deny that I am excited about proper church services coming to Trinity Station. My soul has hungered for worship and the fellowship of believers. Yet, I find myself dreading the effect this development will have on Mr. McAlister, who associates the church so strongly with his grief for Mary.

How strange that a man can possess so many admirable qualities, leadership, responsibility, and courage, even a gruff kind of compassion for those under his care, while simultaneously rejecting the very Source from which such virtues flow. It troubles me.

Rose set down her pencil, reflecting on the complex man who had become such a central figure in her thoughts. Boone McAlister was unlike anyone she had ever known. His strength was evident not just in his physical presence, but in the way he shouldered the tremendous responsibilities of the camp. His intelligence showed in his strategic management of the logging operation and his quick grasp of situations. Even his stubbornness reflected a kind of integrity. Once committed to a course, he followed it with unwavering determination.

Yet, his rejection of faith created a fundamental divide between them that seemed impossible to bridge. Rose believed deeply that true peace could only come through reconciliation with God, something Boone actively resisted.

And why did this trouble her so much? She had encountered nonbelievers before without feeling this persistent concern for their spiritual welfare. What was it about Boone specifically that occupied her thoughts and prayers with such regularity?

The question made her uncomfortable, hinting at feelings she wasn't prepared to examine too closely. She reached for her pencil again, determined to redirect her thoughts.

The children are progressing well in their studies; she wrote. *Even Peter Cooper, who struggled initially, is gaining confidence with his letters. Timmy Wilson shows a remarkable aptitude for mathematics that should be further encouraged. Hannah Abernathy—*

A knock at the door interrupted her writing. Rose closed her journal and moved to answer it, expecting Ethel with a last cup of tea before retiring.

Instead, Ethel stood there with worried eyes, a shawl thrown hastily over her nightdress. "It's Jed," she said without preamble. "He's developed a fever in the last hour. I thought you should know immediately."

Rose was already reaching for her satchel. "How high is the fever?"

"High enough that he's confused and restless."

"Infection," Rose murmured, dread settling in her stomach.

Chapter 15

Rose burst through the door to find Jed thrashing weakly on his cot, his face flushed with fever. Clara stood beside him, pressing a damp cloth to his forehead with worried eyes.

"When did the fever start?" Rose asked, immediately setting her satchel on the small table and opening it.

"About an hour ago," Clara replied, stepping back to give Rose room. "He was fine at supper, even laughed at my jokes. Then he started complaining his leg was burning something fierce. The fever came on after that."

Rose placed her palm against Jed's forehead, feeling the alarming heat radiating from his skin. His eyes fluttered open at her touch, unfocused and glassy.

"Miss Bellamy?" he mumbled, his voice hoarse. "The trees... they're falling..."

"I'm here, Jed," she assured him, already unwrapping the bandages around his leg. "You're safe. The trees can't hurt you."

The wound beneath the bandages confirmed her fears. Angry red streaks extended outward from the gash, and the flesh around the stitches was swollen and hot to the touch. A discharge seeped from the edges of the wound.

"Infection has set in," she told Clara quietly.

"How bad is it?" Ethel asked.

"Bad enough," Rose answered truthfully. "I need clean water, as hot as you can make it, Ethel. And more lanterns, I need to see clearly."

As Ethel hurried to comply, Rose began sorting through her medicinal herbs. "Echinacea for the infection, goldenseal to clean the wound, willow bark for the fever," she murmured, selecting packets with practiced hands. "And yarrow... we'll need plenty of yarrow."

Clara watched her preparations with apprehension. "Will he lose the leg?"

The question hung in the air, heavy with implications. A lumberjack without a leg was a man without a livelihood in this unforgiving territory.

"Not if I can help it," Rose replied with more confidence than she felt. "But we must work quickly. This type of infection can spread rapidly."

Jed moaned, his head rolling from side to side as fever dreams took hold. "Watch out... the widow-maker... run!"

"Should I fetch Mr. McAlister?" Clara asked, wringing her hands. "He'll want to know."

Rose nodded without looking up from her preparations. "Yes, please. And ask him to bring the whiskey."

As Clara slipped out, Ethel returned with steaming water and additional lanterns, which she arranged to cast maximum light on Jed's leg. The increased illumination revealed the full extent of the infection, much worse than Rose had initially thought.

"Lord help us," Ethel prayed.

Rose rolled up her sleeves and washed her hands in the hot water. "We need to reopen part of the wound to drain the infection," she explained, selecting a small, sharp knife from her satchel. "And remove the stitches that are causing problems."

"You've done this before?" Ethel asked, her voice tight with concern.

"Yes," Rose replied, though the truth was more nuanced. She had assisted her grandmother with similar procedures but had never taken the lead herself in a case this severe. Still, she knew the principles and had no choice but to act.

"Hold his shoulders, please," she instructed Ethel. "This will be painful, even in his fevered state."

Ethel positioned herself at the head of the cot, placing her strong hands firmly on Jed's shoulders. Rose took a deep breath, then carefully went to work.

Jed jerked and cried out as she made a small incision to release the built-up infection. Discharge immediately began to seep out, confirming that her decision had been correct.

"That's good," she murmured, pressing gently around the wound to encourage more drainage. "The poison needs to come out."

Heavy footsteps approached, and Rose glanced up to see Boone filling the doorway, his expression dark with concern, the bottle of whiskey in his hand. Simon stood behind him.

"How bad?" Boone asked without preamble, moving into the small room and assessing the situation with a quick glance.

"Infection has taken hold," Rose answered, continuing her work without pausing. "I'm draining the wound now, then we'll clean it thoroughly and apply fresh poultices."

Boone's eyes moved from Jed's flushed face to the infected leg, his jaw tightening. "Will he make it?"

The blunt question reflected the frontier reality they inhabited. No room for false reassurances when lives hung in the balance.

"If the infection hasn't reached his blood, I believe he will survive," Rose replied honestly. "But it will be a difficult night."

Boone nodded once, making a swift decision. "I'll stay and help. Simon, organize the cutting crews in the morning without me. Clara, go home and get some rest. We may need your help tomorrow."

Simon departed with a worried backward glance, taking his wife with him. Ethel remained at Jed's shoulders, murmuring soothing words as Rose continued draining the infection.

"What do you need me to do?" Boone asked, rolling up his sleeves.

"Hold his leg steady while I remove these stitches," Rose directed. "They're trapping infection inside."

Without hesitation, Boone moved to the foot of the cot and grasped Jed's leg firmly but gently. His large hands dwarfed the young lumberjack's calf, but his touch was controlled and precise.

Rose used small scissors to snip the compromised stitches, carefully removing each one while allowing more infection to drain. Jed whimpered and twisted, but Boone's grip kept the leg immobile enough for her to work quickly and safely.

"Easy, boy," Boone murmured, his voice gruff but surprisingly gentle.

The unexpected tenderness in his tone caught Rose's attention, revealing a glimpse of the man beneath the stern foreman's exterior. She continued her work with renewed focus, cleaning the wound with whiskey-soaked cloths that made Jed cry out despite his semi-conscious state.

"Now the goldenseal wash," she announced, reaching for a bowl of yellowish liquid she had prepared. "It will help clean the wound from within."

Boone watched her methodical movements with intense concentration. "Your grandmother taught you this?"

Rose nodded, carefully applying the herbal solution to the open wound. "My mother and grandmother both were known throughout our county for their healing skills. People came from miles around when doctors couldn't help them or weren't available."

"And they trusted them? With herbs instead of proper medicine?" Boone asked, a hint of skepticism in his voice despite the evidence of Rose's competence before him.

"Proper medicine often fails where nature's remedies succeed," Rose replied without defensiveness. "God has provided healing plants for every ailment, if we know how to use them."

She expected Boone to bristle at her mention of God, but he remained focused on Jed, his expression troubled.

"I've seen many men die from infections like this," he said. "Out here, a small injury can kill if it festers."

"Which is why we must be vigilant," Rose agreed, preparing a poultice of mashed echinacea root and yarrow. "This will draw out more infection and help his body fight what's already spread."

Ethel, who had been silent during their exchange, spoke up. "I'll brew willow bark tea for his fever. And perhaps something stronger to help him sleep."

Rose nodded gratefully. "Valerian root would be best if you have any in the kitchen stores."

"I believe I do," Ethel replied, gently releasing Jed's shoulders now that the most painful part of the procedure was complete. She patted his cheek maternally before leaving to prepare the tea.

Alone with Boone, Rose became acutely aware of the small room's intimacy. They worked in close proximity, their hands occasionally brushing as they tended to Jed. The lantern light cast shadows across Boone's face, emphasizing the strong lines of his jaw and the worry etched around his eyes.

"You don't have to stay," Rose told him as she carefully applied the poultice to Jed's leg. "I can manage with Ethel's help."

"I'm responsible for every man in this camp," Boone replied firmly. "Jed was injured while working under my direction. I won't leave him now."

The statement revealed more about Boone's character than perhaps he intended. His sense of responsibility ran deep, possibly too deep, taking on the weight of events beyond his control.

Rose secured the poultice with fresh bandages, her movements efficient but gentle. "There. Now we wait and watch. The fever is the greatest concern now."

Boone dragged a wooden stool next to the cot. "Then we wait together."

Jed stirred restlessly, mumbling incoherent phrases. Rose dipped a cloth in cool water and placed it on his forehead, trying to bring down the dangerous fever.

"Tell me about Jed," she said, hoping the conversation might distract Boone from his evident worry. "I know so little about him, except that he seems quite young for such dangerous work."

Boone leaned forward, elbows on his knees, watching Jed's flushed face. "He's twenty-four. Came from a failed homestead north of here. His father died of pneumonia three winters ago, leaving Jed to support his mother and two sisters. They moved to Oregon City, where the sisters could find work as seamstresses."

"And Jed came here," Rose finished, understanding dawning. "To send money home to them."

Boone nodded. "He's a good worker. Quick to learn, not reckless like some young men. This accident wasn't his fault."

Rose refreshed the cool cloth on Jed's forehead, noting with concern that his fever hadn't abated.

"His mother and sisters must be worried about him," she mused.

"They don't know yet," Boone replied. "Mail travels slow out here. By the time they hear of this, he'll either be recovering or..." He left the grim alternative unspoken.

"He will recover," Rose stated with quiet conviction. "We must have faith."

Boone's expression hardened slightly at her words, but he didn't argue. Instead, he reached for the whiskey bottle and took a small swig before offering it to Rose.

She shook her head. "No, thank you."

"Not for drinking," he clarified. "For your hands."

Rose accepted the bottle and poured a small amount of whiskey over her hands, rubbing them together to distribute it. The sharp scent filled the small room, mingling with the herbal aromas of her medicines.

Ethel returned with a steaming cup of tea. "Willow bark and valerian with a touch of honey," she said, placing it on the small table.

"Perfect," Rose acknowledged. "Thank you, Ethel."

"Can I do anything else?" the cook asked, her eyes moving between Jed's restless form and Boone's tense figure.

"Perhaps some coffee for Mr. McAlister and myself, if you wouldn't mind," Rose suggested. "It will be a long night."

After Ethel departed again, Rose carefully lifted Jed's head, trying to get him to drink some of the tea. Most of it dribbled down his chin as he turned away, lost in fever dreams.

"Come now, Jed," she coaxed gently. "This will help you feel better."

"Here," Boone said, moving to help. He supported Jed's shoulders, holding him at a better angle. "Try again."

With Boone's assistance, Rose managed to get several swallows of the medicinal tea into Jed. The young man coughed and spluttered but kept the liquid down.

"Good," Rose murmured, returning the cup to the table.

Boone carefully lowered Jed back to the pillow, his movements surprisingly tender for such a large man, and he returned to his stool

"You've done this before," Rose observed. "Watched over the sick."

"Logging camps breed accidents and illness. I've sat with many men through difficult nights."

Jed's fever remained. His thrashing became more violent, his delirious mumblings more frantic. "The trees! They're falling! Run, Mary! RUN!"

Boone flinched visibly at the name, his knuckles whitening as he gripped his knees. Rose glanced at him with concern.

"We need to cool him down," she said. "His fever is too high."

"Cold water from the spring," Boone suggested, already rising. "I'll fetch it."

While he was gone, Rose prayed over Jed, her lips moving in wordless supplication as she continued applying cool cloths to his forehead. The infection was fighting back hard, and she feared it might already have reached his bloodstream.

"Lord, guide my hands," she whispered. "Give me wisdom to heal this young man."

Boone returned quickly with a bucket of icy spring water. "Do you think this will help?"

"Yes. We'll soak cloths in it and place them on his pulse points—wrists, neck, and behind his knees. The cold will help lower his core temperature."

They worked together, Boone wringing out the cloths in the frigid water and handing them to Rose, who positioned them strategically on Jed's burning body. The young man shivered violently but didn't wake from his fevered state.

"We need to reduce his coverings. Can you help me sit him up to remove his shirt completely?"

Boone nodded, moving to support Jed's weight while Rose carefully pulled the sweat-soaked shirt over his head. The young lumberjack's chest was flushed with fever, his breathing rapid and shallow.

"Now just a light sheet," Rose instructed as he laid him back down. "We need the cool air to reach his skin."

As they worked, Jed began muttering again, his words more distinct in his delirium. "Not my fault... the ground gave way... didn't see it coming... Mary said watch the widow-makers...the log rolled."

Boone went completely still, his face draining of color. "What did he say?"

Rose paused in her ministrations, looking up at Boone with concern. "He's delirious. Fever patients often mix up memories and dreams."

"No," Boone insisted, his voice tight. "What did he say about Mary?"

Before Rose could answer, Jed continued his fevered ramblings. "Mary warned us... look up... always look up in the forest... widow-makers..."

Boone sank back onto his stool, his expression stricken. "He must be mixing up the accidents," he said hoarsely. "His and... Mary's."

Understanding dawned on Rose. "He knew Mary well?"

Boone nodded, his eyes never leaving Jed's face. "Yes. He was there that day. One of the youngest on the crew. He helped... helped move the fallen tree branch off... He's been haunted since that day."

The revelation added new layers to the intensity of Boone's concern for Jed. This wasn't just about responsibility for a worker. It was about a shared trauma, a connection to the most painful day of Boone's life.

"I'm sorry," Rose said softly. "I didn't realize."

Boone's jaw tightened as he visibly gathered his composure. "It doesn't matter now. What matters is keeping him alive."

They returned to their task, applying cool compresses and monitoring Jed's breathing. Ethel brought coffee and then retired for the night, leaving Rose and Boone alone with their critically ill patient.

The hours crept by slowly. Midnight came, marked only by the distant call of an owl and the occasional pop of the lantern wick. Jed's fever remained dangerously high, his brief periods of lucidity becoming less frequent. Rose refreshed the herbal poultice on his leg, noting with growing concern that the red streaks had continued to spread upward toward his thigh.

"This isn't working," she admitted, her voice tight with worry. "The infection is advancing despite our efforts."

Boone's expression was grim in the lantern light. "What else can we try?"

Rose hesitated, considering possibilities she had only heard about but never attempted. "There's one remedy my grandmother used for the most severe infections. A poultice of crushed garlic and honey. It's potent and painful, but it might be our last resort."

"Do you have the ingredients?"

"Ethel will have garlic in the kitchen. And honey."

"I'll find them," Boone said, rising immediately.

While he was gone, Rose checked Jed's pulse, rapid and thready. His breathing had become more labored.

"Please, Lord," she prayed aloud, clutching Jed's limp hand. "Spare this, young man. Guide my hands to heal him. Give me wisdom beyond my experience."

She was still praying when Boone returned with several garlic bulbs and a small crock of honey. He paused in the doorway, watching her bent head and moving lips with an unreadable expression.

"Your prayers won't stop blood poisoning," he said as he approached, his voice tight with suppressed emotion. "Only action will save him now."

Rose accepted the ingredients without responding to his challenge. She quickly crushed the garlic cloves in a small wooden bowl, mixing them with honey to form a thick paste. The pungent aroma filled the small room.

"This will be extremely painful," she warned as she prepared to apply the mixture directly to the open wound. "You will need to hold him down."

Boone positioned himself at Jed's shoulders, his strong hands ready to restrain the young man. "Do what you must."

Rose took a deep breath, said a silent prayer, and applied the garlic-honey mixture directly to the infected wound.

The effect was immediate. Jed's entire body went rigid with pain, a hoarse scream tearing from his throat despite his weakened state. Boone held him firmly as he began thrashing, speaking low, calming words that seemed to penetrate even Jed's fever-addled mind.

"Easy, boy. Easy. It's for your own good. Miss Bellamy is helping you. Hold still now."

Rose worked quickly, covering the entire wound with the potent mixture before wrapping it with fresh bandages. By the time she finished, Jed was exhausted from the pain and still burning with fever.

"Now we wait again," she said, washing her hands in the remaining cool water. "If this doesn't turn the tide..."

She didn't finish the sentence. She didn't need to. Boone's grim expression showed he understood the stakes perfectly.

The night deepened around them. Rose prepared more willow bark tea, managing to get a few swallows into Jed's parched mouth. Boone maintained his vigil, occasionally rising to pace the small confines of the room before returning to his post on the stool.

"You should rest," he told Rose around two in the morning. "I can watch him."

Rose shook her head, stifling a yawn. "I need to monitor the progression of the infection. If it worsens, we may need to take more drastic measures."

"More drastic than garlic and honey that made him scream?" Boone asked.

"If the infection reaches higher..." Rose's voice trailed off.

Boone's expression darkened. "It won't come to that."

"I pray you're right."

"Prayer," Boone repeated, a bitter edge to his voice. "Always prayer."

Rose looked up from checking Jed's pulse, meeting Boone's stormy gaze directly. "Yes, Mr. McAlister. Prayer. Along with every medical skill I possess and every herb known to help. I use all the tools available to me, including faith."

"Faith didn't save my Mary," he said.

The raw pain in his voice stilled Rose's immediate defense. This wasn't an abstract theological argument anymore, it was the cry of a wounded soul.

"I'm sorry about Mary," she said. "Truly. I can't imagine your loss."

Boone looked away, but not before Rose glimpsed the sheen of moisture in his eyes. "She was everything good in my life," he said, his voice so low Rose had to lean forward to hear him. "Everything kind and gentle and hopeful. And none of it, not her goodness, not her faith, and not her prayers, protected her from a falling tree branch that crushed the life out of her while I watched, unable to help her in time."

The confession hung in the air between them, more revealing than anything Boone had shared before. Rose felt the weight of his grief as if it were a physical presence in the small room.

"Sometimes I think we aren't meant to understand why terrible things happen," she ventured carefully. "Only to trust that God's mercy extends beyond what we can see."

"Mercy," Boone repeated, the word flat and lifeless on his lips. "Where was mercy when Mary was dying? Where is mercy for Jed now, burning with fever because he was doing the job I asked of him?"

"Perhaps mercy is sitting right here with us," Rose suggested gently. "In the knowledge of herbs that might save him, in the clean water to cool his fever, in the hands that tend his wounds. Perhaps mercy doesn't always prevent suffering but walks alongside us through it."

Boone looked at her then, really looked at her, as if seeing beyond the schoolteacher-healer to the woman beneath. Something shifted in his expression, not agreement, not yet conviction, but perhaps the smallest crack in the wall of his resistance.

"Check his fever again," he said, changing the subject. "His thrashing has lessened."

Rose touched Jed's forehead, then his neck, a cautious hope rising within her. "It may be breaking," she said. "He feels slightly cooler."

Together, they checked the bandaged leg. Rose unwrapped it carefully, both of them holding their breath as the final layer came away.

The angry red streaks had not advanced. The skin around the wound, while still inflamed, had lost the frightening darkness.

"The infection is receding," Rose breathed, relief washing through her. "Thank God."

For once, Boone didn't bristle at her gratitude to the divine. His focus remained on Jed, whose breathing had become more regular, his rest more natural than the fever-induced stupor of hours before.

"He'll live?" Boone asked, needing the confirmation.

"I believe so," Rose nodded. "If the improvement continues." She prepared a fresh poultice, gentler this time, with healing comfrey added to the mix and reapplied it to Jed's wound.

As she worked, Rose realized how exhausted she was. Her hands trembled slightly, and the room seemed to tilt momentarily before she steadied herself against the edge of the cot.

"You need rest," Boone observed, his tone brooking no argument. "You've been at this for hours."

"So have you," Rose countered.

"I'm accustomed to long nights," Boone replied.

Rose finished bandaging Jed's leg and straightened, wincing as her back protested the movement after hours bent over her patient. "I should stay with him."

"I'll watch him," Boone insisted. "You can make a pallet there in the corner to lie on with these extra blankets. If his condition changes, I'll wake you immediately."

The idea was inviting to Rose's exhausted body.

"We should take shifts," she suggested. "You need rest too."

"I'll wake you in an hour to trade places," Boone agreed.

Too tired to argue further, Rose nodded and moved to the corner and arranged the blankets on the floor. She didn't even remove her shoes, simply stretching out and pulling a thin blanket over herself.

"Promise you'll wake me if he worsens," she murmured, her eyes already closing.

"I promise," Boone replied, his deep voice the last thing she heard before sleep claimed her.

Chapter 16

Rose dreamed of forests and falling trees, of running through endless pines, searching for someone just beyond her reach. A voice called her name, urgent and familiar, pulling her from the depths of slumber.

"Miss Bellamy. Rose."

She opened her eyes to find Boone leaning over her, his face taut with concern. For a moment, disorientation clouded her mind. The unfamiliar room. The lantern's low light. Boone's proximity.

"Is it Jed?" she asked, instantly alert despite her confusion. "Has he worsened?"

"No," Boone assured her quickly. "Quite the opposite. His fever has broken. He's sleeping normally now."

Relief flooded through her as the night's events came rushing back. She sat up, noting the gray predawn light seeping around the edges of the curtained window. "How long have I slept?"

"About four hours," Boone admitted. "I didn't have the heart to wake you."

Rose pushed aside the blanket, surprised and touched by his consideration. "You should have. You need rest too."

"I've managed," he replied, though the shadows under his eyes spoke otherwise. "But I'll take that rest now, if you're ready to watch him."

Rose moved to check on Jed, finding exactly what Boone had reported. The young lumberjack's skin was cool and slightly damp, the characteristic aftermath of a broken fever. His breathing was deep and even, his rest peaceful rather than the tortured unconsciousness of earlier.

"The worst has passed," she confirmed, relief evident in her voice. "Thank God."

This time, Boone made a small sound that might have been agreement. "Your herbs worked," he acknowledged. "That garlic mixture saved his leg, possibly his life."

"Knowledge passed down through generations," Rose said. "My grandmother would be pleased to see her teachings put to such good use."

Boone nodded, already moving toward the pallet on the floor Rose had vacated. "Wake me if you need anything. Or if his condition changes."

"I will," she promised.

As Boone stretched his tall frame out on the pallet, Rose busied herself tidying the medical supplies and preparing fresh tea for when Jed awakened. The danger had passed, but he would need careful nursing and nourishment to regain his strength.

Ethel appeared at the door shortly after, her anxious expression giving way to relief when she saw Jed sleeping peacefully.

"He made it through," she whispered. "When I left you last night, I feared the worst."

"It was a close thing," Rose admitted. "But the infection is receding now. He'll need good food when he wakes... broth to start, then heartier fare as he recovers strength."

Ethel nodded, her gaze moving to Boone's sleeping form. "Never thought I'd see the day... him sleeping while others work."

"He kept watch all night," Rose defended him quietly.

"And how did the two of you manage, alone, all those hours?"

Rose felt her cheeks warm at the implication. "We tended to Jed. There was nothing improper."

"I didn't suggest there was," Ethel replied with a small smile. "But shared trials have a way of bringing people closer, whether they intend it or not."

"He's a complicated man," she said. "But beneath the gruffness, there's goodness and care."

"I've always thought so," Ethel agreed. "Just needed the right person to draw it out again."

Jed stirred on his cot, his eyes fluttering open. He looked around in confusion before focusing on Rose.

"Miss Bellamy?" he croaked, his voice dry from fever. "What happened?"

"You developed an infection in your leg, Jed. A bad one. But you're past the worst of it now."

Jed frowned, trying to piece together his scattered memories. "I remember pain... and voices. Someone holding me down."

"That was Mr. McAlister," Rose explained, glancing toward the sleeping foreman. "He stayed with you all night."

Jed followed her gaze, surprise registering on his pale face. "The boss did that? For me?"

"He cares about his men more than he might show," Rose said.

Ethel appeared with a cup of broth. "Think you can manage some of this, young man? You need to rebuild your strength."

With Rose's help, Jed managed to sit up slightly and sip at the warm broth. His hands trembled with weakness, but his eyes were clear and alert, the best possible sign after such a dangerous fever.

"I thought I was dying," he admitted between sips. "I remember dreams of falling trees and running."

"Fever dreams," Rose assured him. "Common during serious illness. But you've come through it now."

"Thanks to you," Jed said, gratitude plain in his voice.

"God guided my hands," Rose replied sincerely. "I merely applied what knowledge my grandmother and mother taught me."

Jed nodded. He finished half the broth before leaning back, exhausted by even this small effort.

"Rest now," Rose instructed, taking the cup. "Your body needs sleep to heal."

As Jed drifted back to sleep, Rose moved to the small window and carefully parted the curtain. Dawn had broken fully over Trinity Station, painting the camp in a soft morning light. Men moved toward the cutting sites, women carried water from the spring, and children played in the cleared spaces between buildings. Life continued its steady rhythm, unaware of the drama that had unfolded through the night in the small room off the cookhouse.

She turned back to find Boone awake, watching her from the pallet on the floor. His eyes, still heavy with sleep, but held none of their usual guardedness.

"He woke briefly," Rose reported. "Took some broth and seems lucid. The infection is definitely receding."

Boone nodded, sitting up and running a hand through his disheveled hair. "You should be proud. Not many would have known what to do."

"I'm just grateful he responded to the treatment. Another hour or two might have made all the difference."

They looked at each other across the small room, the shared experience of the night creating an unexpected intimacy. Rose was acutely aware of Boone's rumpled appearance—shirt half-untucked, and hair tousled. He looked less like the stern camp foreman and simply more like a man, tired, concerned, and relieved.

"You should get some proper rest," she suggested. "In your own bed. I can manage Jed now that the crisis has passed."

Boone stood, stretching his tall frame. "I should check on the cutting crews first. Simon will have organized them, but they'll be wondering what happened."

"Tell them Jed will recover," Rose said. "It will ease their minds."

"I will." He hesitated, seeming on the verge of saying something more, but ultimately deciding against it. "I'll check back later today."

Rose nodded, watching as he straightened his clothing and made himself presentable for the camp's eyes. The armor of the foreman sliding back into place, piece by piece.

Before leaving, Boone paused at Jed's bedside, looking down at the sleeping young man with relief mixed with something deeper, more personal.

"Thank you," he said finally, turning back to Rose. "For saving him."

"You're welcome."

Boone nodded once and departed, leaving Rose with their sleeping patient and the lingering sense that something fundamental had changed during the night's vigil. The wall between them hadn't fallen, but a door had appeared—small, perhaps, but undeniably present where before there had been only solid stone.

As she began preparing fresh bandages for Jed's next dressing change, Rose smiled softly to herself. God worked in mysterious ways indeed, using even a dangerous infection to open pathways between hearts that seemed permanently closed to one another.

"Thank You, Lord," she whispered.

Outside, the camp continued its morning rhythm, unaware that in a small room off the cookhouse, healing had begun for more than just an injured lumberjack's leg.

Chapter 17

Five days had passed since the peak of Jed's infection, each day bringing visible improvement to his wound. Clara and Ethel took turns tending to Jed during school hours, checking his condition and providing companionship to lift his spirits. Rose devoted her time before and after school, as well as her lunch breaks, to tending to his needs. Throughout the nights, Boone remained vigilant, sleeping on the pallet in Jed's room and rousing himself regularly to monitor his friend's progress.

"Am I fit enough for visitors yet, Miss Bellamy?" Jed asked, adjusting himself against the extra pillows Ethel had provided to prop him up.

"Perhaps tomorrow," Rose replied, checking his bandaged leg. "Your body still needs rest to heal properly."

"Rest is all I've been doing," Jed grumbled good-naturedly. "A man could go mad staring at these four walls day after day."

Rose smiled, understanding his restlessness. "Would you like something to read? I could bring a few more books."

"That's kind of you, but…" Jed hesitated, color rising in his pale cheeks. "Truth is, I struggle with reading."

Rose kept her expression neutral, recognizing his embarrassment. "Then perhaps I could read to you for a while each day after school."

Hope brightened his features. "You wouldn't mind?"

"Not at all. It would be my pleasure."

As Rose gathered her medical supplies, Jed cleared his throat. "Miss Bellamy, have you seen Boone today?"

"Not yet," she answered.

"It's just…" Jed looked down at his hands. "He's seemed… different. Distracted-like. Not himself the past couple of evenings."

Rose had noticed the same change. After their night-long vigil during Jed's crisis, Boone had seemed withdrawn. The connection that had formed between them during those tense hours seemed to have evaporated in the light of day.

"I'm sure he's just pre-occupied with work," she offered, though she suspected there was more to his withdrawal.

"Maybe so," Jed agreed without conviction. "But Boone's always busy with work."

Rose nodded thoughtfully. "Perhaps when he comes to be with you this evening. Encourage him to talk."

"I'll do my best, Miss Bellamy."

Leaving Jed with a fresh cup of medicinal tea, Rose stepped into the cookhouse, where Ethel was supervising dinner preparations. The scent of baking bread filled the air as kitchen helpers peeled potatoes and chopped carrots for the evening stew.

"How's our patient?" Ethel asked, wiping flour-covered hands on her apron.

"Improving steadily," Rose replied. "He's eager for company, which is a good sign."

"I'll send Simon in later with a game of checkers," Ethel decided. "That should cheer the boy up."

Rose glanced at the windows, noting the late afternoon light. "I should freshen up before dinner."

"Speaking of dinner," Ethel said, lowering her voice as she moved closer to Rose, "have you seen Mr. McAlister today?"

Rose shook her head. "Not since early this morning when I checked on Jed."

Ethel's expression grew troubled. "He didn't come for breakfast this morning. Nor dinner last night. Simon took food to his cabin, but said Boone barely acknowledged him."

"Is he ill?"

"Not in body," Ethel replied cryptically. "It's the date that's troubling him, I expect."

"The date?"

Ethel glanced around to ensure no one else was listening. "It's been exactly one year today since Mary died."

Understanding dawned, and with it, a wave of compassion. "Oh."

"Few remember the exact day," Ethel said. "Life moves forward, especially in a place like this. But for Boone..." She sighed heavily. "Time hasn't healed that wound much at all."

Rose thought of how Boone had stayed awake all night to help her save Jed, how he had finally spoken of Mary a little, and how something had shifted between them in those quiet hours of shared purpose and concern. Now he had withdrawn again.

"He shouldn't be alone today," Rose decided aloud. "Not with such memories."

Ethel studied her with knowing eyes. "No, he shouldn't. But he won't thank anyone for intruding on his private grieving."

"Even so," Rose said, gathering her resolve, "no one should bear such pain in isolation."

Ethel's expression softened. "You care for him."

It wasn't a question, and Rose didn't deny it. "I care for everyone at Trinity Station," she said instead.

"Mmm." Ethel's noncommittal hum spoke volumes. "Well, if you're determined to check on him, he's not in his cabin. Simon checked a few moments ago."

"Where would he go?"

Ethel hesitated, then spoke deliberately. "There's a small clearing beyond his cabin, through the pines. A place where he might seek privacy today."

Rose nodded. "I'll go and find him and make sure he is okay."

"Go carefully, Rose. Grief makes even the kindest men unpredictable."

With a reassuring smile, Rose departed, her mind already preparing for what might be a difficult encounter. The afternoon had cooled considerably, prompting her to wrap her shawl more tightly around her shoulders as she walked. Trinity Station bustled with activity around her, men returning from the cutting sites, women tending to evening chores, and children playing. Normal, everyday life continued its rhythm while one man marked the most painful anniversary imaginable.

Boone's cabin stood apart from the main cluster of buildings, situated at the edge of camp where the forest encroached on the cleared land. It was larger than the other dwellings but still modest, built of sturdy logs with a small covered porch. Rose had never visited it before. She had never had a reason to approach his private domain.

As Ethel predicted, there was no sign of him. The cabin windows were dark, the door firmly closed. Rose hesitated, uncertain whether to knock or continue her search elsewhere. A narrow path leading into the trees behind the cabin caught her attention, barely discernible, but clearly used regularly by someone.

Rose gathered her skirts and stepped onto the path. It wound through towering pines, their fragrance intensifying as she moved deeper into the forest. Pine needles cushioned her footsteps, creating a hushed quality to the woods that felt almost sacred.

After several minutes of walking, the trees thinned, revealing a small clearing. Rose stopped at the edge, her breath catching at the sight before her.

In the center of the clearing stood a collection of wooden crosses, a cemetery carved from the wilderness. Six crosses in all, each bearing a carved name. And kneeling before one of them, his broad shoulders bent in an attitude of grief, was Boone.

He had placed fresh wildflowers at the base of the cross, delicate white blooms that stood out against the dark earth. His head was bowed, his hands clasped tightly, as if in prayer.

She hesitated, uncertain of her intrusion. This moment was so intensely private that witnessing it felt almost like a violation. She took a step backward, intending to leave him to his solitude, but a dry pine cone cracked beneath her foot.

Boone's head lifted immediately, his body tensing with alert wariness as he turned toward the sound. When he saw Rose standing at the edge of the clearing, his expression registered surprise, then resignation.

"Miss Bellamy," he acknowledged, his voice rough.

"I apologize for disturbing you," Rose said. "I can go."

Boone gazed at her for a long moment, then shook his head slightly. "You've come all this way."

Taking this as permission, Rose approached. The cross before which Boone knelt bore the simple inscription "Mary McAlister," carved with evident care into the wood. The other crosses bore different names and dates, all within the past few years.

"The men who didn't make it," Boone explained, noting her glance at the other markers.

Rose nodded, standing a respectful distance from him. "May I?" she asked, gesturing to a spot nearby.

Boone nodded once, and Rose carefully arranged her skirts to sit on the ground.

"How did you find me?" he asked after a moment.

"Ethel mentioned you might be here," Rose answered honestly. "People are concerned about you."

A muscle ticked in Boone's jaw. "I'm not in need of concern."

"Perhaps not. But concern comes nonetheless when people care about you."

This simple truth seemed to unsettle him. He looked away, back to the cross bearing Mary's name.

"One year," he said. "Exactly one year ago today."

Rose remained silent, letting him speak at his own pace.

"Time should dull it," he continued, running a hand through his hair in a gesture of agitation. "That's what everyone says. Time heals all wounds. But it doesn't feel dulled at all today. It feels... raw. As if it just happened."

"Grief doesn't follow rules or timetables," Rose offered gently. "Some days are harder than others."

Boone picked up a pine cone, turning it absently in his large hands. "Saving Jed brought it all back. Why could I help save him, but not her? Why did his infection respond to treatment, while she..." His voice faltered. "While she died in my arms?"

The pain in his voice was so acute that Rose felt it physically, like a pressure in her chest. "I can't answer that," she admitted. "I wish I could."

Boone stared at the pine cone in his hands. "I've never told anyone exactly what happened that day. Not the entire truth of it."

Rose remained still, hardly daring to breathe, aware that he was on the verge of sharing something he had kept locked inside for a year of solitary grief.

"She came to bring me a midday snack," he began, his voice taking on the distant quality of someone recounting a nightmare. "I was overseeing a cutting site about a quarter-mile from here. We were taking down some massive old-growth pines—dangerous work. I had told her many times not to come to active cutting sites, but she..." A ghost of a smile touched his lips briefly. "She was stubborn. Said a man needed to eat properly to keep his strength up."

He crushed the pine cone in his hand; the segments breaking apart between his fingers.

"I heard it before I saw it. That distinctive crack. Like a rifle shot, but deeper, more solid. Every lumberjack knows that sound. A tree or large branch falling." His breathing had quickened, his eyes fixed unseeing on the crushed pine cone. "I looked up and saw it—a massive limb breaking free. A widow-maker, we call them."

Rose knew the term, a deadly danger in logging loose branches that could fall without warning, killing or maiming those below.

"Mary was walking toward me, carrying a basket. Smiling. She didn't see it coming. I tried to run and shout... it all happened so fast." Boone's voice grew hoarse. "The branch came down... and she was under it."

He squeezed his eyes shut, reliving the moment in all its horror.

"Jed was beside me… he saw it happen as well. We both ran. He got to her first. We moved the branch… it took six men Rose to lift it off her. There was so much blood, but she was still alive. Still conscious." His voice broke on the word. "I picked her up and started running toward camp. Holding her against my chest, telling her to hold on, that she'd be fine, that she just needed to keep breathing."

Rose felt tears prickling her eyes but held them back, knowing Boone needed steady strength, not emotion.

"She knew she was dying," he continued. "She looked up at me with those clear eyes of hers and said she couldn't feel her legs anymore. That it felt cold. I ran faster, praying the whole time… begging God not to take her, promising anything if He'd just let her live."

He looked up at Rose then, his eyes reflecting a pain so deep it seemed bottomless.

"She wasn't afraid," he said, wonder mixing with the grief in his voice. "Even as she was slipping away in my arms, she wasn't afraid. She asked me not to be angry with God. That she'd be waiting for me. That she loved me and always would."

A single tear escaped despite Rose's efforts, trailing down her cheek.

"She died before I reached the camp," Boone concluded, his voice flat with exhaustion. "Her last words were about faith, and she said we'd meet again. And I…" He swallowed hard. "I've failed her, Rose. Because I can't believe anymore. I can't believe in a God who would take her that way, who would ignore my prayers as I ran with her dying in my arms."

Rose took a deep breath, choosing her words with care. "You haven't failed her, Boone. Questioning faith in the face of tragedy isn't failure—it's human."

He looked up at her use of his first name, but didn't comment on it.

"When my parents and grandparents died," Rose continued, "I was angry, too. They all fell ill with diphtheria within days of each other. I prayed constantly, used every herbal remedy my grandmother and mother had taught me. None of it made any difference. They still died, all four of them, leaving me alone."

"I questioned everything I had been taught to believe," Rose continued. "I railed at God, demanded answers, bargained, and pleaded. The silence in response was deafening."

"How did you find your way back to faith?" Boone asked, genuine curiosity in his voice.

Rose considered the question carefully. "It wasn't one moment, but many small ones. A neighbor bringing food when I couldn't think of cooking. The beauty of spring flowers blooming despite my grief. The realization that the skills my mother and grandmother taught me could still help others, even if I couldn't save them."

She met his gaze directly. "I don't claim to understand divine purpose or the reasons behind suffering. I only know that I found peace in accepting that some questions don't have answers we can comprehend."

Boone's expression remained skeptical, but there was a hunger in his eyes, a yearning to believe that Rose understood completely.

"Tell me about her," Rose requested softly. "Not how she died, but how she lived. Who was Mary?"

The question seemed to catch Boone off guard. He looked back at the cross bearing his wife's name, and for a moment, Rose feared she had pushed too far. But then he spoke, his voice warming with memory.

"She loved to laugh," he began. "Not delicate, ladylike laughter, but real, full-throated joy. It used to scandalize some of the more proper women when we lived in Salem before coming here." A small, genuine smile touched his lips. "She was educated... much more than me. She could quote Shakespeare and the Bible with equal ease. But she was practical, too. She could shoot better than most men and wasn't afraid to get her hands dirty."

As he spoke, his posture gradually relaxed, the rigid set of his shoulders easing.

"Trinity Station was her dream as much as mine," he continued. "When the timber company offered me the position, she was the one who pushed me to accept. She had this vision of building not just a logging camp but a real community. A school was her idea from the beginning."

He picked up another pine cone, this time turning it gently in his hands rather than crushing it.

"She collected these," he said, holding it up. "Said each one was unique, like a person. She'd point out the different patterns, the variations in color and shape. I never saw any of that until she showed me."

The tenderness in his voice as he spoke of these small details revealed the depth of their bond and the magnitude of his loss.

"She must have been a remarkable person," Rose said.

"She was." Boone placed the pine cone carefully beside the wildflowers at the base of the cross. "The kind of person who made everyone around her better somehow. She made me a better man."

"Remembering the joy, not just the loss, that's part of healing Boone. Honoring who she was by carrying forward is what I imagine she would want for you."

Boone glanced at her sharply. "Is that why you've pursued the school so determinedly? Because it was her dream?"

"Partly," Rose acknowledged. "When I learned it was her vision, continuing it seemed a way to honor her memory. But teaching has always been my calling. I came here to teach Boone. Learning about

Mary's dreams and her vision... well, it only seemed proper to follow her wishes."

"She would have liked you," Boone said. "Your determination. Your willingness to fight for what you believe in. She never backed down from a challenge either."

"I wish I could have known her."

"So do I," Boone replied simply.

They sat in companionable stillness; the light beginning to fade as afternoon yielded to early evening. In the distance, a woodpecker tapped rhythmically against a tree trunk, the sound echoing through the clearing.

"That night with Jed," Boone said abruptly, "watching you fight for his life with such certainty, such purpose... it reminded me of who I used to be. Before."

Rose waited, sensing there was more he needed to say.

"Your faith isn't just words," he continued. "It's in your actions, your skills, the way you care for people. It's..." He struggled to articulate what he meant. "It's real in a way I can see and understand, even when I don't share it."

"Faith without works is dead," Rose quoted softly. "Belief means little if it doesn't change how we live."

Boone nodded slowly. "That's what Mary believed, too. She never just talked about her faith, she lived it."

A light breeze stirred the clearing, carrying the scent of pine and wildflowers. The white blooms at the base of Mary's cross trembled slightly.

"What are they?" Rose asked, gesturing to the flowers.

"White trillium," Boone answered. "They were Mary's favorites. She said they were like tiny stars fallen to earth."

"They're beautiful."

Boone gazed at the small flowers, his expression softening. "They only bloom for a short time. I thought I'd missed them this year, but I found these on the north slope this morning. Like they were waiting for today."

The image struck Rose as poignantly apt—nature itself offering a small gift of remembrance.

"Boone," she ventured carefully, "what is your greatest fear now? After a year of grief?"

He didn't answer immediately, and Rose worried she had pushed too far. But when he spoke, his voice was steady, though quiet.

"That opening my heart again... to faith, to community, to any-one—means risking this kind of loss a second time." He gestured to the cross, to the physical representation of his grief. "I'm not sure if I would survive it."

The raw honesty of his admission hung in the air between them.

"Isn't a life without connection already a kind of loss?" Rose asked gently.

"Perhaps," he acknowledged. "But it's a predictable one. Controllable."

"And is that what Mary would want for you? A controlled, predictable life without risk or connection?"

A flash of pain crossed his features. "No. She'd hate that. She always pushed me to take chances, to reach out, and to build relationships."

"Her spirit lives on in this place," Rose said, gesturing to encompass not just the clearing but Trinity Station beyond. "In the school, and in the community, she helped envision. In the memories you carry."

The light had faded significantly as they talked, the clearing now bathed in the soft gray of approaching dusk. Boone finally stood, brushing pine needles from his trousers. After a moment's hesitation, he extended his hand to help Rose up.

She accepted, feeling the strength in his calloused palm as he pulled her easily to her feet. The brief contact sent a warmth through her that had nothing to do with physical exertion.

"Thank you," Boone said. "For finding me. For not letting me be alone with this today."

"You're never truly alone. Even when it feels that way."

He didn't agree or disagree, but his expression had lost some of its earlier bleakness. "We should head back before it gets too dark to see the path."

They walked together through the trees. Boone moved with the confidence of someone who had traveled this route countless times, guiding Rose around obstacles with occasional murmured warnings about roots or low branches.

As they neared the edge of the forest, Boone paused beside a small clump of trillium growing in the shelter of a massive pine. He bent down and carefully picked a few of the delicate white flowers.

"Mary used to say that beautiful things should be shared," he said, holding the trillium out to Rose. "That keeping beauty to yourself diminished it somehow."

Rose accepted the flowers, understanding the significance of this small gesture. Boone sharing not just a bloom but a piece of Mary's wisdom, a fragment of the memories he had kept closely guarded for so long.

"Thank you. I'll press these in my Bible to preserve them."

Boone nodded, and they continued walking toward the lights of Trinity Station. They didn't speak again until they reached the clearing where his cabin stood.

"Will you join us for dinner at the cookhouse?" Rose asked as they approached the main camp. "Ethel was concerned when you missed meals."

Boone considered the invitation. "I suppose I should make an appearance. The camp notices when its foreman disappears."

"They care about you," Rose corrected gently. "Not just as their foreman, but as a person."

"I'll come shortly," he agreed. "After I've washed up."

They parted at the crossroads between his cabin and the path leading to the cookhouse. Rose clutching the delicate white trillium carefully in her hand as she walked toward the welcoming glow of lanterns and the murmur of voices gathering for the evening meal.

As she reached the cookhouse steps, she glanced back once. Boone stood watching her from the distance, a solitary figure no longer bent by grief but standing straight, his gaze fixed on her with an expression she couldn't quite interpret. He raised his hand in acknowledgment when he saw her turn, and she returned the gesture before entering the cookhouse.

Ethel spotted her immediately, hurrying toward her, concern etched on her face. "There you are! I was beginning to worry. Did you find him?"

"Yes," Rose replied simply, not wanting to betray Boone's confidence by sharing the details of their conversation.

Ethel's sharp eyes noted the trillium in Rose's hand. "Mary's favorites," she said.

Rose nodded. "He'll be joining us for dinner shortly."

A look of profound relief crossed Ethel's weathered features. "That's more than I hoped for, truth be told. I knew this day would be dark for him."

"He's carrying a heavy burden," Rose said. "But perhaps he's beginning to see he doesn't have to carry it alone."

Ethel studied her with knowing eyes. "You're good for him, Rose Bellamy. Whether he realizes it yet or not."

Rose felt her cheeks warm. "We're friends, that's all. He's still devoted to Mary's memory."

"As he should be," Ethel agreed. "But the heart is a remarkably expansive thing. It can hold past loves and present connections without diminishing either."

The cookhouse door opened, and conversations hushed momentarily as Boone entered. He had indeed washed up, changing into a clean shirt, his hair still damp at the temples. His gaze immediately sought Rose across the room, a brief nod acknowledging her presence before he moved to take his usual place at the head of the table with Simon and the other senior lumberjacks.

Conversations resumed, though Rose noticed many curious glances directed Boone's way.

"He'll be all right now," Ethel predicted in a low voice meant only for Rose's ears.

"He has a long way to go," Rose cautioned. "Grief like that doesn't heal in a single conversation."

"No," Ethel agreed. "But every journey begins with a single step."

As the evening meal progressed, Rose occasionally caught Boone looking her way, his expression thoughtful. Once, when their eyes met directly, he didn't look away as he might have done in the past. Instead, he held her gaze steadily across the crowded room.

Later, as she prepared for bed in her small room off the cookhouse, Rose pressed the trillium between the pages of her Bible, specifically in Psalm 34:18: "The Lord is close to the brokenhearted and saves those who are crushed in spirit."

A fitting verse, she thought, for a man beginning the long journey from crushing grief toward healing and, perhaps, eventually, toward faith once more.

"Guide him, Lord," she prayed softly, closing the Bible with the trillium safely preserved within its pages. "And guide me in helping him find his way back to You."

Chapter 18

"Class, who can tell me what this plant is used for?" Rose held up a sprig of dried yarrow, turning it so all the children could see the feathery leaves and tiny clustered flowers.

Eliza's hand shot into the air, waving enthusiastically. "It stops bleeding, Miss Bellamy!"

"That's correct, Eliza," Rose smiled. "Yarrow is excellent for stopping bleeding and helping wounds heal. Native Americans called it 'life medicine' because it's so useful."

Peter Cooper raised his hand next. "My ma puts it in tea when we get fevers."

"Your mother is very wise," Rose acknowledged. "Yarrow tea can indeed help reduce fevers by making you sweat out the sickness."

She turned to the slate board behind her and wrote "YARROW" in neat letters. "Now, who can think of another healing plant we've discussed?"

Several hands rose, but Rose's attention shifted as the schoolhouse door opened. Boone ducked through the entrance. The children turned at the sound, a ripple of whispers spreading through the room.

"Mr. McAlister," Rose greeted him, her pulse quickening. "Welcome."

Boone removed his hat, holding it awkwardly in his large hands. "Miss Bellamy. I hope I'm not interrupting."

"Not at all. We're just finishing our lesson on medicinal plants." Rose turned to the children. "As you know, Mr. McAlister promised to speak with us today about logging safety."

Timmy straightened in his seat. "Are you going to tell us about widow-makers, sir?"

A flash of pain crossed Boone's features, but he quickly masked it. "Yes, Timmy."

Rose gestured toward the front of the classroom. "Children, let's welcome Mr. McAlister properly."

The students chorused, "Good morning, Mr. McAlister," with varying degrees of enthusiasm and volume.

"Morning," Boone replied gruffly, moving to the front. He stood stiffly beside Rose's desk, clearly uncomfortable with eighteen pairs of eyes fixed on him.

"Perhaps you could start by explaining what a logging operation entails," Rose suggested gently, recognizing his discomfort.

Boone cleared his throat. "Right. Well..." He glanced around the classroom, his eyes settling on the boys in the back row. "Logging is dangerous work. Not a game. Every day, men risk their lives to harvest timber that builds homes and businesses throughout Oregon Territory and beyond."

As he spoke about his work, his voice gradually lost its stiffness. Rose observed with interest how his posture relaxed, his gestures becoming more natural as he explained the complex process of felling trees safely.

"The most important rule in the forest is awareness," Boone continued, his deep voice filling the small schoolhouse. "You must always know what's around you, above you, and even below you. The ground can give way unexpectedly, especially after heavy rains."

He moved to the slate board, picking up a piece of chalk with hands that dwarfed it. With surprising precision, he sketched a simple tree.

"When we cut a tree, we don't just start chopping anywhere," he explained, adding marks to his drawing. "We make a face cut on the side where we want the tree to fall. Then a back cut on the opposite side, leaving what we call a hinge."

The children leaned forward, captivated by his explanation. Even James Riley, who typically struggled to focus, watched with rapt attention.

"The hinge controls the fall," Boone continued, drawing lines to demonstrate. "Get it wrong, and the tree could barber-chair—split upward—or fall in an unexpected direction."

Hannah raised her small hand. "What's a widow-maker, Mr. McAlister?"

Rose watched Boone's face carefully, seeing the momentary tightening around his eyes before he answered.

"A widow-maker is a broken limb, a branch, or even a leaning tree that gets caught in the canopy of other trees," he replied steadily. "It can hang there, seemingly secure, then fall without warning when the wind blows or another tree is cut nearby." His voice remained professional, betraying none of the personal anguish Rose knew he associated with that term.

"My pa says to always look up in the forest," Samuel added.

Boone nodded approvingly. "Your pa is a wise man, Samuel. Looking up can save your life."

Rose watched with growing admiration as Boone fielded questions from the children, his natural aptitude for teaching becoming increasingly evident. He simplified complex concepts without talking down to them, used analogies they could understand, and maintained their attention with occasional anecdotes about logging mishaps that had important lessons but weren't too frightening.

"What's the biggest tree you ever cut down?" Timmy asked eagerly.

A genuine smile crossed Boone's face, transforming his features. "About four miles north of here, we felled a Douglas fir so wide that eight men holding hands couldn't reach around its base. Took nearly two days just to cut through it."

The children gasped appreciatively.

"Did it make a big crash when it came down?" Peter asked, eyes wide.

"Like thunder right next to your ear," Boone confirmed. "Shook the ground so hard we felt it in our boots."

As the children peppered him with more questions, Rose observed how different Boone looked when speaking about his profession with obvious passion. The stern, closed-off foreman had been replaced by an animated, knowledgeable man who clearly took pride in his work and understood how to convey that knowledge to others.

When Abby Wilson asked a question about identifying different types of trees, Boone pulled a small leather pouch from his pocket and emptied its contents onto Rose's desk. Various pieces of bark, pine needles, and small pine cones tumbled out.

"The forest speaks its own language," he explained, picking up a piece of reddish bark. "This is from a cedar. Smell it."

He passed the bark around, each child taking a careful sniff.

"The scent is as distinctive as its appearance," Boone continued. "Once you learn to recognize these signs and scents, the forest becomes easier to understand and navigate."

Rose was touched by this unexpected side of him. The man who collected bark samples in a pouch was not the same grim, closed-off figure who had initially resisted her presence at Trinity Station. This was a glimpse of the Boone who existed before grief hardened him, the man who noticed and appreciated the unique patterns of pine cones Mary had pointed out to him.

When he finished his presentation, the children applauded enthusiastically. Boone looked surprised and somewhat embarrassed by their response.

"Thank you, Mr. McAlister," Rose said. "That was incredibly informative."

Catching sight of the sun's position through the window, she turned back to the class with a smile. "It seems we've reached our lunch hour. Please enjoy your break and be back in sixty minutes. We'll resume our exploration of arithmetic, then."

The children gathered their lunch pails, filing out of the schoolhouse with excited chatter about Boone's presentation. Several boys stopped to thank him personally, clearly impressed by his knowledge.

When the last child had departed, Rose turned to Boone. "You have a natural gift for teaching. I don't think I've ever seen James Riley sit still for that long."

Boone looked genuinely surprised. "I've never done something like that before."

"You wouldn't know it," Rose replied, organizing papers on her desk. "You explained complex concepts clearly and kept their attention completely. That's no small feat with eighteen children of varying ages."

"It was... easier than I expected," Boone admitted, collecting the tree samples and returning them to his pouch. "They ask good questions."

"They're curious about everything, especially the work their fathers do. I appreciate how you handled Hannah's question about widow-makers. I know that must have been difficult."

Boone's expression sobered. "Children deserve honest answers, even about difficult subjects." He paused, then added, "Mary believed that too."

"I was planning to check on Jed during the lunch break," she said. "Would you like to come along?"

Boone nodded. "I'd like that."

They left the schoolhouse together, walking side by side along the path toward the cookhouse. The camp was alive with midday activity: men carrying supplies, women tending to chores, and children playing.

"The school is coming along well," Boone remarked. "Even Simon mentioned his daughter is reading now."

"Clara's mentioned that too," Rose smiled. "Penny is particularly quick with letters. She's already helping the younger children."

They walked in silence for a few paces before Boone spoke again, his voice more hesitant. "I didn't think the school would matter so much. To the camp, I mean."

Rose waited, sensing he had more to say.

"When you first arrived," he continued, "I saw education as a luxury we couldn't afford. But I was wrong. The children needed more. They need..." he gestured vaguely, searching for the right word, "...hope. A future beyond timber."

"I agree. Education opens doors to possibilities they might never otherwise imagine."

"Mary understood that," Boone said. "She saw what Trinity Station could become, not just what it was."

Rose chose her next words carefully.

"She must have been very forward-thinking."

"She was," Boone confirmed. "Always looking ahead and planning improvements. The school was just the beginning of what she envisioned."

"What else did she hope for?" Rose asked.

Boone's pace slowed as he considered the question. "A proper church building. A small general store so families wouldn't have to travel so far for supplies. A permanent doctor someday."

"All excellent goals," Rose said. "Trinity Station has good bones for a permanent settlement."

"You think so?" Boone asked, genuine interest in his voice.

"Absolutely. The location is strategic, access to water, good timber, and a defensible position. With the right investment and vision, it could grow beyond just a logging camp."

"Joshua Campbell wants to expand operations here. Build more permanent structures, possibly even bringing in families specifically for support roles rather than just logging."

"That would be wonderful," Rose said enthusiastically. "More children for the school, more diverse skills in the community."

They reached the cookhouse, where delicious aromas wafted through the open windows. Inside, several lumberjacks were already eating their midday meal at the long tables.

"Rose, Boone!" Ethel called when she spotted them. "Jed's been asking for you both. Clara's sitting with him now."

"How is he doing?" Rose asked.

"Restless," Ethel replied. "He's tired of being confined to bed. Getting downright cantankerous about it."

"Sounds like he's recovering well, then," Boone commented with a hint of dry humor.

Ethel chuckled. "Indeed. I'll bring food for all of you shortly."

Rose and Boone made their way to the small room where Jed was. They found Clara reading aloud from one of Rose's books, while Jed listened from his propped-up position on the cot.

"Visitors!" Jed exclaimed with obvious relief when they entered. "Please tell me you've come to rescue me from this prison."

Clara closed the book with a mock-stern expression. "That's gratitude for you. I read until my throat's dry, and you call it imprisonment."

"The reading's fine, Mrs. Blackwood," Jed assured her quickly. "It's being stuck in this bed that's driving me mad."

"The price of healing properly," Rose replied, moving to his bedside. "Let me check your leg, and then we can discuss when you might be allowed up for short periods."

Clara stood, surrendering her chair to Rose. "I'll help Ethel with the food. Simon said to tell you he'll stop by after the afternoon cutting, Jed."

After Clara departed, Rose carefully removed the bandages from Jed's leg. The wound looked remarkably better. The angry redness had subsided, and healthy pink tissue was forming along the healing edges.

"Good progress," Rose noted approvingly. "The infection is completely gone."

"So I can get up?" Jed asked hopefully.

"Short periods," Rose decided. "With help. No weight on this leg yet."

Jed's face fell. "But—"

"No arguments," Boone interrupted firmly, taking the chair Clara had vacated. "You'll follow Miss Bellamy's instructions exactly. That's an order."

Despite his stern tone, Rose caught the underlying concern in Boone's voice. Jed must have heard it too, because he nodded without further protest.

"Yes, sir. I just..." Jed's voice trailed off, his expression frustrated.

"You're worried about your position," Boone stated matter-of-factly. "About your mother and sisters, depending on your wages."

Jed nodded, not meeting Boone's eyes. "Can't earn my keep lying in bed."

"Your position is secure," Boone assured him. "Your pay continues while you recover."

Jed looked up, surprise and relief washing over his features. "The company agreed to that?"

"I didn't ask the company," Boone replied simply. "It's the right thing to do."

Rose, applying a fresh poultice to Jed's wound, glanced up at this statement.

"I don't know what to say," Jed murmured.

"Say you'll follow Miss Bellamy's instructions so you can return to work properly healed," Boone replied.

"I will," Jed promised fervently. "Every word."

Rose began re-wrapping the leg with clean bandages. "The worst is behind you now, Jed. Your body is healing well. Another couple of days of rest getting up with assistance and no pressure on this leg, then perhaps light duties that don't require standing."

"I could sharpen tools," Jed suggested eagerly. "Or help with planning the next cutting areas."

Boone nodded approvingly. "Good thinking. We'll find ways to keep you useful without risking that leg."

The door opened, and Ethel entered, carrying a large tray laden with bowls of steaming stew, thick slices of bread, and mugs of hot coffee.

"Midday meal for our patient and his visitors," she announced, setting the tray on the small table. "Venison stew today... William Wilson brought down a buck yesterday."

"It smells wonderful," Rose said, completing Jed's bandaging and washing her hands in the basin by the bed.

Ethel helped arrange the meal so Jed could eat comfortably from his position on the cot. "Need anything else before I head back to the kitchen?"

"This is perfect, Mrs. Hayes," Jed replied appreciatively. "Thank you."

After Ethel departed, the three of them ate. Jed's appetite had returned with a vengeance, a good sign of healing.

"Mr. McAlister gave us a lesson on logging safety today in school," Rose told Jed. "The children were fascinated."

"Were they now?" Jed grinned, glancing at Boone. "I'd have paid good money to see that."

"It wasn't anything special," Boone muttered.

"He drew diagrams on the slate board," Rose continued, "and brought samples of different tree barks for the children to examine. Even James Riley paid attention the entire time."

"That restless boy?" Jed laughed. "Now I really am impressed."

Boone changed the subject. "Tell me what's happening with the old Henderson tract. Simon mentioned they have started clearing it? Tell me your thoughts on this."

As the men discussed logging matters, Rose observed their interaction with interest. Boone treated Jed with a respectful camaraderie that spoke of genuine regard, not merely a foreman's obligation to an injured worker. For his part, Jed clearly admired Boone, looking to him for approval and advice.

The conversation eventually turned to the impending visit from Joshua Campbell and Reverend Parker.

"Simon says they're expected within the week," Jed remarked. "Folks are excited about having proper church services."

"Yes, many in the camp have missed regular worship," Boone said.

"Will you attend the services, boss?" Jed asked.

The directness of the question hung in the air. Rose held her breath, knowing how difficult this topic remained for Boone.

"I haven't decided," Boone replied after a pause. "But I won't stand in the way of others attending."

It wasn't a yes, but neither was it the firm refusal he'd given earlier. Rose counted this as progress, however small.

"Rose, are you looking forward to proper services?" Jed asked.

"Very much," she admitted. "I've missed the fellowship of worship, and the singing of hymns together."

"You have a pleasant voice," Boone remarked unexpectedly. "I've heard you singing with the children in your classroom and to yourself when you think no one is listening."

Rose felt a flush of warmth at realizing he had noticed such a detail. "My mother always sang while working. I suppose I inherited the habit."

"My Mary sang too," Boone said, surprising both Rose and Jed with the casual mention. "Not always on key, mind you, but with great enthusiasm."

Jed chuckled. "I remember. She'd sing while gathering kindling, loud enough to scare off any wildlife within a hundred yards."

Instead of withdrawing from these memories, Boone actually smiled. "She claimed the bears were music critics and deserved to be warned off."

Rose watched this exchange with quiet amazement. Boone was speaking of Mary not with raw grief but with fond remembrance. Their conversation in the forest clearing had perhaps helped him begin to separate memories of Mary's life from the tragedy of her death.

"Speaking of wildlife," Jed said, "did you tell Miss Bellamy about the time Mary tried to rescue that bear cub?"

Boone grimaced. "That was a disaster waiting to happen."

"What happened?" Rose asked.

"We had just finished building this cookhouse and Mary heard whimpering in the underbrush out back and found what she thought was an abandoned bear cub."

"Her heart was bigger than her common sense sometimes," Jed added fondly.

"She carried this squalling cub into camp, determined to nurse it back to health," Boone continued. "I was checking the river landing when Simon came running, shouting that my wife had lost her mind and was asking Ethel for milk for a bear."

Rose laughed, picturing the scene. "What did you do?"

"What could I do? By the time I got back, she had the thing wrapped in her shawl like a baby," Boone said, shaking his head at the memory. "I had to explain that mama bear was likely nearby and extremely unhappy about her missing cub."

"The look on her face when she realized," Jed chuckled. "Half horrified, half disappointed she couldn't keep her new pet."

"We returned the cub to where she found it and watched from a distance," Boone said. "Sure enough, mama bear showed up within the hour to collect her offspring."

"Mary insisted on naming it anyway," Jed added. "Called it, Theodore, and made us all promise not to cut trees in that section of forest for a month to give them peace."

"And did you?" Rose asked.

"Of course," Boone replied, as if it were obvious. "You didn't argue with Mary when she had her mind set on something."

The affection in his voice was palpable. Rose glanced at Jed, who was watching Boone with a mixture of surprise and approval. They were both witnessing something remarkable—Boone reclaiming happy memories of Mary without being overwhelmed by grief.

"She sounds like a force of nature," Rose said.

"She was," Boone agreed. "Completely unpredictable and impossible to resist."

The conversation flowed easily after that, with Jed sharing more stories of the early days at Trinity Station. Rose listened intently, building a clearer picture of the community before she arrived and of the woman whose vision for the camp had inspired her own efforts.

Eventually, Jed began to show signs of tiring, his responses becoming shorter as his energy waned.

"We should let you rest," Rose said, noticing his drooping eyelids. "Remember, the more you rest now, the faster you'll heal."

"I'm not tired," Jed protested weakly, even as he stifled a yawn.

"Of course not," Boone replied dryly. "You're just resting your eyes while talking to us."

Jed grinned sheepishly. "Maybe I am a bit worn out."

Rose collected the empty dishes onto the tray. "Sleep is medicine too. I'll check on you again this evening after school."

"I'll be back this evening as well," Boone promised, standing to leave. "We can discuss the Henderson tract cutting plan, then."

Jed's face brightened at the prospect of being involved in work matters despite his confinement. "I'd like that, boss."

Rose and Boone took their leave, carrying the tray back into the main cookhouse. Ethel was busy directing the cleanup from the midday meal, her helpers washing dishes and wiping down tables.

"How's our patient?" she asked as they approached.

"Healing well," Rose replied. "But tiring easily, as expected."

"That's normal," Ethel nodded. "His body's working hard to mend itself."

"I should head back to the schoolhouse. The children will be returning soon," Rose said.

"I'll walk with you," Boone offered. "I'm heading to the north cutting site, and it's on the way."

They bid Ethel goodbye and stepped outside into the crisp afternoon air. The sky was clear, a vivid blue that made the green of the surrounding pines seem even more intense.

"Jed looks much better today," Boone remarked as they walked.

"He's young and strong," Rose replied. "And he has excellent motivation to recover quickly."

"His family," Boone nodded. "He takes that responsibility seriously."

"As do you," Rose observed. "Your concern for him goes beyond duty as his foreman."

"I suppose it does. The men in this camp, they're more than just workers. After a while, they became..." He hesitated, seemingly uncomfortable with sentiment.

"Family?" Rose suggested.

"Of a sort," Boone acknowledged. "Men who risk their lives together develop a bond. It's not something easily explained."

"It doesn't need an explanation," Rose assured him. "I see it in how you interact with them, how they look to you for more than just work orders."

"Thank you," he said abruptly.

"For what?"

"For saving Jed's life," Boone replied. "And for... the other day. For finding me in the cemetery."

Rose glanced at him, noting the effort it took for him to express gratitude about something so personal. "You're welcome. Though I believe Jed would have fought his way through, regardless. He's remarkably resilient."

"Even so, your knowledge made the difference." Boone paused, then added quietly, "And the other day... speaking about Mary, about what happened... I haven't been able to do that with anyone else."

"Sometimes an outside perspective helps. Someone who didn't know her but can still honor her memory."

Boone nodded slowly. "Perhaps. Whatever the reason, it felt... necessary. Overdue."

They had reached the schoolhouse. Children were already gathering outside, playing in small groups, as they waited for afternoon lessons to begin.

"Will you speak to the class again sometime?" Rose asked. "Perhaps about other aspects of logging or frontier life? The children were truly engaged."

Boone looked surprised but not displeased by the invitation. "I could, yes. If you think it would be helpful."

"Very helpful," Rose assured him. "And perhaps others could too. William might explain blacksmithing, and Simon or Tom could demonstrate woodworking."

"Bringing practical knowledge into their book learning," Boone mused. "Mary would have approved."

"I believe she would."

The children had noticed their approach and were watching curiously, perhaps wondering if Boone would join their lessons again.

"I should return to work," Boone said, seeming suddenly aware of the many eyes upon them.

"Of course," Rose agreed. "Thank you again for speaking to the children. It meant a great deal to them."

Boone nodded, replacing his hat. "Good afternoon, Miss Bellamy."

"Good afternoon, Mr. McAlister."

As Boone walked away, several of the boys ran up to Rose, full of questions about when he might return to teach them more about logging. She smiled at their enthusiasm, promising that Mr. McAlister would likely visit their classroom again soon.

Gathering her students, Rose led them back into the schoolhouse for the afternoon session. As she began the arithmetic lesson, her mind kept returning to the changes she'd witnessed in Boone over the past few days. The wall around his heart hadn't collapsed, but definite cracks had appeared, small openings through which glimpses of his true nature could be seen.

It was progress, Rose thought as she directed the children to their slate work. Slow progress, like Jed's healing leg. Painful at times, requiring patience and careful attention, but moving steadily in the right direction.

Chapter 19

Rose ushered the excited children toward the forest's edge, each of them clutching small buckets or baskets. The morning air carried a crisp pine scent as eighteen pairs of eager feet trampled the undergrowth at the forest boundary.

"Remember what we discussed in class?" Rose called over the chatter. "Stay within sight at all times and touch nothing unless I've identified it first."

"Yes, Miss Bellamy," the children chorused, their faces bright with anticipation of this unusual school day.

Eliza hurried to Rose's side, her long braids bouncing. "Will we find yarrow like you showed us yesterday?"

"I hope so," Rose replied, smiling at the girl's enthusiasm. "It often grows near the edges of clearings. Keep your eyes open for the feathery leaves and flower clusters."

"I want to find something to help my pa's cough," Samuel announced, swinging his wooden bucket determinedly.

"Then we'll look for horehound or coltsfoot," Rose promised. "Both excellent for coughs."

Rose had planned this expedition carefully, selecting an area of forest close enough to camp for safety but diverse enough to showcase the botanical treasures she wanted to introduce. After days of teaching from dried specimens and drawings, she'd decided her students needed hands-on experience with living plants in their natural environment.

"Miss Bellamy, look!" Hannah pointed excitedly toward a splash of purple blooms partially hidden beneath a fallen log.

Rose knelt beside the discovery. "Excellent spotting, Hannah. These are violets. They're not just pretty. Their leaves and flowers can be used to ease headaches and soothe coughs."

The children crowded around, their faces revealing varying degrees of skepticism that something so delicate could have healing properties.

"Can we pick some?" Timmy asked.

"Just a few leaves and perhaps two blossoms from each plant," Rose instructed. "We must never take too much. God provides these healing plants, but we must harvest respectfully."

As the children carefully selected leaves under Rose's guidance, a twig snapped sharply in the forest behind them. Rose turned quickly, instinctively stepping between the sound and her students.

Boone emerged from between two towering pines, his axe resting casually on one shoulder. His expression shifted from surprise to concern as he registered the scene before him.

"Miss Bellamy," he called, striding toward them. "What are you doing out here with the children?"

Rose met his approach with a calm smile, despite her racing heart at his sudden appearance. "Good morning, Mr. McAlister. We're having a practical lesson on medicinal plants. The children are learning to identify useful herbs in their natural setting."

Boone scanned the group of children, who had paused in their collecting to watch this unexpected interaction. His brows drew together. "This far from camp? Without an escort?"

"We're barely two hundred yards from the school," Rose pointed out reasonably. "Still within hearing distance of the camp."

"That doesn't mean it's safe," Boone countered, lowering his voice so only she could hear. "These woods harbor mountain lions, bears, and occasionally less savory human visitors. A lone woman with eighteen children would make an easy target."

Rose hadn't considered the possibility of human threats, and her expression must have revealed this oversight. Boone's stern look softened marginally.

"I assume you have a route planned for your... botanical expedition?" he asked.

"Yes. I intended to follow the stream for a short distance, then loop back through that clearing." She pointed to a sunny spot visible through the trees.

Boone studied the proposed path, then rested his axe against a tree trunk. "I'll accompany you."

It wasn't a request, but Rose didn't object. His concern was legitimate, and his knowledge would certainly enhance their safety. Besides, the children were watching this exchange with undisguised interest, and she didn't wish to undermine his authority in their eyes.

"We would welcome your expertise, Mr. McAlister," she said sincerely.

He nodded once. "Children," he addressed the group, "stay close together. No wandering off alone, regardless of what interesting plant you spot. Understood?"

"Yes, Mr. McAlister," they responded, some looking intimidated, others clearly excited by his addition to their expedition.

Rose resumed their lesson, leading the group toward a cluster of plants growing near the base of a large oak. "This is plantain," she explained, kneeling beside the broad-leaved plant. "Not the fruit that grows in tropical climates, but an extremely useful herb that often grows right under our feet."

"It looks like a weed," James observed skeptically.

"Many of God's most useful creations appear humble," Rose replied. "This 'weed' can draw poison from insect stings, stop bleeding, and heal wounds."

"My grandmother used to chew it and put it on bee stings," Boone added unexpectedly. "Works faster than anything from a doctor's bag."

The children turned to him with newfound interest, and Rose gave him an appreciative smile. "Exactly right, Mr. McAlister. Would you like to show them how to identify it properly?"

Boone hesitated only momentarily before kneeling beside Rose. He gently turned over one of the leaves. "See these strong fibers running through it?" he demonstrated, pulling slightly, so the children could see the strings that remained intact. "That's one way to know true plantain. And the seed stalks grow straight up, like tiny spears."

Rose watched with pleasure as the children gathered closer to observe Boone's demonstration. He handled the plant with surprising gentleness, his large hands deftly pointing out the identifying characteristics with an assurance that spoke of practical experience.

"Let's continue along the stream," Rose suggested after they had collected a small amount of plantain. "Water-loving plants often have different properties."

As they walked, Boone naturally took position at the rear of the group while Rose led the way, creating a protective formation that kept the children safe between them. Rose appreciated his silent vigilance, his eyes constantly scanning their surroundings as they moved deeper into the forest.

"Miss Bellamy!" Peter called excitedly, pointing toward a tree ahead. "Are those berries good to eat?"

Rose followed his pointing finger and immediately shook her head. "No, Peter. Those are baneberries—highly poisonous. This is an excellent lesson for everyone." She beckoned the children closer. "Those shiny red berries might look tempting, but they can cause severe stomach pain or even death if eaten."

"How do you tell which berries are safe?" Abby asked, eyeing the bright red clusters with newfound wariness.

"An excellent question," Rose replied. "Mr. McAlister, would you care to share your knowledge? I imagine you've spent more time foraging in these woods than I have."

Boone stepped forward, directing the children's attention to the plant's structure. "Notice the shape of the leaves and how the berries connect to the stem. With baneberries, the stem attaches to each berry with a noticeable thickening, almost like a tiny red globe holding up each fruit. Safe berries like huckleberries or elderberries don't have that."

"A good rule in the wilderness," he continued, "is to never eat anything unless you're absolutely certain it's safe. Some poisonous plants look very similar to edible ones."

Timmy looked at the surrounding forest with new respect. "So the woods can be dangerous?"

"Like most things in life," Boone replied, "the forest provides both gifts and dangers. The trick is learning to recognize which is which."

Rose was struck by the philosophical nature of his response.

"Mr. McAlister is showing us how to be safe, just like you do, Miss Bellamy," Hannah observed innocently.

Rose noticed a subtle change in Boone's expression at the child's words—not the pained withdrawal she might have expected weeks ago, but something softer, almost contemplative.

They continued along the stream bank, with Rose and Boone alternating in identifying plants. The children's baskets gradually filled with carefully selected specimens: mint for stomach ailments, willow bark for pain and fever, and rose hips rich in vitamins that would help ward off winter illnesses.

When they reached a small sun-dappled clearing, Rose announced it was time for a brief rest. The children settled on fallen logs and rocks, opening the lunch pails they had brought along.

Boone remained standing at first, his habitual vigilance keeping him on guard at the clearing's edge. But as the children's chatter filled the space with normalcy, he gradually relaxed, eventually accepting a space on a fallen log near where Rose sat.

"You have quite an extensive knowledge of plants," Rose said, offering him an apple from her lunch basket.

Boone accepted it with a nod of thanks. "Necessity, mostly. Men who work in the wilderness either learn which plants can help them or suffer unnecessarily."

"Who taught you?" Rose asked.

"My mother knew a fair amount about wild plants. After she died, I learned more from various camp cooks and old-timers. Men who'd survived decades in the forests usually knew which plants could save their lives."

Rose listened attentively. "My grandmother was my first teacher," she offered in return. "She could identify hundreds of plants and knew multiple uses for each one. My earliest memories are of walking through fields with her, learning to recognize helpful herbs."

"The older generation is often the best to learn from," Boone said.

Rose nodded. "She and my mother both were the unofficial healers in our entire county. People would come from miles around when doctors couldn't help them."

"They must have been proud of you carrying on their knowledge," Boone observed.

"They were," Rose confirmed, a wistful smile crossing her features. "My father called it our family's special ministry, healing through God's green gifts. He built my mother and grandmother a special drying shed for their herbs."

Boone studied her expression. "You miss them."

"Every day. But I'm grateful for the time we had and the knowledge they shared. Using those skills to help others keep their memory alive."

Boone nodded, understanding evident in his eyes. Their gazes held for a moment, recognizing the shared experience of loss despite the different ways they had processed their grief.

"Miss Bellamy," Eliza interrupted, approaching with her nearly full basket. "Where shall we look next?"

Rose broke away from Boone's gaze, returning her attention to the lesson at hand. "I think it's time we collected some evergreen needles. Pine, spruce, and fir all have different properties."

"Can we really use tree needles for medicine?" James asked doubtfully.

"Absolutely," Boone answered before Rose could. "Pine needle tea is rich in vitamins that prevent scurvy, which is a disease sailors and winter-bound settlers often suffered from without fresh vegetables."

Rose nodded appreciatively. "Mr. McAlister is exactly right. The indigenous peoples of this region have long used conifer needles to maintain health through long winters."

After their brief rest, Rose directed the children to collect their belongings and prepare to continue their expedition. As they moved through the forest now, she noticed how naturally she and Boone had fallen into a teaching rhythm—she explaining the medicinal properties of plants they encountered; he adding practical wilderness knowledge about identification and preparation.

"This reminds me of botanical walks with my father," Boone remarked quietly as they paused to let the children examine a patch of wild mint. "He knew every tree species by the smell of its wood alone."

"Was he a logger too?" Rose asked.

"Yes. Taught me everything I know about timber." Boone watched the children carefully harvesting mint leaves. "He believed in understanding the forest, not just cutting it down. Said a man who didn't respect what he harvested wouldn't last long in the business."

"Wise words," Rose commented. "Did you always know you would follow in his footsteps?"

Boone shook his head. "For a while, I considered becoming a shipwright. I was fascinated by the vessels that carried our timber down the coast. The idea of building something that could cross oceans appealed to me."

Rose tried to picture a younger Boone, dreams of shipbuilding filling his imagination. "What changed your mind?"

"My father died when I was sixteen. Left my mother and two younger sisters to provide for." His matter-of-fact tone couldn't quite mask the old pain. "Logging was the skill I had, so logging it was."

"That was a tremendous responsibility to shoulder so young," Rose said.

Boone shrugged. "Many do the same or worse. Life on the frontier doesn't allow for extended childhood."

"What about your sisters? Are they nearby?" Rose asked.

"Both married now. One in Salem, one in California. They write occasionally." His expression suggested this topic had reached its natural conclusion.

Rose respected his boundary, turning her attention back to the children. "I think our baskets are nearly full," she called out. "Let's identify three more plants, then head back to prepare our specimens properly."

As the children searched the nearby undergrowth for new discoveries, Rose noticed Boone watching her with an expression she couldn't quite interpret.

"What is it?" she asked.

"You're good with them," he said simply. "The children. You have a way of making learning seem like an adventure."

The unexpected compliment warmed her. "Thank you. I believe God gives each of us gifts to share. Teaching happens to be mine."

"And healing," Boone added. "Don't discount that skill. It's rarer and more valuable out here than book learning."

"Perhaps they work best in tandem," Rose suggested. "Knowledge of plants without understanding their properties would be incomplete, just as recognizing symptoms without knowing treatments would be insufficient."

"A balanced approach," Boone agreed, respect flickering in his eyes.

"Miss Bellamy!" Samuel called urgently from a few yards away. "Is this plant good or bad? It has three leaves."

Rose and Boone exchanged alarmed glances before hurrying toward the boy. Boone reached him first, pulling Samuel back from the plant he'd been about to touch.

"That's poison oak," Boone explained firmly. "Remember, it by this: 'Leaves of three, let it be.' Touching it causes painful blisters and itching that can last for weeks."

The other children gathered around, staring at the innocent-looking plant with newfound respect.

"This is an important lesson," Rose told them. "Some of the most useful plants in God's creation grow right beside some of the most troublesome. We must learn to distinguish between them."

"Like people," Eliza observed sagely. "Pa says some folks look nice enough but cause nothing but trouble."

Rose and Boone chuckled at this straightforward wisdom.

"Your father is a perceptive man," Rose agreed. "Discernment is valuable whether we're dealing with plants or people."

As they made their circuit back toward the camp, Rose walked alongside Boone, the children spread out before them but still within safe range.

"Did you ever encounter poison oak as a child?" she asked conversationally.

A rueful smile crossed Boone's face. "Once. I was about eight, trying to impress an older boy by claiming I knew all the forest plants. Made the mistake of grabbing a handful to prove it wasn't harmful."

Rose winced sympathetically. "That must have been a painful lesson."

"Three weeks of misery," Boone confirmed. "My mother tried every remedy she knew. Finally, an old trapper suggested a paste of jewelweed, which helped somewhat. I never forgot how to identify it after that."

"The most effective lessons often come through experience. Though preferably less uncomfortable ones."

"What about you?" Boone asked. "Any childhood misadventures with plants?"

Rose smiled at the memory his question evoked. "I once mistook water hemlock for Queen Anne's lace and started to make a flower crown with it. My grandmother saw what I was doing from across the field and came running faster than I'd ever seen her move. She knocked it from my hands and made me wash immediately in the creek."

"Water hemlock is deadly," Boone said seriously. "Your grandmother likely saved your life."

"She certainly did. She turned it into a teaching moment, showing me the differences between the two plants in great detail. I've never confused them since."

As they neared the edge of the forest, the sounds of the logging camp became audible. The rhythmic ring of axes, men's voices calling to one another, and the creak of wagon wheels. The familiar sounds seemed to pull Boone back into his role as foreman, his posture straightening subtly.

"I should get back to the river landing," he said. "The men will be sending logs downstream soon."

"Of course," Rose nodded. "Thank you for accompanying us. Your knowledge added tremendously to our lesson."

Boone glanced at the children, their baskets full of carefully collected specimens. "They learned a lot today. Practical knowledge that might serve them well someday."

"Would you consider joining us again?" Rose asked. "Perhaps for a lesson specifically about tree identification? You mentioned your father taught you to recognize them by the scent of their wood."

Boone appeared surprised by the invitation. "I... could do that, yes."

"The children would be delighted," Rose assured him. "As would I."

Something in her tone caused Boone to study her face more carefully. Whatever he saw there made him nod slowly, thoughtfully. "I'll make time, then."

As he turned to leave, Rose called after him. "Mr. McAlister?"

He paused, looking back at her.

"When I was young, my father built a press for preserving plant specimens," she said. "I've been thinking of asking William Wilson if he could construct something similar for the school. Would you... would you help me design it? To ensure it's sturdy enough for daily use?"

It was a small request, but Rose understood it for what it was—an invitation to further collaboration, another thread in the slowly strengthening connection between them.

"I'd be happy to," he replied. "Perhaps tomorrow evening, after your classes?"

"Perfect," Rose agreed. "I'll sketch some ideas before then."

With a final nod, Boone retrieved his axe and headed toward the river landing. Rose watched him go for a moment before turning her attention back to her students, who were arranging their collected specimens on the tables outside the schoolhouse.

"Now comes the important part," she told them, moving among the tables to examine their finds. "We must learn to preserve these plants properly so they maintain their healing properties."

"Like our mothers do with vegetables for winter?" Abby asked.

"Very similar," Rose confirmed. "Some we'll dry, others we might prepare as tinctures or salves."

"Will Mr. McAlister help us again?" Hannah asked hopefully. "He knows lots about plants, too."

Rose smiled at the child's enthusiasm. "He may join us for future lessons, yes. He has agreed to teach us about identifying different types of trees."

The children's excited chatter confirmed their approval of this plan. Rose guided them in sorting their specimens, explaining which plants should be hung to dry and which required immediate processing. As they worked, she reflected on how naturally Boone had integrated into their educational expedition.

For a man who claimed to have little patience for book learning, he had shown a remarkable aptitude for teaching practical knowledge. More importantly, she had witnessed something significant today, Boone speaking about Mary without pain clouding his features. When Hannah had innocently compared his safety instruction to Rose's teaching, he hadn't withdrawn or changed the subject. Progress, slow but steady.

Chapter 20

Rose adjusted the last sprig of yarrow on the drying frame while eighteen pairs of eager eyes watched her technique. The afternoon light slanted through the schoolhouse windows, illuminating the collection of plants spread across every available surface.

"Remember to separate the stems far enough apart," she instructed, demonstrating with gentle fingers. "If they touch, they might mold instead of drying properly."

Eliza raised her hand. "Miss Bellamy, how long until they're ready to use?"

"Most will need at least a week in this dry air," Rose explained, securing a string to hang another frame. "The thicker stems might take two weeks. We'll check them daily and turn them to ensure even drying."

Samuel held up a willow branch. "Pa's cough is bad. Can we make medicine before the bark dries?"

Rose nodded, moving to his side. "Yes, we can prepare willow bark tea immediately. It's one of the few remedies that works better fresh.

Let me show you how to strip the bark carefully without damaging it."

The children clustered around as Rose demonstrated, their faces intent with concentration.

"Fold the bark inward like this," she continued. "The inner layer is where the medicine—"

The rumble of wagon wheels outside interrupted her demonstration. The children's heads swiveled toward the window and the open door in unison, distraction immediate and complete.

"Wagons!" Timmy announced unnecessarily, already abandoning his herb bundle and rushing outside. "Two of them! With people, we don't know!"

"Visitors?" James added, joining him. "Is it the reverend? Ma said he was coming soon!"

"Children, please step back from the windows. Let's maintain some dignity while we investigate." She smoothed her apron, making a swift assessment of her appearance after their forest excursion. "We'll continue our lesson tomorrow. For now, let's see who's arrived."

She led the orderly procession of students outside, where the camp had already sprung to life with unusual activity. Men paused in their work, women emerged from cabins, and within moments, a crowd gathered in the central clearing as two wagons rolled to a stop.

The first wagon carried a man Rose assumed was Joshua Campbell, the company agent who had hired her. Beside him sat a slender man in simple but dignified black clothing that marked him unmistakably as Reverend Parker. The second wagon, driven by an older man with a weathered face, appeared loaded with supplies and trunks.

Boone materialized from the direction of the river landing, his expression carefully neutral as he approached to greet the visitors.

"McAlister!" Campbell called heartily, jumping down from the wagon with an energy that suggested hours of sitting had taxed his patience. He was a man of medium height with an ambitious gleam in his eyes, dressed practically, but with a quality that spoke of his position. "Good to see you again! The camp looks excellent."

Boone shook the offered hand. "Campbell. You're a day earlier than I expected."

"Fair weather and good roads hastened our journey," Campbell replied, gesturing to his companion, who was descending more carefully from the wagon. "Allow me to introduce Reverend Noah Parker."

The reverend approached with a calm dignity. He appeared younger than Rose had expected, perhaps in his early thirties, with thoughtful eyes and a gentle but confident bearing. Nothing about him suggested the fire-and-brimstone preaching some frontier ministers favored.

"A pleasure, Mr. McAlister," Reverend Parker said, extending his hand. "I've heard much about Trinity Station and its foreman."

Boone accepted the handshake with formal courtesy. "Welcome, Reverend. I trust you had a safe journey."

"Indeed, though I confess I'm not accustomed to such rough roads," the reverend replied with a self-deprecating smile. "My posterior may never be the same."

The unexpected humor earned appreciative chuckles from the gathering crowd, and Rose noticed a slight relaxation in Boone's rigid posture.

Campbell's gaze swept over the assembled community until it found Rose at the edge of the crowd, surrounded by her students. His face brightened with recognition.

"And you must be Miss Bellamy!" he exclaimed, striding toward her. "I see you've wasted no time establishing the school we discussed."

Rose stepped forward, offering her hand. "Mr. Campbell, it's a pleasure to finally meet you in person. Your letter brought me to a wonderful community."

"From what I hear, you've done remarkable work here," Campbell replied, shaking her hand with genuine enthusiasm. "Teaching, healing... I couldn't have hoped for a better representative of the company's interests."

"The community made it possible," Rose answered honestly. "They've embraced education with tremendous spirit."

Campbell beamed, turning to introduce her to the reverend, who approached with a warm smile. "Reverend Parker, this is Miss Rose Bellamy, our schoolteacher, and apparently Trinity Station's resident healer as well."

"Miss Bellamy," the reverend greeted her. "What a blessing to meet you. I understand you've been involving the children in bible learning as well?"

"Simple Bible readings and hymns during their school day," Rose clarified. "Nothing that would presume upon your authority, Reverend."

"On the contrary, I'm grateful," he assured her. "Faith flourishes when nurtured by dedicated believers, not just clergy. I look forward to seeing the foundation you've established."

Campbell clapped his hands together, addressing the gathered community. "Friends! I bring exciting news and prospects for Trinity Station's future. After we've had a chance to refresh ourselves, I'd like to share these plans with everyone." He turned to Boone. "Perhaps in the cookhouse after dinner? I believe we all have much to discuss."

Boone nodded once. "I'll inform Ethel to prepare accordingly."

"Excellent!" Campbell exclaimed. He turned back to Rose. "Miss Bellamy, I'd love to see the schoolhouse. Perhaps you could show me what you've accomplished?"

"I'd be honored," Rose replied, gesturing toward the building. "The children were just finishing a practical lesson in herbal medicine when you arrived."

"Herbal medicine?" Campbell's eyebrows rose appreciatively. "What a wonderfully practical skill to teach. This is precisely the kind of innovative education I envisioned."

As Campbell, Reverend Parker, and Rose walked toward the schoolhouse, she couldn't help glancing back at Boone. He stood watching them, his expression unreadable. When their eyes met briefly, she offered a small, encouraging smile. The slight nod he returned might have been imperceptible to others, but to Rose, it communicated volumes.

Inside the schoolhouse, Campbell examined everything with admiring attention. The simple benches, the slate board on the wall, the drying herbs, and especially Mary's lesson plan book that resided on her Rose's desk.

"This is remarkable," he said, genuine respect in his voice. "When I sent the letter inviting you to Trinity Station, I never imagined such a transformation in such short a time here."

"Miss Bellamy has a gift," Reverend Parker observed, examining the children's slate work sitting on the benches. "These compositions are wonderful."

"The credit belongs to the children," Rose insisted. "They're eager to learn, and their parents have been tremendously supportive."

Campbell picked up a book from Rose's desk. "And what of Foreman McAlister? Has he been supportive as well?"

The direct question surprised Rose. She considered her answer carefully. "Mr. McAlister is dedicated to this camp's welfare. Once he saw how education benefited the community, he provided practical assistance." She gestured to the sturdy floor beneath their feet. "He ensured the children had a safe, warm place to learn."

"Interesting," Campbell mused. "When I proposed expanding Trinity Station beyond a simple logging operation, Boone was... resistant. He preferred keeping it focused solely on timber production."

"Mr. McAlister understands the dangers of this environment better than anyone," Rose replied diplomatically. "His caution comes from responsibility."

"True enough," Campbell conceded. "But a man must look beyond immediate concerns to build something lasting." He set the book down decisively. "Which is precisely what I intend to discuss tonight."

***

Later, as Rose left the schoolhouse to prepare for dinner, she encountered Ethel hurrying toward the cookhouse with an armload of tablecloths.

"There you are!" Ethel exclaimed. "Everyone's talking about Campbell's plans. He's brought architectural drawings and everything!"

"Do you know what he's proposing?" Rose asked, falling into step beside her.

"Bits and pieces from Martha," Ethel replied. "She was helping unpack the wagons. Apparently, there's talk of permanent structures, more family housing, a proper church..." She lowered her voice. "And possibly an infirmary. You might finally have a proper place to practice your healing, not just my back storeroom."

Rose's heart quickened at the possibilities. "That sounds wonderful. Trinity Station could become a real town."

"If Boone agrees," Ethel cautioned. "Campbell may represent the company, but nothing happens here without Boone's cooperation." She studied Rose's expression. "How do you think he'll respond?"

"I'm not certain," Rose admitted. "He's been more open recently to the camp's growth, but change doesn't come easily to him, it seems."

Ethel nodded knowingly. "Especially changes that feel like moving forward without Mary." She adjusted her burden of linens. "Would you mind checking on our guests? Make sure they have fresh water for washing before dinner? I'm overwhelmed with preparations."

"Of course," Rose agreed, changing direction toward the small cabin where Campbell and Parker were staying.

As she approached, she heard male voices in conversation. The reverend's gentle tones contrasted with Campbell's more animated speech. Rose was about to announce her presence when Campbell's words froze her in place.

"Boone McAlister is the key, Reverend. His cooperation determines whether Trinity Station flourishes or remains merely a temporary logging operation. The man has been stuck in grief for a year. It's time he moved forward."

"Grief follows no timetable, Mr. Campbell," the reverend replied mildly. "Especially when accompanied by guilt."

"Perhaps. But Mary's dreams for this place are worth pursuing. She and I discussed them at length during my visits here."

"And you believe Miss Bellamy might help persuade him?" the reverend asked.

Campbell's laugh was short, but not unkind. "Anyone with eyes can see Boone McAlister is warming to our schoolteacher. She's already accomplished what I thought impossible—establishing education here. Perhaps her influence extends further."

Rose stepped back quietly, unwilling to eavesdrop further. The conversation troubled her, not because of its content necessarily, but because of the implication that she might be used as leverage against Boone. She believed in Trinity Station's potential for growth, but not at the expense of manipulating a man still healing from profound loss.

She knocked firmly on the cabin door, dispersing her troubled thoughts behind a pleasant expression.

"Miss Bellamy," the reverend greeted her upon opening the door. "What a pleasant surprise."

"Mrs. Hayes asked me to ensure you have everything you need before dinner," Rose explained.

"Most thoughtful," Campbell replied, rolling up what appeared to be architectural drawings. "We're quite comfortable, though I confess I'm eager to share these plans with everyone."

"The community is excited to hear them," Rose assured him. "Dinner will be ready shortly. May I escort you to the cookhouse?"

Chapter 21

The cookhouse had been transformed. Extra tables had been arranged, clean cloths covered their rough surfaces, and Ethel had somehow produced candles for additional lighting. The space hummed with anticipation as families filed in, dressed in their nicest clothing for the important occasion.

Boone arrived last. His gaze swept the room with a foreman's assessment before settling briefly on Rose. His expression prompted her to offer an encouraging smile. The slight easing of tension around his eyes suggested he'd received her unspoken support.

Dinner proceeded with unusual formality by Trinity Station standards. Ethel had outdone herself, preparing a venison stew with extra vegetables, fresh bread and butter, and even apple cobbler for dessert. Conversation remained politely superficial as everyone waited for the promised presentation. When the meal concluded, Campbell rose from his place at the head of the table.

"Friends," he began, surveying the attentive faces. "When Wilderness Timber Company established this camp three years ago, we envisioned a temporary operation, cutting the best timber, and then moving on. But Trinity Station has demonstrated remarkable durability and productivity under Foreman McAlister's leadership."

Approving murmurs rippled through the gathering.

"More importantly," Campbell continued, "you've begun establishing a true community here. Families are putting down roots, a school, and the beginnings of a church congregation." He gestured to Rose and Reverend Parker in turn. "Trinity Station deserves investment beyond a simple logging operation."

He unrolled large drawings across the cleared table. People leaned forward or stood eagerly to see the architectural renderings of substantial wooden buildings arranged in an organized layout.

"I present to you the future of Trinity Station," Campbell announced, his voice resonating with conviction. "Permanent family housing, constructed of milled lumber, not rough logs. A proper general store to reduce dependence on supply runs to distant settlements. A large schoolhouse with glass windows and a bell tower."

Children gasped with delight at this last detail, and Rose couldn't suppress her own surge of excitement at the prospect of a purpose-built educational space.

"Additionally," Campbell continued, "a small infirmary for treating injuries and illness, and eventually, a real church building." He nodded respectfully to Reverend Parker.

Rose's gaze shifted to Boone, who stood with arms crossed, studying the drawings with unreadable intensity. His jaw tightened almost imperceptibly at the mention of the church.

"This plan," Campbell said, his voice softening as he addressed Boone directly, "represents exactly what Mary envisioned for Trinity Station. She spoke often of creating a permanent settlement where logging families could build stable lives."

A hushed stillness fell over the room at Mary's name. All eyes turned to Boone, awaiting his reaction to this direct invocation of his wife's dream.

Boone remained silent for a long moment, his gaze still fixed on the drawings. When he finally spoke, his voice was controlled, revealing nothing of his inner struggle.

"The company is prepared to finance these improvements?"

"Yes," Campbell confirmed. "The quality and quantity of timber harvested here have exceeded expectations. This investment ensures continued productivity through workforce stability."

"And the timeline?" Boone pressed.

"Construction would begin within the month," Campbell replied. "Starting with expanded family housing, the general store, and the infirmary. The church and additional structures would follow next spring."

Boone nodded once, his expression remaining neutral. "We should discuss the operational details privately."

"Of course," Campbell agreed readily. "But I wanted everyone to share in the vision. After all, this affects the entire community."

The response was immediate and enthusiastic. Families clustered around the drawings, pointing and exclaiming over details relevant to their interests. Children jumped excitedly at the prospect of a proper schoolhouse bell they could ring. Women discussed the practical advantages of more substantial housing.

Rose observed it all with a mixture of excitement and concern. The improvements would genuinely benefit Trinity Station, but Campbell's deliberate mention of Mary's vision had been calculated to pressure Boone. The tension in his posture confirmed he felt it, even as he maintained his composure.

As the evening progressed, Rose found herself engaged in conversation with Reverend Parker, while Boone and Campbell withdrew to discuss business matters.

"How do you find frontier life, Miss Bellamy?" the reverend asked. "Quite different from Pennsylvania, I imagine."

"Very different," Rose acknowledged, "but rewarding in unexpected ways. There's a directness here, a clarity of purpose, that I find refreshing."

"I've observed the same during my travels," Noah agreed. "Faith often thrives in these challenging environments, stripped of unnecessary adornment and focused on essentials."

"I agree," Rose responded. "Though I admit I've missed formal worship services."

"I understand, yet, I assume your scripture reading and hymns during school have helped and enriched the lives of the young ones?" When Rose nodded, he continued, "That's precisely the kind of faithful stewardship these communities need. Not everyone is called to ordained ministry, but all believers are called to nurture faith where they're planted."

"That's kind of you to say, Reverend," Rose replied. "I worried I might be overstepping."

"Not at all," he assured her. "In fact, I hope you'll continue this practice even after I establish regular services. Your connection with these children and their families is clearly strong and valuable."

Their conversation shifted to practical matters of organizing Sunday worship in the cookhouse until permanent church facilities could be constructed. Throughout their discussion, Rose found herself repeatedly glancing toward the door where Boone and Campbell had disappeared.

"You're concerned about him," Reverend Parker observed gently, following her gaze.

Rose hesitated, uncertain how much to share with this insightful but still unfamiliar minister. "Mr. McAlister carries tremendous responsibility for this camp," she said carefully. "These changes, while positive, will increase that burden."

"And reawaken painful memories," Noah added. "Mr. Campbell briefed me on the tragedy." He studied Rose's expression. "You've formed a connection with him, haven't you?"

"We've developed a mutual respect," Rose acknowledged, choosing her words with care. "Mr. McAlister has suffered a profound loss that intersects with my presence here in unexpected ways."

"Mary's teaching ambitions," Noah nodded understandingly. "Mr. Campbell mentioned you've fulfilled her educational vision for the camp."

"I discovered her plans after arriving," Rose explained. "Implementing them seemed the right thing to do, honoring her memory while serving the community's needs."

"And Boone's response to this continuation of his wife's work?"

Rose considered the complex evolution of their relationship. "Initially resistant, then accepting, and now... supportive, in his way. He's a man of few words but meaningful actions."

Noah nodded thoughtfully. "Grief often manifests as resistance to change, particularly changes that feel like moving forward without the loved one." He spoke with the quiet authority of someone who had guided many through such struggles. "Sometimes the hardest spiritual challenge isn't maintaining faith through difficulty, but allowing joy to reenter our lives afterward."

"That's very insightful, Reverend," Rose said.

"Experience teaches harsh lessons," Noah replied with a sad smile. "I lost my brother in similar circumstances, a logging accident when I was younger. I understand something of what Mr. McAlister endures."

This revelation surprised Rose. "I'm sorry for your loss. Does Boone know about your brother?"

"Not yet. Some connections are best revealed naturally when trust has been established." Noah's gaze moved to the door again. "Speaking of which…"

Boone and Campbell had returned to the main room. The contrast in their expressions was striking. Campbell appeared pleased and energized, while Boone's face bore the controlled neutrality Rose had come to recognize as his public mask for private turbulence.

Campbell moved immediately to address the gathering again, but Boone hung back, his eyes scanning the room until they found Rose. Without fanfare, he made his way to her side.

"How did the discussion go?" she asked quietly as he reached her.

"The plans are sound," Boone replied, his voice low enough that only she and Reverend Parker could hear. "The company's commitment appears genuine."

"That's positive news," Rose said, studying his expression for clues to his personal feelings about the development. "The improvements will benefit everyone here."

"Yes," Boone agreed simply, though something in his tone suggested complexity beneath the single syllable.

"Mr. McAlister," Reverend Parker interjected gently, extending his hand. "We haven't had a proper opportunity to speak. I want to assure you that I understand this community has experienced significant loss and change. My role isn't to disrupt, but to support."

Boone accepted the handshake with an evaluative gaze. "Reverend. Trinity Station has managed without formal religious leadership until now."

"Indeed it has," Noah agreed readily. "That speaks to the spiritual resilience already present." He glanced at Rose. "Miss Bellamy has clearly nurtured that admirably in my absence."

Before Boone could respond, Campbell's voice rose commandingly from the center of the room. "Friends, I have excellent news! After reviewing operational considerations with Foreman McAlister, we've agreed that construction will begin immediately on the first phase of improvements!"

Cheers erupted from the gathered families, drowning out any possibility of continued private conversation. Boone's jaw tightened marginally, suggesting to Rose that "agreement" might be overstating his position.

"The initial focus will be expanded family housing," Campbell continued when the noise subsided somewhat. "Followed by the infirmary, which Miss Bellamy will presumably oversee alongside her teaching duties."

Rose blinked in surprise at this announcement, having not been consulted about additional responsibilities. She glanced at Boone, whose raised eyebrow indicated he was equally unaware of this plan.

"Presumption seems to be Mr. Campbell's specialty," Boone muttered under his breath, just loud enough for Rose to hear. Unexpectedly, a corner of his mouth quirked upward briefly, a fleeting moment of dry humor that Rose found reassuring.

Campbell was outlining construction timelines when Hannah Abernathy tugged at Rose's skirt.

"Miss Bellamy," she whispered loudly, "will you still be our teacher when the new school is built? Papa says it might have a real bell we can ring!"

Rose knelt at the child's level. "Of course I will. And yes, I believe there are plans for a proper bell."

"And will Mr. McAlister still come to teach us about trees and logging?" Hannah persisted, looking up at Boone with innocent expectation.

"I expect Mr. McAlister will be very busy with all the new building work," Rose began carefully, offering him an escape.

"I'll make time," Boone said, surprising Rose. "Someone needs to ensure you know which trees are safe to climb."

Hannah beamed up at him. "Thank you, Mr. McAlister! Papa says you know everything about trees, even how they talk to each other!"

"Trees don't actually talk, Hannah," Boone corrected gently.

"But Papa said they communicate through their roots," Hannah insisted. "That's talking, isn't it? Just without words."

A genuine smile briefly touched Boone's lips. "I suppose that's one way to look at it."

Rose watched this exchange with quiet amazement.

The evening continued with excited discussions about Trinity Station's future. Campbell circulated through the gathering, answering questions and elaborating on details. The reverend engaged various family groups, clearly building relationships that would serve his ministry.

Rose was drawn into conversations about the educational implications of the expansion. Parents eagerly discussed additional subjects that might be taught in a proper schoolhouse, while children peppered her with questions about the promised bell.

Throughout it all, she remained aware of Boone's movements around the room. Unlike Campbell's gregarious networking, Boone's interactions were briefer and more focused, typically addressing practical concerns raised by the men who worked under his supervision. Yet, he didn't withdraw from the gathering, maintaining a presence that gradually shifted from obligation to genuine engagement.

As the evening wound down, families began departing with excited conversations about the future. Rose helped Ethel gather empty plates, carrying them to the washing area.

"Quite an evening," Ethel commented, scraping leftover food into a bucket. "I haven't seen this much excitement since... well, a very long time."

"The improvements will make a tremendous difference," Rose said, stacking plates. "Especially the infirmary. Proper treatment space would have made caring for Jed much easier."

"Speaking of which," Ethel lowered her voice, "what do you make of Campbell volunteering you for medical duties without asking? Seems presumptuous."

"It was unexpected," Rose acknowledged, "though not unwelcome. I've been providing what care I can, anyway."

"Still, a man ought to ask before assigning additional work," Ethel insisted. "Even Boone looked surprised by that announcement."

"I'll speak with Mr. Campbell tomorrow," Rose assured her. "To clarify expectations on both sides."

Ethel nodded approvingly. "Good. You've earned that respect." She glanced toward the main room, where Boone was speaking with Simon near the door. "He's handling this better than I expected."

Rose followed her gaze. "Yes. The mention of Mary's vision could have been difficult."

"Was difficult," Ethel corrected. "I know that man's expressions better than most. But he didn't retreat." She gave Rose a meaningful look. "Some might say your influence has been beneficial in that regard."

Boone approached them.

"Miss Bellamy," he said, "Campbell mentioned you might have questions about the proposed infirmary. If you'd like to discuss it, I have the preliminary drawings."

Rose wiped her hands on a nearby towel. "I would, actually. I hadn't realized medical duties would be formally part of my responsibilities."

"Neither had I," Boone replied dryly. "Campbell tends to make plans first and consider implementation details afterward."

Ethel shooed them both away from the washing area. "Go on, then. I've got plenty of help here." She nodded toward Martha, Clara, and Beth, who were already tackling the mountain of dishes.

Boone led Rose to a quieter corner of the cookhouse, where several drawings lay spread on a small table. Most of the crowd had dispersed, leaving only a few scattered conversations continuing in the main area.

"Here's the proposed infirmary," Boone said, indicating a detailed sketch of a modest but well-designed building. "Two treatment rooms, a dispensary area, and living quarters attached." He glanced at her. "Campbell assumes you'll relocate from your current room to live adjacent to the infirmary once it's built."

Rose studied the drawing with professional interest, noting the practical layout and thoughtful details like a covered porch for waiting patients. "It's well-designed," she acknowledged. "Though this represents a significant expansion of my duties beyond teaching."

"That was my concern as well," Boone said. "Formalizing both roles might stretch you too thin."

The fact that he'd considered her workload touched Rose unexpectedly. "I appreciate that concern," she said. "Though I've managed both informally thus far."

"With limited resources and facilities," Boone pointed out. "Proper facilities might increase demands on your time. More families will come with the expansion, bringing more children and more potential patients."

"You're right, of course. Perhaps eventually we'll need a dedicated teacher and a dedicated healer or doctor, but for now..." She traced the outline of the proposed building with one finger. "This would certainly improve care for injuries like Jed's."

Boone watched her studying the plans, his expression thoughtful. "What do you think of Campbell's overall vision?" he asked after a moment. "Beyond the infirmary."

The question surprised her with its directness. Rose chose her words carefully. "I believe Trinity Station has potential beyond logging. These improvements could create something lasting, something that serves families for generations." She looked up at him. "But changes of this magnitude affects everyone, especially those with leadership responsibilities. Your concerns matter too."

Boone's eyes held hers, appreciation for her balanced response evident in his expression. "Campbell mentioned that you and Mary share similar visions for education here."

"Perhaps," Rose acknowledged. "Though I never had the privilege of knowing her thoughts directly. I've tried to honor what I learned of her intentions."

"You have," Boone assured her. "More than honored them. You've expanded them." He looked down at the drawings again. "Mary would have been pleased with what you've accomplished."

The simple statement carried enormous weight coming from him, not just acknowledgment but a genuine connection between his past and present. It represented a bridge Rose hadn't dared hope.

"Thank you," she said. "That means a great deal coming from you."

Something vulnerable flickered in Boone's eyes, quickly masked as Campbell approached them, still riding the wave of excitement from his successful presentation.

"Ah, reviewing the infirmary plans?" Campbell observed cheerfully. "What do you think, Miss Bellamy? Suitable for your medical practice?"

"The design is excellent," Rose replied. "Though I'm curious about the assumption that I'll manage both teaching and formal medical duties. We hadn't discussed such an arrangement previously."

Campbell looked momentarily taken aback by her direct question. "I assumed... given your existing healing work... but of course, nothing is definite without your agreement." He recovered quickly, offering an apologetic smile. "I should have consulted you first. A presumption on my part."

"I'm not opposed to the idea," Rose clarified. "But proper planning requires a clear understanding of expectations on all sides."

"Absolutely right," Campbell agreed readily. "Perhaps we could discuss details tomorrow? I'm eager to hear your thoughts on what supplies and equipment would be necessary."

"That would be fine," Rose agreed. "Sometime in the morning would be best."

"Perfect," Campbell said. He turned to Boone. "I've been meaning to ask—will Reverend Parker be staying with me indefinitely, or have other arrangements been made?"

"The cabin you're using has two rooms," Boone answered. "I assumed you'd both stay there. After you return to Portland, the reverend is welcome to call the cabin his own. The previous man who was living in it before you came has agreed to stay on at the bunkhouse."

"Excellent, excellent," Campbell nodded. "Though I should warn you, the reverend rises early for prayer. I may need to adjust my sleeping habits accordingly while I'm here." He chuckled good-naturedly. "Speaking of whom, I should find him and retire for the evening. Tomorrow brings much planning!"

After Campbell departed, Rose and Boone stood in momentary silence, both processing the evening's developments.

"He's enthusiastic," Rose observed neutrally.

"Relentlessly so," Boone agreed, with a hint of the dry humor that occasionally surfaced in private conversation. "Though not without reason. The company stands to profit significantly from a stable, permanent operation here."

"And the community benefits as well," Rose added. "It seems a fair exchange."

Boone nodded slowly. "If implemented properly." He began rolling up the drawings with careful precision. "Campbell sometimes envisions results without fully considering the process required to achieve them."

Rose recognized the subtle criticism from a man who valued methodical planning and realistic assessment. "Like assuming I'd naturally take on formalized medical duties alongside teaching?"

Boone nodded, securing the rolled plans with a leather tie. "His vision isn't wrong, but his timeline and assumptions need tempering with practical experience."

"Which is why your input is essential," Rose observed. "You understand what's truly feasible here."

Boone paused in his task, studying her with unexpected intensity. "You think I should support these plans, then?"

Rose sensed Boone was genuinely seeking her perspective, not just making conversation. This trust represented significant progress in their relationship.

"I think Trinity Station deserves the chance to become something permanent," she answered thoughtfully. "Not just for the current families, but for future generations. Mary saw that potential." She hesitated, then added gently, "Supporting that vision doesn't mean leaving her memory behind. It means carrying it forward."

Boone absorbed her words, his expression revealing nothing of his internal response. After a moment, he simply nodded and resumed securing the drawings.

"It's growing late. You must be tired after your forest expedition with the children this morning and all the commotion this evening."

"It was a full day," Rose acknowledged. "Though a rewarding one. The children learned valuable skills this morning."

"Your knowledge of medicinal plants is impressive," Boone said as they walked toward the cookhouse door. "Few teachers I've encountered would consider such practical instruction essential."

"My grandmother would say book learning without practical application is only half an education," Rose replied with a smile. "Children remember what they discover with their own hands far better than what they merely hear."

"True of adults as well," Boone agreed, holding the door open for her as they stepped outside.

The night air felt refreshingly cool. Most of the camp had settled for the evening, with only a few lanterns still glowing in distant windows. The quiet felt particularly welcome after the excitement and tension of the community gathering.

"I wanted to thank you for speaking to Hannah earlier," Rose said as they walked. "About continuing your lessons on trees, even with the changes coming."

"I made a commitment to the children," Boone replied simply. "Changes to the camp don't alter that."

"Will you address the camp tomorrow about the expansion plans?" Rose asked. "After Campbell's announcement, I'm sure people will have many questions."

"At breakfast," Boone confirmed. "The men need clear information before rumors take root." He paused, seeming to weigh his next words. "Your observation about carrying Mary's vision forward rather than leaving it behind... I appreciate that perspective."

"I believe she would want Trinity Station to flourish," Rose said gently. "Everything I've learned about her suggests she saw possibilities where others saw only timber."

Boone nodded slowly. "She did." After a brief silence, he added, "Rest well, Miss Bellamy. I look forward to helping you design the press for preserving plant specimens tomorrow evening."

"I'm glad you remember that. Good night, Mr. McAlister," Rose replied. "And thank you for considering my thoughts on the matter."

Rose reflected on the day's extraordinary developments as she entered the cookhouse again and made her way to her room. From the morning's botanical expedition to the evening's ambitious plans for Trinity Station's future, change was clearly accelerating in this remote community.

Yet amidst all the external changes, the more significant transformation might be the internal one she'd witnessed in Boone tonight. His willingness to discuss Mary's vision without withdrawing, his genuine consideration of Rose's perspective, and his commitment to the children all represented healing progress.

In her small room, Rose lit her lamp and opened her journal to record the day's events. As she wrote about Campbell's plans and Boone's measured response, she found herself adding a prayer for wisdom—for herself, for Boone, and for the entire community facing this pivotal moment in Trinity Station's development.

The proposed expansion represented more than buildings and infrastructure. It embodied hope for a sustainable future, one where logging families could put down permanent roots rather than following transient timber operations. It offered the possibility of civilization's comforts without sacrificing the frontier spirit that made Trinity Station unique.

Rose closed her journal and prepared for bed, her mind still processing all she had witnessed. As she extinguished her lamp, one thought remained foremost: Trinity Station stood at a crossroads, and the decisions made in the coming days would shape not just its physical landscape but its very character for years to come.

Tomorrow would indeed bring new challenges, but also new possibilities. With that thought, Rose drifted toward sleep, her dreams filled with schoolhouse bells, Boone McAlister, and the image of a community blossoming from a simple logging camp into something permanent and enduring.

Chapter 22

Rose tightened the leather straps on her woven gathering basket, adjusting it to hang comfortably at her side. The early morning air carried the scent of pine and wood smoke as she stepped out of the cookhouse, mentally cataloging the herbs she needed to replenish. Jed's recovery had depleted her yarrow supply.

The day stretched before her, a Saturday, with no lessons to prepare for and a full day ahead of her.

As she passed the central clearing of the camp, movement caught her eye. Boone sat alone on his cabin porch, hands busy with a small carving knife and piece of wood.

Rose hesitated, then adjusted her course toward his cabin. He looked up at her approach, setting aside his carving.

"Good morning, Mr. McAlister," she called.

"Miss Bellamy." He nodded, watching her with a quiet assessment.

"I'm surprised to see you not working," Rose said, stopping at the foot of his porch steps. "No logging today?"

"No, with the arrival of Campbell, the men have the day off," Boone explained.

Rose noted the tension in his shoulders despite his casual posture. "I'm heading to gather herbs, yarrow especially, after using so much on Jed. Would you like to join me? I could use the extra hands, and you know the forest better than I do."

Boone's expression shifted from surprise to consideration.

"Where were you planning to go?" he asked.

"The clearing near Eagle Ridge has excellent yarrow," Rose replied. "Though I'm open to suggestions if you know better locations."

"There's a meadow beyond the north cutting with more medicinal plants than anywhere else I've seen. Yarrow, mullein, even wild ginger in the shadier spots."

"That sounds perfect," Rose said, unable to hide her enthusiasm. "Is it far?"

"About an hour's walk," Boone replied, disappearing briefly into his cabin. He emerged with a canteen and a small pack. "The trail's rough in spots."

"I'm not afraid of rough trails," Rose assured him, adjusting her basket.

A hint of amusement flickered across his face. "I imagine you wouldn't be."

They set off toward the northern forest, leaving the bustle of camp behind. The well-worn logging path eventually narrowed into a game trail that wound through increasingly dense trees. Boone walked slightly ahead, occasionally holding branches aside for Rose to pass.

"Campbell seems determined to start construction immediately," Rose observed after they had walked in silence for several minutes.

"Too determined," Boone replied. "He's thinking like a business-man, not a builder. These things take time, especially with limited manpower."

"Will you have to reassign men from logging to construction?"

Boone nodded. "Some. William has carpentry experience. Simon too. But it means reduced timber production."

"Which the company won't appreciate," Rose surmised.

"Exactly. Campbell sees the expansion as complementary to logging operations, but initially, it will compete for resources." Boone ducked under a low-hanging branch. "He's arranging for additional workers from Portland, but they won't arrive for weeks."

Rose considered this practical challenge. "Could the families help? Many of the women have building experience from establishing their own homes."

"That's worth considering," Boone acknowledged. "Though I hesitate to add to their already considerable workload."

"Perhaps if presented as community effort rather than obligation," Rose suggested. "Many would gladly contribute to improvements that benefit everyone."

Boone glanced back at her with unexpected appreciation. "That's a practical suggestion. I'll propose it at the next camp meeting."

The trail narrowed further, forcing them to walk single file through a dense patch of undergrowth. As they emerged into a slightly wider section, their hands accidentally brushed. Rose felt the brief contact like a spark against her skin and noticed Boone's step faltering momentarily before he continued forward.

"The permanent settlement will change everything," Rose said. "Families putting down roots rather than following timber operations."

"For better or worse," Boone agreed.

"You don't sound entirely convinced it's for the better."

Boone was quiet for several steps. "Change brings uncertainty. The men know logging. It's straightforward—dangerous but predictable in its way. A permanent settlement brings different challenges."

"And opportunities," Rose added. "Children with consistent education. Families with stable homes. A true community with shared purpose."

"Mary believed that too," Boone said.

They walked in silence for a while, the forest alive with bird calls and the rustle of small creatures in the underbrush. Rose noticed Boone seemed distracted, his attention only partially on their surroundings despite his habitual vigilance.

"Is something troubling you about the expansion beyond the practical concerns?" she asked finally.

Boone's pace slowed slightly. "Campbell's motives are primarily financial. The company sees profit in stability, not community for its own sake."

"Does the motive matter if the outcome benefits everyone?"

"It matters in implementation," Boone replied. "When profits conflict with people's needs, I know which the company will prioritize."

The path widened as they approached a small stream. Boone offered his hand to help Rose cross on stepping stones. His grip was firm and steady, his calloused palm warm against hers. She noticed he didn't immediately release her hand when they reached the other side; the contact lingering a heartbeat longer than necessary.

"We're nearly there," he said, finally letting go. "Just beyond that ridge."

As they crested the small rise, a beautiful meadow spread before them, vibrant with wildflowers and herbs. The open space was ringed by towering pines, creating a natural sanctuary bathed in morning light.

"Oh!" Rose exclaimed, her breath catching at the sight. "It's magnificent."

Boone watched her reaction with quiet pleasure. "Mary called it the medicine cabinet. She discovered it our first spring here."

Rose looked at him, touched by his willingness to share this connection to Mary. "Thank you for bringing me here."

Boone nodded once, then gestured toward a patch of feathery plants with tiny flower clusters. "There's your yarrow."

Rose moved eagerly toward the plants, kneeling to examine them. "Perfect specimens," she said, opening her basket. "The flowers are just reaching their peak potency."

Boone knelt beside her, watching as she carefully selected stems for harvesting. "How do you choose which to take?"

"Never the youngest or oldest plants," Rose explained, demonstrating with her small harvesting knife. "And never more than one-third from any single area. That ensures regrowth."

"Sustainable harvesting," Boone observed. "Like selective timber cutting."

Rose smiled, pleased by the comparison. "God provides abundantly, but we must harvest with respect and foresight."

She demonstrated the proper cutting technique, then handed Boone her spare knife. "Would you like to try?"

He accepted it with a nod, carefully mimicking her technique on a nearby plant. His large hands moved with surprising delicacy, the same precision she'd observed when he handled tree samples for the children.

"My grandmother would approve," Rose said, watching him work. "She was particular about proper harvesting."

"My mother was the same with berry picking," Boone replied. "Said greedy hands left empty bushes for winter."

They worked side by side, gradually filling Rose's basket with carefully harvested yarrow. As they moved to a new patch, Rose spotted purple flowers nestled among rocks at the meadow's edge.

"Wild violets!" she exclaimed, moving toward them. "Excellent for coughs and fever."

The ground was uneven, with loose rocks hidden among tall grass. As Rose reached for a particularly fine specimen, her foot slipped on a moss-covered stone. She pitched forward with a startled cry.

Boone was beside her instantly, his strong arm catching her around the waist before she fell. "Careful," he murmured, his voice close to her ear.

Rose steadied herself against his chest, acutely aware of his proximity, the solid strength of him. "Thank you," she managed, her voice slightly breathless. "I didn't see that loose stone."

His arm remained around her waist a moment longer than necessary for mere stability. When he finally stepped back, Rose noticed a slight flush beneath his tan.

"The ground's treacherous here after rain," he said, clearing his throat. "Better stick to the clearer areas."

Rose nodded, trying to calm her racing pulse as she carefully gathered the violets she'd been reaching for. They continued harvesting, moving methodically across the meadow to collect various herbs.

"This mullein will help with coughs," Rose said, carefully cutting the soft, fuzzy leaves of a tall plant. "Boiled with honey, it soothes irritated throats."

"My grandmother used it with whiskey for my grandfather's winter cough," Boone recalled, examining the plant with newfound interest.

"A common addition," Rose acknowledged with a smile. "Though not one I typically recommend for children."

A comfortable rhythm developed between them as they worked. Rose would identify a plant and explain its properties, while Boone often added practical knowledge about where similar specimens could be found or how the indigenous peoples had used them.

The first drop of rain caught Rose by surprise, landing cool against her cheek. She looked up to see dark clouds gathering overhead, having missed their approach while absorbed in her work.

"The Weather's turning," Boone observed, glancing at the rapidly darkening sky. "Summer storms move quickly here."

More drops followed, fat and cold, rapidly increasing in number. Rose hurriedly secured her filled basket as the gentle shower transformed into steady rainfall.

"There's shelter this way," Boone said, taking her elbow and guiding her toward the edge of the meadow. They hurried across the open space as the rain intensified, reaching the protective canopy of a massive pine trees just as the downpour began in earnest.

The ancient tree's dense branches created a relatively dry space beneath its sprawling limbs. Rose pressed her back against the rough trunk, catching her breath as she watched sheets of rain transform the beautiful meadow into a misty watercolor.

"That came suddenly," she said, brushing droplets from her sleeves.

"Typical Oregon weather," Boone replied, setting down his pack. "Unpredictable."

The enclosed space beneath the pine created an unexpected intimacy, forcing them to stand close together to avoid the rain dripping through thinner sections of the canopy. Rose became acutely aware of Boone's presence.

"Will it pass quickly?" she asked, trying to focus on practical matters.

"Hard to say. Summer showers sometimes last minutes, sometimes hours." Boone leaned against the trunk beside her, their shoulders nearly touching. "Are you cold?"

"A little," Rose admitted, rubbing her arms where the rain had dampened her sleeves.

Boone opened his pack and withdrew a folded oilcloth, the type lumberjacks used to protect supplies. He draped it around her shoulders without ceremony.

"Thank you," Rose said, pulling the water-resistant material closer. "You came prepared."

"Living in these mountains teaches preparation," he replied. "Or harsh lessons."

They stood watching the rain transform the landscape, turning vibrant greens deeper and more intense. The gentle patter on pine needles above created a soothing rhythm, punctuated occasionally by heavier drops finding their way through the canopy.

"Something's still troubling you, I sense," Rose observed quietly after a while. "Beyond Campbell's plans and the practical challenges of expansion."

Boone remained silent, his profile still as he gazed out at the rain.

"Campbell asked me yesterday about your intentions regarding Trinity Station."

The statement surprised her. "My intentions?"

"Whether you planned to stay permanently or move on eventually." Boone's voice remained neutral.

"I see. And what did you tell him?"

"That he should ask you directly." Boone turned to face her. "But I realized I wanted to know the answer myself."

The admission hung between them, weighted with more significance than the simple words conveyed. Rose met his gaze directly.

"I came to Trinity Station believing God called me here," she said. "Nothing has happened to change that belief. If anything, the need for both education and medical care has only become clearer. I have no intention of leaving unless circumstances force it."

Something in Boone's expression eased, a tension releasing that she hadn't fully registered until it disappeared.

"That's... good to hear," he said simply.

"Was that truly what was bothering you?"

Boone looked away. "Not entirely," he admitted after a long pause. "I've been... confused lately."

"About the camp's future?"

"About my own." The words seemed difficult for him. "About feelings I didn't expect to have again."

Rose's heart quickened. "What kind of feelings?"

Boone met her eyes. "Feelings for you, Rose. That's what's been troubling me."

The use of her first name, rare from his lips, emphasized the personal nature of his confession. Rose took a careful breath, aware they had reached a pivotal moment.

"I understand why that would be troubling. Given your loss."

"It feels like betrayal," Boone admitted, the words emerging with difficulty. "Like I'm forgetting her. Replacing her."

"Is that possible?" Rose asked. "To forget someone who was so deeply part of your life? To replace what you shared?"

Boone shook his head slowly. "No. That's what makes this so confusing. Mary remains... Mary. Nothing changes that. But these feelings for you exist alongside, not instead of."

"Perhaps that's how it should be," Rose suggested carefully. "The heart expands rather than exchanges. New feelings don't invalidate what came before."

"The reverend said something similar when we spoke yesterday," Boone admitted. "That honoring Mary's memory doesn't require sacrificing my future happiness."

"You spoke with Reverend Parker about this?" Rose asked, surprised.

"He approached me after Campbell's presentation, mentioned losing his brother in a logging accident. Said grief can become a prison if we let it." Boone's expression grew distant. "He asked if Mary would want me locked in that prison forever."

"And what did you answer?"

"That she wouldn't. Mary embraced life too fully to wish its absence on anyone, especially me."

Rose nodded, touched by this insight into the woman whose vision had shaped Trinity Station. "That sounds like the Mary I've come to know through others' memories."

"She would have liked you. Your determination. Your faith. Your practical kindness."

"I would have liked her too, I'm sure."

They stood in silence for a moment; the rain continuing to fall around their sheltered space.

"I don't know what to do with these feelings," Boone admitted finally. "I wasn't prepared for them."

"Feelings can simply be recognized and allowed to exist while we discern their meaning."

Boone studied her face. "You're not surprised."

A small smile touched Rose's lips. "I've had my own confusing feelings to consider," she admitted. "And more time to reflect on them."

"You have feelings for me also?" he asked, his voice carefully controlled.

"Yes, Boone. I do."

Boone's shoulders relaxed slightly, his expression softening.

"I don't know what happens next," he said honestly.

"Neither do I. But perhaps we don't need to know every step of the path to begin walking it."

"Faith," Boone observed, but without the dismissiveness that might have colored such a comment weeks earlier.

"Yes. But also practical wisdom. Some journeys reveal themselves only in the taking."

The rain began to ease, transitioning from a steady downpour to gentle patter. Droplets clung to pine needles and leaves, catching what light filtered through the clouds.

"The storm's passing," Boone noted, glancing upward through the branches.

Rose nodded, reluctant to break the intimacy of the moment yet aware they needed to return to camp eventually. "We should gather the rest of the yarrow before heading back."

"I'll help you finish," Boone offered. "Then perhaps... if you have time... we could work on the plant press design this afternoon?"

"I'd like that."

They emerged from beneath the pine to find the meadow transformed by rain. Colors appeared more vibrant, and the air felt freshly scrubbed. They completed their harvesting in companionable ease, working together with a new awareness of each other.

As they prepared to leave, Rose took a final look at the beautiful meadow. "I'd like to bring some of the older children here someday. There's so much they could learn from this place."

"We could arrange that," Boone said.

The use of "we" didn't escape Rose's notice. A small thing, perhaps, but significant in its implication of shared future plans.

The return journey passed more quickly than the outward trek. Their conversation flowed naturally between practical matters and occasional personal observations. Once, when Rose stumbled slightly on the path, Boone's hand came to her elbow to steady her—a simple touch that now carried new meaning for both of them.

"The plant press," Boone said as they approached the edge of camp. "I've been thinking about the design. A simple screw mechanism would apply even pressure without damaging delicate specimens."

"That sounds perfect," Rose agreed. "The schoolhouse would be a good place to work on it. I need to arrange these herbs for drying, anyway."

They parted briefly at the camp's edge—Rose to deliver a portion of yarrow to Ethel for Jed's continued treatment, Boone to his cabin. They agreed to meet at the schoolhouse in an hour.

Chapter 23

Rose pushed open the schoolhouse door to find Boone already there. He stood at her desk, examining several sheets of paper with pencil sketches of plant press designs. His shirtsleeves were rolled up to his elbows, revealing tanned, muscular forearms. He looked up as she entered, and the quiet intensity of his gaze made her pulse quicken.

"You've been busy," she observed, setting down her basket.

"I had some ideas after we parted," he said, gesturing to the sketches. "I wasn't sure how detailed your drawings might be."

Rose moved to stand beside him.

"These are excellent," she said, genuinely impressed by the precise technical drawings. "Far more detailed than my rough sketches."

Boone's design showed a wooden frame with adjustable screw mechanisms at each corner, creating even pressure across layers of absorbent paper where plants would be pressed.

"The screws allow for adjusting pressure based on the delicacy of the specimen," he explained, pointing to specific details. "And I've designed it so additional frames can be stacked as needed."

Rose traced the careful lines with her fingertip. "You have unexpected talents, Mr. McAlister. These could be professional drafting plans."

A ghost of a smile touched his lips. "Not so unexpected. I originally wanted to be a shipwright, remember? Design was part of that dream."

"The precision shows," Rose said. "William will have no trouble following these plans."

Their hands nearly touched on the paper, and neither moved away. The schoolhouse was quiet except for the distant sounds of camp activity filtering through the open windows.

"How much lumber will we need?" Rose asked.

"Not much. I've noted the dimensions here." Boone indicated the margin of his sketch. "Oak would be ideal for durability, but pine will serve if that's what's available."

"The specimens will need absorbent paper between layers," Rose added. "I have some, but we'll need more if the children are to make their own plant collections."

Boone nodded. "I'll add it to the supply order going to Portland within the week. Unless you'd like to discuss it with Campbell yourself. He's eager to support your educational initiatives."

Rose sighed, moving to arrange her herbs on the drying frames. "Mr. Campbell is certainly enthusiastic. Sometimes overwhelmingly so."

Boone's expression darkened slightly. "He tends to see people as pieces in his grand vision. Useful but interchangeable."

"Is that why you've been hesitant about his expansion plans?" Rose asked, carefully laying yarrow stems on a frame.

"Partly." Boone came to stand beside her, automatically helping arrange the herbs in neat rows. "Campbell sees Trinity Station as a business opportunity first, a community second. I worry about the consequences when those priorities conflict."

Rose nodded, appreciating his concern for the camp's welfare. "Yet, the expansion would benefit everyone here."

"If done right," Boone agreed. "Which is why I requested oversight of the construction process rather than leaving it to Portland contractors who've never lived in these conditions."

Rose glanced at him with new respect. "That was wise."

"Necessary," he corrected. "These will be homes for people I'm responsible for, not just company assets."

As they worked side by side preparing the herbs for drying, Rose considered how naturally they fell into a rhythm together. Boone's hands were large and calloused from years of axe work, yet they moved with surprising gentleness among the delicate plant stems.

"You mentioned faith earlier," Rose said, recalling their conversation in the forest. "About pathways revealing themselves in the taking."

"I did."

"That's different from how you spoke of faith when I first arrived."

"Many things are different from when you first arrived."

"The reverend hopes you'll attend services tomorrow, as do I," she ventured, testing the boundaries of this new territory between them.

"I know."

"Will you?"

He didn't answer immediately, and Rose let the question hang between them, not pressing for a response she knew must come from his own conviction.

"I haven't decided," he finally said. "Part of me wants to. Part of me remains... resistant."

"Because of Mary?"

"Because of what happened to her," he clarified. "Because I prayed while running with her in my arms, and those prayers went unanswered."

Rose moved to stand directly across from him, meeting his eyes over the drying frame. "What if they weren't unanswered, but answered differently than you hoped?"

"She died, Rose. What different answer could possibly justify that?"

"I don't presume to know God's purposes. I only know my own experience. That sometimes what feels like abandonment becomes something else when viewed through time's perspective."

"Like what?"

"Like how losing my family brought me to Trinity Station? To this place where I could be useful. To these children who needed teaching. And to you."

The simple words, a truth too important for either to look away from. Boone held her gaze, a questioning in his expression.

"I'm not suggesting Mary's death had a purpose that makes it acceptable," Rose clarified. "Only that God's presence doesn't end when tragedy strikes, even when it feels like it does."

"I want to believe that."

"I know," Rose said. "Faith isn't always a comfort, Boone. Occasionally, it's a wrestling match."

A corner of his mouth lifted slightly. "Genesis 32. Like Jacob with the angel?"

Rose smiled, pleased he remembered the biblical reference. "Exactly like that. And sometimes we walk away with a limp."

Boone nodded thoughtfully. He gathered several stems of yarrow, placing them carefully on the drying frame. "When Mary died, I was angry at God. Furious, really. For letting it happen. For not answering my prayers. For taking the one person who brought light into my life."

He arranged the yarrow with methodical precision before continuing.

"But lately, I've been thinking that refusing to acknowledge God doesn't hurt Him. It only hurts me. Keeps me locked in that prison Reverend Parker mentioned."

"And now?"

"Now I'm considering attending services tomorrow. Not because I've resolved all my questions, but because staying away hasn't resolved them either."

"That's courage, Boone. Real courage."

"It doesn't feel like courage. It feels like... surrender."

"Sometimes those are the same thing."

Their eyes met across the frame of drying herbs, and Rose felt a deepening connection beyond mere attraction or friendship.

"I should check these plant press measurements with William," Boone said after a moment, moving back toward the desk where his drawings lay. "Make sure they're feasible with the materials we have on hand."

"Of course. I can finish arranging these herbs."

"I'll return shortly," he promised, gathering his sketches.

Chapter 24

Boone's large frame filled the schoolhouse doorway, his presence announced by the creak of the hinges before Rose even looked up from her herbs. But it wasn't his return that made her hands still over the yarrow—it was what he carried. Balanced in his arms was a wicker basket covered with a white cloth, and tucked alongside it were several wildflower blooms, their delicate petals stark against the light weave.

"I thought you were checking measurements with William," Rose said, setting down the herbs she'd been arranging.

Boone stepped fully into the schoolhouse. He glanced down at the basket.

"I did speak with William. He said the press design is sound." Boone cleared his throat. "Ethel mentioned you skipped breakfast."

Rose moved closer, curious. "And she sent you with lunch?"

"Not exactly." A hint of color appeared high on his tanned cheeks. "I asked her to prepare it. For both of us."

Rose's eyes widened slightly.

"I know a place," he continued, his words measured as if carefully chosen. "Not far from camp. With a view of Trinity Station that I'd like to show you." He extended the small bunch of wildflowers toward her. "I thought perhaps we could continue our conversation there. If you're amenable."

Rose accepted the flowers, their stems still cool and damp from wherever he'd collected them.

"That sounds lovely," she replied, unable to keep the pleased warmth from her voice. "Let me just secure these herbs so they'll dry properly."

She moved quickly around the room, adjusting the drying frames and gathering her shawl from where she'd draped it over her chair. All the while, she felt Boone's gaze following her movements, patient yet intent.

"There," she said, returning to where he stood. "Everything's arranged."

Boone nodded, then extended his free arm to her in a gentlemanly gesture that seemed both natural and surprising coming from him. "Shall we?"

Rose placed her hand lightly on his forearm, feeling the solid muscle beneath the fabric of his sleeve. The simple contact sent a flutter through her chest that she hadn't experienced since her youth, except this was deeper somehow, more grounded in reality than girlish fantasy.

They stepped outside into the afternoon light, and Rose was immediately aware of Martha standing near the community well, her curious gaze following them. News would spread quickly in the close-knit camp, but Rose found she didn't mind.

"Which way?" she asked.

Boone guided her toward a narrow trail that branched away from the main logging paths. "It's about a fifteen minutes' walk. Not too strenuous."

The trail wound upward through stands of pine and fir, occasionally opening to offer glimpses of Trinity Station below. Rose noticed how Boone subtly adjusted his pace to match hers, and how his hand occasionally came to her elbow when the terrain grew uneven, steadying her with a touch that was both protective and respectful.

"I never realized the camp was so visible from up here," Rose remarked as they rounded a bend that offered a particularly clear view of the clearing below.

"Few do. Most trails lead away from camp into cutting areas." Boone paused, pointing toward where men were visibly setting up stakes near the edge of the cleared land. "Looks like Campbell's already marking boundaries for the new structures."

"He certainly doesn't believe in delaying progress. Though I admire his enthusiasm."

"Enthusiasm without planning leads to poorly built homes and wasted lumber," Boone replied, though his tone lacked the sharp edge it might have held days earlier. "I'll review his marked boundaries tomorrow."

"To ensure they're practical for the terrain?"

Boone nodded. "And for safety. Campbell understands business but knows little about building in these mountains and forests."

They continued along the trail, which narrowed as it curved around a massive boulder. Boone's hand moved to the small of her back, a brief guiding touch that sent warmth spreading through her.

They emerged suddenly into a small clearing perched on an outcropping that offered a breathtaking view. Below, Trinity Station sprawled like a miniature village, smoke rising from cook fires and the glint of the river visible beyond. All around, the forest stretched to distant mountains, an endless tapestry of green in varying shades.

"Oh," Rose breathed, momentarily stunned by the vista. "It's magnificent."

Boone's expression softened as he watched her reaction. "I named this Eagle's Rest. I found it my first month here, before the camp was even half-built."

He set down the basket and shook out a wool blanket he'd carried tucked under his arm, spreading it over a relatively flat space near the edge of the clearing. The domesticity of the gesture, coming from this typically stoic man, touched something deep in Rose's heart.

"May I help?" she asked.

"All set," he replied, kneeling to unpack the basket. "Ethel was generous with provisions."

Rose settled on the blanket, arranging her skirts as Boone revealed the contents of the basket: thick slices of fresh bread, cold roasted venison, a jar of preserved peaches, two apples, and a small jug that appeared to contain cider.

"This is quite a feast," Rose said, accepting a tin plate from him.

"Ethel insisted we needed sustenance after our morning of herb gathering." A flicker of amusement crossed his features as he added, "She may have been matchmaking."

Rose couldn't help but laugh. "She's not particularly subtle about it."

"No," Boone agreed, arranging food on Rose's plate before serving himself. "Though in this case, I can't fault her intentions."

Rose took a bite of bread to give herself time to compose her thoughts.

"Did you come to this spot often?" she asked finally. "With Mary?"

Boone considered the question, slicing the venison with his pocketknife. "Occasionally. Mostly in that first year when the camp was being established. It offered perspective when challenges seemed overwhelming."

"And after she died?"

"Not until today." His voice remained steady, though his hands paused momentarily in their task. "It didn't feel right somehow."

"Thank you for sharing it with me," she said quietly.

Boone nodded once, passing her a portion of the venison. Their fingers brushed during the exchange, a brief contact that seemed to linger in the air between them.

"So, tell me, was teaching always your ambition?" Boone asked.

Rose smiled, remembering her childhood plans. "Not initially. I wanted to be a traveling healer. I daydreamed frequently about visiting remote homesteads throughout our county, treating ailments and delivering babies."

"When did teaching enter the picture?"

Rose took a sip of cider, savoring the sweet-tart flavor. "Our minister's wife operated a small school. When I was sixteen, she asked me to help with the younger children. I discovered I loved watching, understanding dawn on their faces." She paused, remembering. "Grandmother said I'd found my calling—healing minds as she healed bodies."

"She was right," Boone observed. "You have a gift with the children."

"Teaching feels like breathing to me," Rose admitted. "Natural and necessary."

They ate in easy companionship, sharing stories from their respective childhoods. Rose's adventures gathering herbs with her grandmother, and Boone's early experiences timbering with his father.

As they finished eating, Boone gathered the empty plates, repacking them neatly in the basket. His movements were efficient, practiced—a man accustomed to order. Rose leaned back against the trunk of a pine tree at the clearing's edge, watching him with quiet appreciation.

"Campbell's expansion plans," Boone said as he settled beside her. "What do you truly think of them?"

Rose considered the question, recognizing its importance to him. "I believe Trinity Station could become something extraordinary—not just a logging operation, but a true community where families flourish. The plans themselves seem sound, though perhaps ambitious in timeline."

"And the proposed infirmary? That would significantly increase your responsibilities."

"I was surprised by Campbell's assumption, but not opposed to the idea." Rose turned slightly to face him. "Healing and teaching have always been intertwined for me. The infirmary would provide proper space for both aspects of service."

Boone nodded, his gaze thoughtful. "You've become essential to Trinity Station in a remarkably short time."

"I hope useful, at least," Rose replied modestly.

"Far more than merely useful." Boone's voice deepened slightly. "You've brought something this place lacked."

"I'm curious what matters most to you, Boone? Beyond Trinity Station's practical concerns."

He considered the question with characteristic thoughtfulness. "The welfare of those under my responsibility," he answered finally. "Ensuring the men return safely each day. Seeing families established securely. Building something that lasts." He glanced at her. "And you?"

"Faith, first," Rose replied. "Serving where I'm called. Using the gifts I've been given to their fullest purpose." She picked a small wildflower growing at the blanket's edge. "And finding meaning even in difficult circumstances."

Boone watched her twirl the little flower between her fingers. "Your faith guides everything, doesn't it?"

"It does," Rose acknowledged. "Not as rules to follow, but as the foundation everything else rests upon." She met his gaze directly. "It's why your spiritual journey matters to me, Boone. Not just as the camp's leader, but as..." She hesitated, searching for the right word.

"As someone you care about?" he supplied quietly.

"Yes."

Boone shifted, leaning forward to rest his elbows on his knees, his gaze on the distant mountains. "I understand the importance faith holds for you. I respect it, even when I struggle with my own."

Rose turned the flower in her hands, choosing her words carefully. "Faith isn't static, Boone. It grows like this flower... sometimes slowly, sometimes through difficult soil. What matters is that the roots continue reaching downward."

"Even when the evidence suggests otherwise?" There was no mockery in his question, only genuine inquiry.

"Evidence is complex," Rose replied. "When my family died despite my prayers and all my herbal remedies, I questioned everything. The silence felt absolute." She paused, remembering those dark days. "But continuing to live, to use what they taught me to help others... that became its own answer, eventually."

"How did you reconcile your prayers going unanswered?"

"I came to understand they weren't unanswered so much as answered differently than I'd hoped." Rose placed the small flower on the blanket between them. "I prayed for my family's recovery, but perhaps what they received was peace instead of pain. What I received was the strength to carry forward their legacy."

Boone absorbed her words, his expression introspective. "I've been thinking about attending services tomorrow," he said after a moment. "Not just for appearance's sake."

"What changed your mind?"

"Several things." His eyes met hers. "Conversations with you. Reverend Parker's remark about grief becoming a prison. And the realization that my absence affects more than just myself."

"The men look to you," Rose affirmed. "Your example matters."

"Not just the men," Boone said, holding her gaze with quiet intensity. "My spiritual journey, as you called it, affects what might exist between us as well. Doesn't it?"

The directness of the question sent a flutter through Rose's chest. "Yes," she admitted. "It does."

"Because shared faith would be important in a deeper relationship."

"Important, yes." Rose took a breath, choosing honesty over diplomacy. "Essential, even. Not because I require perfection or even certainty, but because faith shapes how I understand everything... purpose, morality, and the future. A life partnership would need that common foundation."

Boone nodded slowly, accepting her answer without visible disappointment. "That's fair. And honest."

"What about for you?" Rose asked. "Would it matter if I didn't share your values or vision for Trinity Station?"

"Absolutely," he replied without hesitation. "Compatibility in core principles is essential." He paused, a hint of dry humor touching his expression. "Though your initial reception suggested we might differ somewhat in that regard."

"We've both adjusted our visions, I think."

"True." Boone glanced toward the camp below, where activity continued as the afternoon progressed. "You've helped me see beyond immediate concerns to longer possibilities. I hope I've contributed some practical perspective in return."

"You have," Rose assured him. "We balance each other well."

Rose felt a deepening awareness of Boone's presence beside her, the breadth of his shoulders, the strength evident even in repose, and the surprising gentleness in his hands as he adjusted the blanket beneath them.

He began gathering the last of their picnic items, and Rose moved to help. As she reached for the cider jug, their hands collided. Boone's fingers wrapped reflexively around hers, warm and steady.

"Rose," he said, his voice lower than before.

She looked up to find his face much closer than expected, his eyes intent on hers. The world narrowed to this moment, his hand around hers, the mingled scent of pine and leather that accompanied him, and the almost imperceptible narrowing of the space between them.

"Boone," she whispered, suddenly aware of the rapid beating of her heart.

His free hand rose, hovering near her cheek without quite touching it. Rose felt herself leaning slightly forward, drawn by something powerful yet gentle between them.

A loud crack echoed through the trees, a branch breaking somewhere nearby, startling them both. Boone straightened, his hand falling away from hers as his gaze swept the surrounding forest with ingrained vigilance.

"Just a branch," he said after determining there was no threat. "The wind's picking up."

Rose took a steadying breath, both disappointed and somewhat relieved at the interrupted moment. They were still learning each other, still navigating the complex territory between friendship and something deeper. Patience was appropriate, even necessary.

"We should head back," Boone suggested, his voice returning to its normal register. "I sense the weather might be changing."

Rose nodded, helping him fold the blanket. The almost-moment lingered between them, acknowledged though unspoken, as they packed the remaining items into the basket.

As they prepared to leave the clearing, Rose bent to pick up the small wildflower she'd placed on the blanket earlier.

"For your collection?" Boone asked, watching as she tucked it carefully into her sleeve cuff.

"A reminder," she replied. "Of a significant conversation."

"Significant. Yes."

They began their descent toward camp; the path requiring single-file walking in many sections. Boone led the way, occasionally turning to offer a hand over trickier portions, each contact a brief connection that reinforced their growing awareness of each other.

As they neared the edge of camp, Rose spotted Martha and Beth hanging laundry. Both women paused in their work to watch Boone and Rose's approach with undisguised interest.

"We have an audience," Rose murmured.

Boone glanced toward the women, nodding a formal greeting that they returned with poorly concealed smiles.

"News travels faster than river water in Trinity Station. By dinner, everyone will know we shared a picnic."

"Does that concern you?"

"No. Though I'm not accustomed to being the subject of camp discussions."

"It's human nature to notice when patterns change. And you bringing me to Eagle's Rest represents a change."

"A deliberate one,"

They walked past the women, whose conversation resumed in animated whispers as soon as they passed. Rose suppressed a smile, remembering similar dynamics in her Pennsylvania community. Some aspects of human behavior remained consistent regardless of setting.

As they approached the cookhouse, they encountered Reverend Parker emerging with Campbell. The two men paused their conversation, Campbell's expression brightening with interest at the sight of them together.

"Miss Bellamy, Mr. McAlister," Reverend Parker greeted them warmly. "Enjoying this fine afternoon, I see."

"We were reviewing Trinity Station's boundaries from Eagle's Rest," Boone replied smoothly.

"An excellent vantage point," Campbell agreed enthusiastically. "I visited it briefly during my last stay. Perfect for visualizing the camp's potential growth." He gestured toward the papers in his hand. "We've been finalizing arrangements for tomorrow's service. Will you be joining us, Boone?"

"Yes, I'll attend."

Satisfaction crossed Reverend Parker's face, though he maintained a neutral tone. "We'll be pleased to have you join us, Mr. McAlister."

"Speaking of tomorrow's service," Campbell continued, "we were hoping you might lead a hymn, Miss Bellamy."

Rose blinked in surprise. "I'd be honored."

"Excellent!" Campbell clapped his hands together. "Service at ten o'clock in the cookhouse. We've arranged for the tables to be moved outdoors in the morning and benches set up in rows inside." He glanced at Boone. "Perhaps we could meet beforehand to discuss the proposed locations for the new structures?"

"Eight o'clock at my cabin," Boone agreed. "Bring the detailed drawings."

With polite nods, the two men continued on their way, Campbell immediately resuming their previous conversation with animated gestures.

Boone and Rose continued toward the cookhouse, where activity suggested dinner preparations were already underway.

"I should help Ethel," Rose said as they reached the steps. "And return her basket."

Boone handed her the picnic basket, but made no move to leave immediately. "I'll see you at dinner, then."

"I look forward to it," Rose replied honestly.

His eyes held hers for a moment longer than necessary. "Thank you for joining me today."

"Thank you for asking me. It was lovely."

He waited as she ascended the steps and opened the cookhouse door, his tall figure resolute in the yard. Rose paused in the doorway, glancing back at him with a smile that carried all the complexity of their afternoon together, gratitude, hope, and the quiet acknowledgment of something deepening between them.

As she entered the cookhouse, Rose tucked the memory of their shared afternoon carefully into her heart, like pressing a delicate flower between the pages of a treasured book.

Inside, Ethel glanced up from the large pot she was stirring, her eyebrows rising expectantly.

"Had a nice picnic, did you?" she asked, not bothering to hide her interest.

Rose smiled, setting the basket on a nearby table. "Very pleasant, thank you. The food was perfect."

"And the company?" Ethel pressed, lowering her voice as Clara entered from the storage room with an armload of potatoes.

"The company," Rose replied softly, "was even better than the food."

Ethel's satisfied smile suggested this was exactly the answer she'd hoped for. "Good. Now, tell me everything while we prepare dinner. Did he actually talk, or was it all meaningful silence?"

Rose laughed, taking the knife and beginning to work on the onions. "He talked quite a bit, actually."

"And the wildflowers?" Ethel nodded toward the flowers Rose had carefully placed on the table.

"They are lovely. I've never received a bouquet from a gentleman before."

Ethel nodded approvingly, returning to her stirring with a satisfied expression. "About time," she murmured, just loud enough for Rose to hear. "About time indeed for both of you."

Rose continued chopping onions, letting their pungent aroma explain the moisture gathering in her eyes. But in truth, it wasn't the onions that brought tears; it was the unexpected fullness of her heart, the sense of standing at the threshold of something precious and fragile and real.

"You're smiling like you've discovered a secret," Ethel observed, interrupting her thoughts.

Rose looked up. "Not a secret," she replied truthfully. "Just a possibility I hadn't dared hope for."

Ethel's expression softened with understanding. "The best kind of discovery," she agreed. "Now finish those onions before they make us both weep like schoolgirls."

Rose laughed and returned to her task, carrying the afternoon's conversation in her heart like a precious gift. One to be unwrapped

again in quiet moments, examined from every angle, and treasured for
the promise it held.

Chapter 25

Boone's fingers fumbled with the unfamiliar collar button, his calloused hands struggling with the small fastening. He muttered under his breath, trying once more to thread the polished button through the starched hole of his seldom-worn dress shirt. The garment felt restrictive, the collar stiff against his neck like a gentle stranglehold.

"Ridiculous," he murmured, finally securing the button and reaching for his one good coat hanging on the peg beside the mirror. The woolen garment smelled faintly of cedar from the chest where it had been stored since Mary's funeral.

He shrugged into the coat, adjusting the sleeves that felt slightly tight across his shoulders. Logging had built more muscle since he'd last worn it. The man looking back at him from the small mirror mounted on his cabin wall was almost a stranger, clean-shaven, hair neatly combed, and dressed like someone headed to a Portland church rather than the foreman of a remote logging operation.

His gaze drifted to the bureau drawer where Mary's Bible resided. For a moment, his hand hovered over the wooden knob, an instinct born of memory rather than conscious thought. He pulled the drawer open, revealing the leather-bound volume nestled among Mary's few remaining possessions that he couldn't bear to part with.

The Bible's cover was worn at the corners, the pages edged with the faint yellowing of frequent use. Mary had read from it every evening, her voice soft in the quiet of their cabin. Boone reached toward it, fingers almost touching the leather, before withdrawing his hand.

A new beginning deserves new actions, not simply carrying old patterns into different circumstances. He closed the drawer firmly.

A knock at his door interrupted his thoughts.

"Boone? Are you ready?" Simon's voice called from outside.

"Coming," Boone responded, casting one final glance at his reflection. The formal clothes felt like a costume, but the decision they represented was genuine enough.

He opened the door to find Simon waiting, similarly dressed in his Sunday best

Simon's eyebrows rose slightly. "Well now, don't you look proper," he remarked, unable to keep the surprise from his voice.

"Don't get used to it," Boone replied dryly, closing his cabin door behind him.

"The men will be glad to see you there," Simon said as they started down the path.

Boone nodded, not quite ready to discuss his reasons for attending. "We need to assist Jed to the services. He shouldn't miss the service just because he can't walk properly yet."

"Good thought," Simon agreed. "Clara mentioned he's been asking about attending. Cabin fever's setting in for that boy."

The morning air carried the promise of another warm day, though a slight breeze rustled the pines surrounding Trinity Station. Camp activity was subdued, as most families prepared for the upcoming service.

When they entered Jed's recovery room, the young man was struggling to pull a clean shirt over his head while balancing on his good leg.

"Need some help with that?" Boone asked, stepping forward.

Jed looked up, surprise written across his features at the sight of his formally dressed foreman. "Boss! You're coming to service?"

"Appears so," Boone replied, helping Jed maneuver his arm through the sleeve without losing balance.

"I'm glad for it," Jed admitted.

"Simon and I will help you get there," Boone said. "Doctor's orders say no weight on that leg yet."

"Miss Bellamy checked it this morning," Jed reported. "Said the healing's clean, but I need another week before trying to walk on it."

"Then we'll get you properly situated," Simon said, moving to Jed's other side. "Between the two of us, you'll float into that service like royalty."

The young lumberjack laughed. "Won't that be a sight? Jed Dawson, carried in like a king." His expression grew more serious as he added, "I appreciate it, boss. Being stuck in here while everyone goes about life... it's been lonesome."

Boone nodded in understanding. Isolation, whether physical or emotional, took its toll. He'd experienced enough of it this past year to recognize the hunger for community in Jed's eyes.

Between them, Boone and Simon managed to transport Jed from his room and into the main area of the cookhouse without jostling his injured leg. The normally bustling building had been transformed for the service. The large tables had been moved outside, where they would later serve for the fellowship meal, and benches arranged in neat rows facing a small pulpit fashioned from stacked crates draped with a clean tablecloth.

Joshua Campbell spotted them immediately, hurrying over with characteristic enthusiasm. "Boone! Excellent to see you attending!" he exclaimed, as if Boone's presence was a personal victory. "And bringing young Jed as well. Perfect, perfect."

Boone merely nodded, helping Simon maneuver Jed toward a bench near the front where his leg could be properly elevated.

As they settled Jed, Boone became aware of ripples of reaction spreading through the gathering crowd. Glances, nods, and small smiles of approval followed him as he moved through the makeshift sanctuary. Tom clasped his shoulder briefly, William offered a respectful nod, and Martha whispered something to her husband that made them both glance Boone's way with apparent approval.

Near the makeshift pulpit, Rose stood in conversation with Reverend Parker, helping arrange hymn sheets on a small table. She wore a dress of deep blue, simpler than the fashions Boone remembered from Salem or Portland, but elegant in its modest styling. Her golden hair was neatly arranged, catching light from the nearby window.

As if sensing his gaze, she looked up. Their eyes met across the gathering crowd, and Rose's face brightened with a smile that affected Boone's breathing in unexpected ways. She excused herself from Reverend Parker and moved toward him, weaving through the incoming families.

"Good morning," she greeted him.

"You look..." he hesitated, searching for an appropriate word that wouldn't reveal too much in such a public setting. "...well," he finished inadequately.

Rose's smile widened slightly. "As do you. I've never seen you in formal attire before."

"Been a while since I've had occasion for it," he admitted.

"Well, it suits you," she said simply. "Though I imagine the collar feels rather confining after work shirts."

Boone couldn't help the small laugh that escaped him. "Like a yoke on a yearling."

Her answering laugh drew attention from nearby families, several of whom exchanged knowing glances that Boone pretended not to notice.

"Reverend Parker will begin shortly," Rose said. "Will you sit with me?"

"I'd like that."

They moved toward an open space on a bench near the middle of the room. Ethel, directing traffic like a seasoned ship's captain, caught Boone's eye and gave him an approving nod before turning back to settling a disagreement between Peter and Paul Cooper and Timmy Wilson over seating arrangements.

Reverend Parker moved to the front of the room, then, raising his hands to quiet the assembled community. The gathering fell silent, expectation filling the air as children were shushed, and final adjustments were made to the seating arrangements.

"Friends and neighbors of Trinity Station," the reverend began, his voice carrying clearly through the room without excessive volume. "What a blessing to gather together in worship this morning. Though we meet in humble circumstances, I'm reminded of our Lord's promise that where two or three gather in His name, He is present with them."

Boone felt Rose shift slightly beside him, her posture straightening with attentive respect. He studied her profile, the quiet confidence in her expression as she focused on the reverend's words. Her faith wasn't rigid or performative, but as natural as breathing, integrated into every aspect of her being.

"Before we begin our hymn, I want to thank you all for the warm welcome extended to me," Parker continued. "I've been particularly impressed by the resilience of this community. Many frontier settlements focus solely on survival, but Trinity Station is clearly building something that transcends mere existence. You're creating a community founded on shared purpose and mutual support."

Murmurs of appreciation rippled through the gathering. Boone noticed Campbell nodding vigorously near the front, clearly pleased with this assessment.

"Now, to begin our worship, I've asked Miss Bellamy to lead us in our opening hymn, 'Amazing Grace,'" Noah announced, extending his hand toward Rose.

She rose gracefully from her seat, moving to stand beside the reverend. Without accompaniment, she began to sing, her clear voice filling the cookhouse with the familiar melody.

"Amazing grace, how sweet the sound, that saved a wretch like me..."

Boone had heard Rose singing with the children or quietly to herself while tending herbs or walking between the schoolhouse and cookhouse, but her voice in this setting carried a clarity and confidence that caught him by surprise. It wasn't trained or operatic, but pure and heartfelt, inviting others to join rather than performing for them.

The congregation began to sing along, first hesitantly, then with growing confidence. Boone remained silent, the words catching in his throat as unexpected emotion welled up inside him. The familiar lyrics about being lost and then found struck him with new meaning as he watched Rose leading the hymn, her face alight with genuine belief.

A memory surfaced—Mary singing this same hymn at a service in Salem before they moved to Trinity Station, her voice blending with the small church choir. The recollection brought a pang, but not the sharp, unbearable pain he'd grown accustomed to. Instead, it carried a bittersweet quality, like pressing on a bruise that had begun to heal.

As the final verse concluded, Rose returned to her seat beside him. Her cheeks were flushed slightly from singing, her eyes bright.

"That was beautiful," he said quietly as she settled beside him.

"The sentiment or the singing?" she asked with a small smile.

"Both," Boone replied honestly.

Reverend Parker led them through several prayers, including special mentions for Jed's continued recovery and thanksgiving for the camp's safety through recent logging operations. Boone followed along with more attentiveness than he'd anticipated, the familiar rhythms of worship gradually loosening something tight within his chest.

When Noah opened his Bible to begin the sermon, Boone noticed Rose retrieving a small notebook and pencil from her pocket. At his questioning glance, she whispered, "I like to note particularly meaningful passages to reflect on later."

This small detail, her active engagement with the message rather than passive listening, struck Boone as characteristically Rose. She approached faith as she did teaching, with thoughtful attention and a desire to incorporate what she learned into practical application.

"Our text today," Parker announced, "comes from Second Corinthians, chapter five, verse seventeen: 'Therefore, if anyone is in Christ, the new creation has come: The old has gone, the new is here!'"

Boone straightened. The verse seemed almost deliberately selected for him, though he knew Noah had likely planned his sermon before knowing Boone would attend.

"Many of us come to the frontier seeking new beginnings," Noah continued, looking around at the gathered community. "We leave behind homes, sometimes painful pasts, often looking for a fresh start in unexplored territory. But true renewal isn't found merely in changing our location, but in allowing God to transform us from within."

Rose wrote something in her notebook, her pencil moving swiftly across the page. Boone caught a glimpse of the words "transformation" and "inner change" before she turned the page.

"What's remarkable about this verse," Noah said, "is what it doesn't say. It doesn't say the past is erased, as if it never happened. It doesn't promise that our histories, with all their joys and sorrows, simply disappear. Rather, it promises a new perspective, a redemptive context in which even our most painful experiences can be transformed into something with purpose."

Boone felt Rose glance at him, but kept his gaze fixed on Noah. The reverend's words resonated with accuracy, addressing the very struggle he'd been facing. How to honor Mary's memory while allowing himself to move forward.

"God doesn't waste our experiences, friends. Not the triumphs, not the failures, and especially not the heartaches." Noah's voice grew gentler. "What feels like an ending may be, in God's economy, merely a painful but necessary transition to something new He is creating in us."

As the sermon continued, Boone increasingly engaged. Noah wasn't preaching abstract theology but practical faith for people who faced real dangers, hard work, and profound loss. His message acknowledged the reality of suffering while offering hope that such experiences could be integrated into a meaningful life rather than simply survived.

When Noah concluded, Boone realized he'd been leaning forward, absorbed in the message in a way he hadn't experienced since before Mary's death. Rose noticed too, giving him a warm smile as they rose for the closing hymn.

After the final blessing, the congregation began moving outdoors, where the tables had been arranged for the fellowship meal that would follow. The men, including Boone, pitched in to carry benches outside, arranging them around the tables while women brought out covered dishes prepared earlier that morning.

Boone helped Simon get Jed situated at a table near the cookhouse entrance, ensuring his injured leg was properly elevated on a stool.

"Looks like you survived the service," Jed commented with a grin once he was settled.

"Appears so," Boone replied dryly.

"Boss," Jed said, his tone growing more serious, "I just wanted to say... it means something to me, seeing you here today... that you're willing to be part of this again."

Before Boone could respond, Campbell approached with rolled-up plans tucked under his arm, his expression bright with the enthusiasm that seemed his perpetual state.

"Boone! Excellent service, wasn't it? I was hoping we might review these boundary stakes I've placed for the infirmary site. I think you'll find—"

"It's Sunday, Campbell," Boone interrupted, not unkindly but firmly. "Business can wait until tomorrow."

Campbell looked momentarily taken aback, then chuckled. "Of course, of course. A day of rest, as the Good Book says."

"We all work hard five to six days a week. We deserve one day without thoughts of cutting quotas and construction timelines."

Campbell raised his hands in good-natured surrender. "Fair enough. Tomorrow, then." He glanced toward where Rose was helping arrange food on the serving table. "Though I suspect your desire for a day of rest might have additional motivations."

Boone didn't dignify the suggestion with a response, but Campbell merely smiled knowingly before moving off to engage Reverend Parker in conversation.

Across the gathering, Rose stood surrounded by a group of women and children. Her blue dress stood out among the more muted colors typically worn in camp, making her easy to track amid the moving crowd. She was laughing at something Clara had said, her head tilted back slightly, the sound carrying across the yard.

Several of the children had begun playing an improvised game of tag, weaving between the adults with the boundless energy of youth. Boone watched them with a mixture of amusement and concern, noticing how their increasingly wild chase was veering dangerously close to the serving table.

"Samuel! James! Slow down!" Beth called, but her warning came too late.

Samuel, attempting to escape James's pursuit, cut sharply around Martha Riley, lost his footing on the uneven ground, and fell heavily. His cry of pain silenced conversations across the gathering as he clutched his knee, blood already visible through his fingers.

Boone moved without conscious thought, reaching the boy at the same moment as Rose. They knelt on either side of Samuel, whose face was contorted with pain and approaching tears.

"Let me see, Samuel," Rose said gently, her hands already reaching for his.

Beth and Tom pushed through the gathering crowd, concerned parental alarm on their faces.

"He'll be alright," Boone assured them, recognizing the fear in their eyes. "Just a scrape, from the looks of it."

"It hurts!" Samuel protested, his lower lip trembling as he fought against tears in front of the gathered community.

"I know it does," Boone said, his voice steady. "But it's nothing to worry about. Miss Bellamy will have you fixed up in no time."

Rose carefully examined the boy's knee, where a significant scrape had torn both his trousers and skin. "A good cleaning and a bandage, and you'll be right as rain," she confirmed, giving Samuel an encouraging smile.

"My medical supplies are inside," she added, looking up at Beth and Tom. "Would you like to bring him in, or shall I?"

"I've got him," Boone said, gathering the boy carefully into his arms. Samuel's weight was nothing to a man accustomed to handling heavy timber, and the child instinctively wrapped his arms around Boone's neck for stability.

"Does this mean I'm brave like Jed?" Samuel asked, his pain momentarily forgotten in the excitement of being carried by the camp foreman.

"Braver," Boone assured him. "Jed cried when he got hurt."

"I did not!" Jed protested from his bench, though his grin belied his indignation.

A ripple of relieved laughter spread through the watching crowd as Boone carried Samuel toward the cookhouse, Rose, and the Abernathy's following close behind.

Inside, Boone set Samuel down carefully on the cot that Jed typically occupied.

"Let's have a look at that knee," Rose said, kneeling before Samuel with a basin of clean water she'd retrieved from the kitchen area. She began gently cleaning the abraded skin, her movements practiced and efficient.

"Will it need stitches?" Samuel asked, wide-eyed at the prospect, torn between fear and the potential for an impressive story to tell his friends.

"No stitches today," Rose assured him. "But it's a good, proper scrape that will make an excellent scar to show your friends."

Boone knelt beside Rose, helping hold Samuel steady while keeping the boy distracted. "So, Samuel, I hear you've been learning about tree identification in school. Can you tell me three ways to tell a pine from a fir?"

Samuel's face brightened at the question, and he launched into an enthusiastic explanation about needle arrangement, cone shapes, and bark texture. His detailed knowledge surprised Boone, who glanced at Rose with raised eyebrows.

"He's one of my most attentive students when it comes to natural sciences," Rose explained, applying a soothing salve to the cleaned wound. "Particularly anything related to the forest."

"Pa says I might be a forester someday," Samuel declared proudly. "Or a sawmill operator."

"Both fine professions," Boone agreed seriously, as if discussing career options with an adult.

Beth watched the interaction with a warm smile. "Thank you both for taking care of him. Most men would have left such things to the womenfolk."

"Logging camps require all hands during emergencies," Boone replied with a shrug. "Even minor ones."

"Still, you work well together," Beth observed, her gaze moving between Boone and Rose with barely concealed approval. "Like you've been doing this for years."

Rose secured a clean bandage around Samuel's knee, her cheeks coloring slightly at Beth's comment. "There we are. All finished. Keep it clean, Samuel, and come see me tomorrow before school so I can check it."

"Can I go play now?" Samuel asked, already sliding off the bench.

"Walking only," his mother instructed firmly. "No more running games today."

Samuel nodded, then impulsively hugged Rose. "Thank you, Miss Bellamy." He turned to Boone, hesitated, then extended his hand formally. "Thank you, Mr. McAlister."

Boone shook his small hand with appropriate seriousness. "You're welcome, Samuel."

Samuel headed for the door, his gait only slightly favoring his injured leg.

Tom placed his hand on his wife's shoulder. "We should make sure he actually walks rather than runs the moment he's out of sight."

"Indeed," Beth agreed with a knowing mother's smile. She glanced back at Rose and Boone. "Thank you again."

In their absence, the room fell into relative quiet, the sounds of the gathering outside filtering through the open doors like distant music. Rose busied herself cleaning up the medical supplies while Boone remained, suddenly conscious of their solitude.

"How was it?" Rose asked finally, turning to face him directly. "Being here today, I mean. At the service."

Boone appreciated her directness. "Difficult," he admitted. "But not in the way I expected." He searched for words to explain the complex emotions he'd experienced. "It was like returning to a house you once lived in. Familiar in structure, but requiring new habits."

Rose nodded, understanding in her gaze. "Faith can be like that after absence. The framework remains, but our relationship to it changes with experience."

"Parker's sermon seemed... relevant," Boone acknowledged.

"I thought so too," Rose said. "Particularly, the part about God not erasing our past, but giving it new context and purpose."

"You think that's possible? That loss can have a purpose without diminishing its pain?"

"I believe so," Rose replied without hesitation. "Not in a way that makes the suffering itself good, but in how we grow through it." She moved closer, her expression earnest. "My parents' and grandparents' death will never be a good thing, Boone. But the person I've become through that experience, the ways I've learned to help others from my own pain... that can be meaningful without betraying their memory."

"Your faith sustained you through that."

"My faith gave me context," Rose corrected gently. "It didn't eliminate the pain or questions, but it provided a framework for understanding that I wasn't abandoned in my suffering."

"That's what I've struggled with most. The feeling of abandonment when Mary died." The words came easier than he expected, flowing from a place that had been tightly sealed for too long.

"I can't claim to understand God's purposes in allowing tragedy. But I do know He doesn't waste our pain, even when we can't see how He's using it."

"Your presence here seems to be part of that... redemptive context, Reverend Parker mentioned."

"I hope so," she replied softly. "I've certainly felt called here in ways I couldn't have anticipated."

"It's more than the teaching or the healing," Boone continued, compelled to articulate what had been growing clearer to him. "Your perspective... your ability to see possibilities beyond immediate circumstances... it's changed how I view Trinity Station. How I view the future."

"The future looks different to me, as well, Boone. Different from I imagined when I first arrived."

Boone fought the urge to reach for her hand, aware of the open door and the community gathered just outside.

"Boone!" Campbell's voice shattered the moment, calling from the doorway. "Sorry to interrupt, but we need your opinion on something. The men are talking about the best location for the church building, and there's quite the debate forming!"

Boone suppressed a flicker of frustration at the interruption. "I'll be right there," he replied, not taking his eyes from Rose's face.

"No rush," Campbell said with a knowing smile that suggested he understood exactly what he'd interrupted. "Though the debate is growing rather spirited." He disappeared back outside, leaving them alone again, but the moment had shifted.

"We should probably join the others," Rose suggested, though her tone conveyed reluctance.

"Probably," Boone agreed, equally unenthusiastic about returning to the gathering.

As they moved toward the door, Boone spoke again, feeling the need to complete the conversation Campbell had interrupted. "Rose, I want you to know that being here today wasn't just about community obligation or setting an example for the men."

She paused, turning back to him with questioning eyes.

"It was also about finding a way forward that honors the past without being imprisoned by it." He took a breath, choosing his words with care. "What's developing between us... it matters to me. More than I expected or felt prepared for."

"It matters to me also, Boone. Very much."

"I can't promise I won't struggle," he continued, needing her to understand. "With faith, with grief, with moving forward. But I am trying."

"I don't need promises of perfection," Rose assured him. "Just honesty and willingness to continue the journey. However, it unfolds."

"That I can offer," Boone said.

Rose's smile held both tenderness and hope, a combination Boone found increasingly essential to his days. "Then that's where we begin."

The sounds of the gathering outside filtered through the open door. Children laughing, adults conversing, and community life continuing its steady rhythm. Standing in the cookhouse with Rose, Boone felt something shift within him, like ice breaking up on a river after a long winter—not a complete transformation, but the definitive beginning of a thaw.

"Campbell will be back if we don't appear soon," Rose said with a small laugh.

Boone nodded, gesturing toward the door. "Shall we?"

Chapter 26

Boone squinted against the afternoon glare, bouncing off the Umpqua River as he directed men positioning logs for the next drive downstream. The familiar sounds of Trinity Station's river operation surrounded him—the grunt of men heaving timber, the splash of logs hitting water, the rhythmic creak of ropes straining under weight. The scent of fresh-cut pine hung in the air, mixed with the earthy musk of the river and the sweat of hard labor.

"Angle it more," Boone called to William and Simon as they maneuvered a massive Douglas fir trunk with pike poles. "Current will catch that end first if you don't counterbalance."

The men adjusted their stance, shifting the enormous log until it aligned properly with the others already floating in the collection boom.

Simon wiped his forehead with his sleeve. "Good catch. Would've broken free downstream."

Boone nodded, his attention already shifting to the next challenge. Supervising the river loading operation required constant vigilance.

One mistake could mean lost timber, or worse, injured men. Yet despite his outward focus, his mind kept drifting to yesterday's events.

The church service, that moment with Rose in the cookhouse after Samuel's injury, and the undeniable shift in their relationship. All of it had left him feeling strangely lighter. Not free of grief, but as though its weight had adjusted, becoming bearable.

Watching William demonstrate proper pike pole technique to a younger logger, Boone permitted himself a brief private moment of reflection. Rose's face came to mind, her expression when he'd admitted his feelings, earnest and hopeful yet patient. She understood his struggle without demanding its immediate resolution. That understanding meant more than he could articulate.

A peculiar stillness interrupted his thoughts. The forest had gone quiet. No birdsong, no chatter of squirrels, just the continuing sounds of men working, oblivious to the unnatural silence. Boone straightened, instinctively scanning the tree line.

"Boss?" Simon approached, noticing his sudden alertness. "Something wrong?"

Boone held up a hand, head tilted slightly as he concentrated. Years in the wilderness had honed his senses to recognize when something wasn't right. This sudden animal silence rarely meant anything good.

Then he caught it. A faint odor carried on the breeze, acrid and sharp. Not the controlled smell of a campfire or cooking smoke, but something wilder, more threatening.

Boone climbed quickly onto a stack of cut timber, gaining height to see over the trees toward camp. His breath caught as he spotted it, a dark plume rising from the direction of Trinity Station's center, thickening rapidly against the sky.

"Fire!" he shouted, jumping down. "Fire in camp!"

The men froze momentarily, then erupted into motion, dropping tools and scrambling up the embankment.

"Where?"

"Looks like the center of camp."

"Move!" Boone ordered, already running. "Simon, get two men to the water barrels. William and Tom, gather every bucket you can find. The rest with me!"

They raced along the river path, the fastest route back to camp. Boone pushed ahead, his longer stride quickly outpacing the others. His thoughts narrowed to immediate necessities: who would need rescuing, what structures might be saved, and how to contain the spread.

Yet beneath these practical calculations ran a current of fear he hadn't allowed himself to feel in months. Not for himself, but for Rose, for the children, and for the vulnerable members of what had become, despite his resistance, his community. His family.

***

Rose circled the outdoor classroom she'd established behind the schoolhouse, listening as Eliza recited the multiplication tables. The mild afternoon had prompted her to move their arithmetic lesson into the fresh air, a decision the children had met with enthusiastic approval.

"Seven times eight is fifty-six, seven times nine is sixty-three," Eliza continued confidently.

Rose nodded encouragement, glancing at the other children seated on logs arranged in a rough semicircle. Most were attentive, though Hannah was distracted by a butterfly fluttering near the wildflowers at the clearing's edge.

"Very good, Eliza," Rose praised as the girl completed the sequence. "Who would like to try the eights table next?"

Several hands shot up, including Timmy, which surprised Rose given his usual reluctance during mathematics lessons.

"Timmy, please proceed with—"

"Miss Bellamy, what's that?" Samuel interrupted, pointing past the schoolhouse toward the center of camp.

Rose turned, following his outstretched finger. A column of dark smoke rose above the tree line, thicker and more ominous than typical cooking smoke. Her stomach tightened as she realized it was coming from the vicinity of the cookhouse.

"Something's burning," Timmy said, standing for a better view.

The children rose in unison, craning to see, murmuring among themselves with growing alarm.

"It's the cookhouse!" Eliza cried, fear edging into her voice. "Mama's there helping Ethel with dinner!"

Rose's teacher instincts took over immediately, pushing aside her own rising panic. "Children," she called firmly, gathering their attention. "We need to remain calm and stay together."

"But my mama—" Eliza began, her voice rising.

"We'll make sure everyone is safe," Rose assured her, projecting confidence she didn't entirely feel. "First, I need all of you to stay right here. Timmy, you're in charge until I return."

The oldest boy straightened at the responsibility, nodding solemnly. "Yes, ma'am."

"I'm going to check on what's happening. All of you must stay here together. Do not follow me, understand? This is very important."

The children nodded, wide-eyed and solemn, clustering closer together as Rose picked up her skirts and ran toward the front of the schoolhouse.

Rounding the building, she had a clear view of the cookhouse. Thick black smoke poured from the windows where the kitchen was located. Even from this distance, she could see flames beginning to lick at the eaves.

The camp erupted into action. Men shouting, women running with buckets, and the alarm bell clanging urgently. Rose spotted Boone sprinting from the direction of the river, outpacing a group of lumberjacks behind him. Even in crisis, seeing him sent a jolt of relief through her.

Her mind raced through the implications. Monday afternoon—Ethel would be in the kitchen with several women preparing the evening meal. Jed would be resting in the small storage room where he'd been recovering. All her medical supplies and belongings were in her room.

But most importantly, people she cared about were in danger.

Rose rushed toward the cookhouse, then remembered the children behind the schoolhouse. She couldn't leave them alone, but she needed to help.

Reverend Parker appeared, hurrying from his and Campbell's cabin. "Rose! What's happening?"

"Fire in the cookhouse," she called. "The children are behind the schoolhouse. Please take them to safety, away from the smoke!"

The reverend nodded. "Of course. And you?"

"I need to help. Jed can't walk, and Ethel—"

"Go," he urged. "I'll take care of the children."

Rose hesitated only long enough to see him headed toward the schoolhouse before racing toward the growing commotion. The smoke grew thicker as she approached, stinging her eyes and catching in her throat.

A crowd had gathered, but maintained distance from the building, where flames now visibly danced along the roofline. The kitchen side of the cookhouse was fully engulfed. Orange fire licking hungrily at the seasoned timber.

"Has anyone seen Ethel?" Rose called as she reached the gathering.

"She's out," Martha pointed to where Ethel stood with Clara and Beth. "They got out when the fire first caught, but—"

"Jed's still inside!" Ethel shouted, pushing through the crowd toward Rose. Soot streaked the cook's face, and her apron was singed along one side. "The fire spread so fast..."

Beth sobbed nearby, her hands covering her face.

Rose scanned the burning building. The main entrance still appeared clear of flames, though smoke billowed from the open door. The kitchen at the side was fully ablaze, but Jed's recovery room was in the back. There might still be time.

A thundering voice cut through the chaos. "Get that bucket line formed NOW!" Boone reached the scene, taking command instantly. Men scrambled to obey, forming a chain from the well to the cookhouse.

Boone's gaze locked with Rose's across the yard, relief visibly washing over his features before his attention snapped back to the crisis. He strode to Ethel, grasping her shoulders. "Who's still inside?"

"Just Jed," Ethel gasped. "We tried to reach him, but the smoke—"

Without hesitation, Boone yanked his shirt over his head and dunked it in the nearest water bucket.

"What are you doing?" Simon grabbed his arm.

"Getting Jed out." Boone wrung out the shirt and tied it around his face to cover his nose and mouth.

"That roof's going to collapse," William warned, pointing to where the flames were eating through the supporting beams.

Rose pushed forward. "I'm coming with you."

Boone shook his head sharply. "Absolutely not."

Rose grabbed a nearby bucket, soaking her shawl and wrapping it around her face.

"Rose—" The conflict in Boone's eyes was clear even through the chaos surrounding them.

"There's no time to argue," she stated firmly.

Something shifted in Boone's expression—not acquiescence, but recognition of her resolve. He nodded once, curtly. "Stay close to me. If I say get out, you get out immediately. Understand?"

"Yes." Rose tucked the wet ends of her shawl more securely.

"Simon!" Boone called. "Keep that bucket line going. Focus on the north wall to keep the fire from reaching the sleeping quarters. William, be ready at the door!"

Taking a deep breath, Boone grabbed Rose's hand, and they plunged through the entrance.

Inside, the smoke hung thick as wool, reducing visibility to mere feet. Heat pressed against them from the kitchen area, where the roar of flames grew louder with each passing second. Boone kept low, tugging Rose toward the small alcove where Jed was.

"Jed!" she called, voice muffled through the wet fabric. "Jed, can you hear us?"

A weak coughing response guided them to the right. Rose felt along the wall, finding the doorway to the room. Inside, Jed's face was streaked with soot, his eyes red and watering.

"B-Boss?" he choked out.

"We've got you." Boone reached the bed in two strides, already pulling Jed's arm over his shoulders. "Can you put any weight on that leg?"

"Some," Jed gasped. "Not much."

"Lean on me," Boone ordered, taking the young man's weight. "Rose, get what you need and meet us at the door in thirty seconds!"

Rose nodded, already moving to the room she was staying in. The smoke was thickening rapidly, making each breath a struggle even through the wet shawl. She pushed through the door, eyes watering so badly she could barely see.

Feeling along the shelves. Her fingers brushed leather—there! She yanked the heavy bag free, then grabbed her bible and journal from the lower shelf. The heat was intensifying, and a loud crack from the ceiling sent her heart racing.

"Rose!" Boone's voice, urgent and strained, called from the main room.

"Coming!" She clutched the precious supplies to her chest and turned for the door just as a burning timber crashed down, blocking her exit with flaming debris.

Rose staggered back, mind racing. The window. She dropped to her knees, crawling beneath the worst of the smoke. The window was tiny, barely large enough for her shoulders, but it might be her only chance.

Outside, she heard Boone's voice, desperate now. "ROSE!"

She fumbled with the window latch, coughing violently as smoke filled her lungs despite the wet cloth. The simple wooden frame refused to budge, swollen shut from years of humidity.

Panic fluttered briefly in her chest, but Rose pushed it away. She grabbed a heavy jar from a nearby shelf and smashed it against the window frame. The glass shattered outward, leaving jagged edges around the frame.

Using her satchel to protect her hands, she knocked away the remaining shards. Fresh air rushed in, momentarily clearing her head.

The heat at her back grew unbearable as flames moved closer. Rose hoisted herself up, squeezing through the narrow opening. The rough wood scraped her sides, tearing her dress and scratching her ribs, but she pushed forward, wiggling until her torso was through.

Hands grabbed her from outside. Clara and Tom pulling her the rest of the way. She tumbled to the ground, gasping clean air into her burning lungs.

"Boone," she choked out. "Jed—"

"They made it out the front," Clara assured her, helping Rose to her feet. "William's got Jed. Boone went back in looking for you!"

Rose's heart seized. "No—he has to get out!" She staggered toward the front of the building, Clara supporting her arm.

They rounded the corner in time to see William and Simon forcibly restraining Boone at the main entrance, which was now belching thick black smoke.

"She's out!" Clara shouted. "Rose is here!"

Boone's head snapped toward them, his soot-blackened face transforming with relief. He shook off the men's restraining hands and rushed to Rose, grabbing her shoulders as if to assure himself she was real.

"You're hurt," he growled, noticing the blood seeping through her torn sleeve.

"Just scratches." Rose pressed her hand to his cheek, leaving a smudge in the soot. "I'm fine."

A thunderous crack split the air as the cookhouse roof began to cave in. Boone pulled Rose away from the building as lumberjacks redoubled their efforts with the bucket line, trying to prevent the fire from spreading to nearby structures.

"My satchel," Rose remembered suddenly.

"Here." Beth appeared beside them. "Clara handed it to me. Everything's safe."

Another section of roof collapsed with a shower of embers. The bucket line worked furiously, but it was clear the cookhouse couldn't be saved. Boone kept his arm around Rose's shoulders, both watching as the flames consumed the heart of Trinity Station.

"We need to check everyone for smoke damage," Rose said, her practical nature asserting itself despite her shaking hands. "Jed especially."

Boone nodded, reluctantly releasing her.

"It happened so fast," Ethel joined them, watching her domain burn with remarkable composure. "One moment I was stirring the beans, the next the whole wall was aflame."

"Dry timber," Boone said grimly. "We're lucky it didn't spread to other buildings."

Rose squeezed Ethel's hand. "We'll rebuild it better than before."

"True enough," Ethel sighed.

Jed appeared supported between William and Simon. His face was gray beneath the soot, and his breathing came in labored wheezes.

Rose immediately shifted to her healer role. "Bring him to the schoolhouse. I need to check his lungs."

Boone caught her arm as she turned to follow. "You need tending to."

"I'll be fine. Others need—"

"Rose." His voice dropped. "You could have died in there."

"But I didn't," she said. "And neither did you."

Boone's eyes held hers, communicating what words couldn't in the midst of crisis. "We'll talk later. Get those scratches cleaned while you're tending the others."

"I will if you will," she countered, nodding to the angry red burn on his forearm he hadn't even noticed in the rush of events.

A half-smile flickered across his grim features. "Agreed."

Simon called for Boone's direction about the water barrels.

"Go," Boone said, releasing her arm. "I'll find you when this is under control."

Rose nodded, already turning toward her patient, but the look they exchanged carried promise and relief that transcended the crisis surrounding them.

Chapter 27

Hours later, Rose finished binding the last of the minor burns and smoke-related injuries. The schoolhouse had been transformed into an impromptu medical station.

Jed rested on a pallet on the floor, his breathing eased by a steam treatment with herbs from Rose's salvaged collection. An herbal poultice covered the worst of the burns Tom had suffered while fighting the fire, and Beth had finally stopped coughing after Rose's honey and mullein mixture soothed her irritated throat.

"You should rest," Ethel advised, appearing at Rose's side with a cup of water. "You've been tending to everyone else for hours."

Rose accepted the drink gratefully. "Speaking of rest... we need to figure out sleeping arrangements. It will be dark soon. We need space for you, myself and Jed. I suppose we could sleep here in the schoolhouse."

"We have already worked that out," Ethel reported. "Jed will go back to his bed in the bunkhouse. The men staying there can assist him if he needs anything. I will stay with the Abernathy's. Boone offered his spare room for you."

Rose nearly choked on her water. "I beg your pardon?"

"Nothing improper," Ethel hastened to add. "He will stay with Joshua and the Reverend until other arrangements are made. He thought you might prefer privacy to sleeping on the schoolhouse floor."

Rose considered the offer. She was bone-weary, her ribs ached from squeezing through the window, and the thought of a quiet space to process the day's events was tempting. Still...

"People would talk," she said carefully.

Ethel snorted. "People already talk. Besides, these are extraordinary circumstances. Even Reverend Parker suggested it might be sensible, given your injuries need tending and Boone's cabin has a water supply nearby."

"The reverend suggested it?"

"Insisted on it, more like. After Boone made the offer." Ethel patted Rose's hand. "Your reputation is safe, dear. Everyone saw how you both risked your lives today. If anything, they're wondering when the wedding will be."

Heat that had nothing to do with the fire crept up Rose's neck. "Ethel!"

The older woman just laughed. "Go get some rest. I packed a few things the women have gathered for you." She said as she handed Rose a basket that held a clean dress, a bar of soap, a comb, and other necessities.

Rose accepted the basket, suddenly overwhelmed by the kindness surrounding her. "Thank you. For everything."

"We take care of our own," Ethel said simply. "Now go. I believe your escort is waiting."

Rose turned to see Boone standing in the schoolhouse doorway. Despite the chaos and destruction of the day, Rose's chest fluttered at the sight of him.

She crossed to join him.

"Are you okay?" Boone asked, voice roughened by smoke. His eyes took in her bandaged arms and the soot still smudging her face.

"I'm fine," she began automatically, then amended at his skeptical look. "Tired. Sore. But grateful everyone survived."

Boone nodded, understanding completely. "Ethel mentioned my offer?"

"She did." Rose glanced back at the crowded schoolhouse. "It's very kind, but I don't want to impose."

"It's no imposition." Boone's voice remained neutral, but his eyes conveyed more. "You need rest, Rose. Proper rest."

"Thank you. I accept."

Relief flickered across his features. He took her satchel and the basket and offered his arm with formal propriety that would have made her smile under different circumstances. As they stepped outside, the night air felt cool against her skin. Rose could see the still-smoldering remains of the cookhouse silhouetted against the darkening sky.

"How bad is the damage?" she asked as they walked toward Boone's cabin.

"The cookhouse is a total loss. We salvaged some cast iron cookware and metal implements, but all the rest is gone. We've secured emergency supplies from the river storehouse. Campbell is already talking about expediting the construction plans, starting with a new dining hall and kitchen."

"At least no one was seriously hurt," Rose offered. "Buildings can be replaced."

Boone's pace slowed, his profile somber in the fading light. "When I couldn't find you..." He stopped walking entirely, turning to face her. "Rose, I thought—"

"I know." She touched his arm, feeling the tension in his muscles. "I'm so sorry for frightening you. The burning timber fell so suddenly."

"I never want to feel that kind of fear again."

"I'm here," she said. "We both are... and we're both fine."

Boone drew a deep breath, visibly composing himself.

They resumed walking, crossing the central clearing toward Boone's cabin. A few camp members nodded respectfully as they passed.

Boone's cabin appeared ahead, sturdy and welcoming, with light glowing from the windows. He had clearly been back already. The front step was swept clean, and a lantern burned beside the door outside.

"I prepared the room earlier," Boone explained, opening the door. "It's small, but private."

Rose stepped inside.

Boone's living quarters were tidy, books stacked neatly and surfaces wiped clean.

"Through here." Boone led her to a narrow door off the main room. Beyond it lay a small chamber with a narrow bed with fresh linens, a small table with a basin of clean water, a towel, and a piece of soap. A lantern provided gentle light, and a tiny window near the ceiling afforded both ventilation and privacy.

"This is perfect," Rose said honestly, touched by the simple comforts he'd arranged. "Thank you."

Boone set her satchel and basket on the floor. "I'll be with Campbell and the Reverend should you need anything. The water's clean—I fetched it from the spring, not the well. Better for washing wounds."

The thoughtfulness of this gesture affected Rose deeply. "Now, let me see that burn on your arm."

Boone started to protest, but Rose fixed him with a stern look that brooked no argument. With a sigh that might have contained a hint of amusement, he rolled up his sleeve to reveal an angry red mark along his forearm.

"This is a second-degree burn."

Rose cleaned the burn thoroughly before applying a salve from her supplies. "This will ease the pain and help prevent scarring," she explained, spreading the creamy mixture over the damaged skin. "But you'll need to keep it clean and reapply the salve morning and night."

"Yes, ma'am," Boone replied.

She glanced up to find him watching her, his expression soft in the lantern light. Their eyes held.

The events of the day, the terror of the fire, the fear for each other's safety, and the relief of survival, seemed to crystallize at that moment, creating a clarity neither could deny.

"I thought I lost you today," Boone said quietly.

"I know," Rose replied, her hand still resting lightly on his arm. "I felt the same when they told me you'd gone back inside looking for me."

"It made me realize something." Boone covered her hand with his own. "Life doesn't offer guarantees, Rose. Mary's death taught me that much. But avoiding connections and being a part of other people's lives doesn't protect us from loss, it just prevents us from experiencing what matters most."

Rose held her breath, hardly daring to hope she understood his meaning.

"I don't want to wait anymore," he continued, his voice gaining certainty. "Not for some perfect moment when all my doubts are resolved and all my grief is processed. Those things may take years, and I don't want to waste another day not moving forward. Not with you."

"Boone," Rose began, but he gently squeezed her hand, asking her to let him finish.

"I care for you, Rose Bellamy. Deeply. In ways, I didn't think possible again. I'm still figuring out how that fits alongside what I felt for Mary, but I know with absolute certainty that I would like to discover the answer with you beside me. Not someday, but now."

Rose felt tears gathering, the emotional weight of the day finally breaking through her careful composure. "I care for you, too. So much."

Boone reached up to brush a tear from her cheek, his touch infinitely tender. "After today, I would rather not waste time with a slow courtship ritual. Life is too uncertain, too precious. If you'll have me, imperfect and still healing as I am, I want to court you properly. Openly."

Rose covered his hand with her own, turning her face into his palm. "Yes," she whispered. "Yes, to all of it."

The simple acceptance seemed to release something in Boone, his shoulders loosening as if shedding a heavy burden. Slowly, giving her every opportunity to pull away, he leaned forward and pressed his lips to her forehead in a kiss of such gentle reverence that fresh tears sprang to Rose's eyes.

When he pulled back, his own eyes shimmered with emotion in the lantern light. "You should rest now. It's been a long day."

Rose nodded, suddenly aware of the bone-deep exhaustion settling over her. "Will you be all right? You need rest too."

"I'll be fine," Boone assured her. "I want to check on the men standing fire watch tonight to make sure the building doesn't re-ignite, then I'll sleep."

"Goodnight, Boone, and be safe," she said.

"Goodnight, Rose. Sleep well."

He withdrew, closing the door quietly behind him. Rose listened to his footsteps moving about the main room, then the sound of the front door opening and closing as he went to make his final rounds.

She changed into a nightgown she found in the basket, the simple task requiring monumental effort in her exhausted state. As she slipped beneath the clean sheets of the narrow bed, Rose realized she felt no awkwardness about staying in Boone's home. Instead, she felt protected, cared for, and strangely at peace, despite the day's dangers and destruction.

Rose's last conscious thought before sleep claimed her was a prayer of thanksgiving, not just for physical survival, but for the precious gift of life and new beginnings rising from the ashes of what had been lost.

Chapter 28

The smell of smoke clung to Rose's hair as she bolted upright in the unfamiliar bed, her heart hammering. For a moment, panic gripped her as she tried to place her surroundings in the dim light filtering through the small window. This wasn't her room at the cookhouse. Then reality flooded back. The fire, the desperate escape, Jed's rescue, and finally, Boone's declaration.

Rose touched her bandaged arms, wincing at the sting of scratches from her window escape. Her throat felt raw from the smoke, and her muscles protested even simple movements. But she was alive. They all were.

She slipped from beneath the clean sheets of the narrow bed in Boone's spare room, her bare feet meeting cool wooden floorboards. The events of yesterday tumbled through her mind. The terror of the flames, her window escape, and Boone's words.

"I care for you, Rose Bellamy. Deeply. In ways, I didn't think possible again."

Rose knelt beside the bed, folding her hands in prayer as the morning light strengthened.

"Lord," she whispered, "thank You for protecting this community through yesterday's fire. Thank You for sparing lives and for giving us strength to face what comes next. Guide me in this new path with Boone. Grant us both wisdom as we navigate these waters together. Help me be patient with his journey back to faith. And Lord, please guide our hands as we rebuild what was lost."

She remained on her knees a moment longer, drawing strength from the stillness of morning prayer. When she rose, Rose felt steadier, more prepared to face the day's challenges.

The dress she'd worn yesterday was ruined, torn from her escape through the window and reeking of smoke. She turned to the basket Ethel had given her last night, finding a simple green dress. It was slightly loose around the waist, but otherwise fit well enough.

After washing her face and hands in the basin of water Boone had left, Rose braided her hair and pinned it neatly. She hesitated at the small mirror hanging on the wall, noticing the smudge of soot she'd missed along her jawline. Scrubbing it away, she studied her reflection. The woman who looked back appeared different somehow. Perhaps it was just exhaustion, or perhaps it was the knowledge that yesterday had changed something fundamental in her life.

Rose gathered her few possessions, making the bed with careful precision before leaving the cabin.

The morning air still carried the acrid scent of the burnt cookhouse, but it was diluted by the familiar smells of pine and earth. As Rose closed the cabin door behind her, she spotted something on the porch step. A small bunch of white trillium flowers, carefully arranged and tied with a piece of twine, underneath a note:

Rose,
Meeting at 8 o'clock near the schoolhouse to organize today's efforts.
Rest today if you need to.
—B

Rose tucked the note in her pocket and the flowers in her basket before heading toward the center of camp.

***

Trinity Station hummed with activity as Rose approached the schoolhouse. A crowd had gathered in the clearing between the school and the smoldering ruins of the cookhouse. The blackened skeleton of the building stood stark against the morning sky, wisps of smoke still rising from the collapsed roof.

Joshua Campbell stood atop an overturned crate, gesturing emphatically as he addressed the gathered community. "We'll expedite construction of the new dining hall immediately! I've already drafted revised plans, expanding the initially proposed building by twenty percent to better serve the camp's needs."

Boone stood near Campbell, arms crossed over his chest. His gaze moved systematically across the crowd until it found Rose. The moment their eyes met, his posture subtly shifted, shoulders relaxing minutely.

"While Campbell's plans have merit," Boone stated, "our immediate concern is establishing a functional cooking area immediately. Today, Simon, William, and Tom will construct a temporary outdoor kitchen."

"We've retrieved most of the cast iron cookware," Simon confirmed, gesturing to a collection of scorched but serviceable pots and Dutch ovens. "Ethel says they just need a good scrubbing."

Rose watched Boone as he continued outlining practical arrangements. His leadership style remained direct and efficient, but she noted subtle changes in how he addressed the community, more inclusive, acknowledging various needs beyond mere survival, and incorporating suggestions rather than simply issuing directives.

Reverend Parker stepped forward as Boone concluded. "If I might suggest, a brief prayer for our community would be appropriate before we disperse to our tasks."

Boone nodded. "Please lead us, Reverend."

The entire community bowed their heads as Noah offered a simple prayer for safety, wisdom, and unity in their rebuilding efforts. Rose watched Boone through barely lowered lashes. His head was respectfully bowed, his expression solemn but no longer resistant.

As the prayer concluded, Boone began assigning specific tasks, directing groups with calm authority. Rose moved toward Ethel and the other women to coordinate medical checks and clothing distribution.

"Miss Bellamy!" Eliza called, running up with Samuel, hobbling behind on his injured knee. "Is it true you're living with Mr. McAlister now?"

The innocent question carried clearly across the suddenly quiet gathering. Rose felt heat rise to her cheeks as several heads turned their direction.

"Eliza," Beth scolded, hurrying over. "That's not appropriate."

"But Papa said Miss Bellamy slept at Mr. McAlister's house," Samuel added helpfully.

Tom appeared behind his children, looking mortified. "I only mentioned that Mr. McAlister had offered his spare room temporarily after the fire," he explained hastily. "Children, Miss Bellamy needed a safe place to rest after helping save Jed's life."

"And Mr. McAlister slept with Reverend Parker and Mr. Campbell," Timmy announced with absolute certainty, compounding the awkwardness.

A strangled sound that might have been suppressed laughter came from Simon's direction. Even Boone's ears had reddened, though his expression remained admirably composed.

"Mr. McAlister kindly offered me shelter for one night while he stayed elsewhere," Rose explained gently.

"Oh," Eliza looked disappointed by this mundane explanation. "I thought maybe you were getting married."

This time, the laughter couldn't be contained. Several of the lumberjacks chuckled openly while Beth looked skyward, as if seeking divine intervention.

"Children, that's quite enough," Reverend Parker intervened kindly. "Run along now and play."

As the children scampered off, the gathering naturally broke into smaller working groups.

Martha appeared at Rose's elbow. "Well, if you wanted the courtship to remain private, that ship has sailed," she observed dryly.

"Apparently so," Rose agreed, adjusting her sleeve to better cover her bandaged arm. "Though I'd hardly call it a courtship yet."

Martha raised an eyebrow. "Not what I heard from Clara, who heard from Simon, who overheard Reverend Parker telling Campbell that Boone specifically mentioned courtship intentions."

"The camp grapevine works with remarkable efficiency," Rose commented, unable to suppress a smile.

"Faster than the telegraph," Martha agreed cheerfully. "Now, shall we see about those clothing supplies?"

***

By midday, the immediate crisis had evolved into organized activity. Boone supervised the construction of a temporary cooking shelter while monitoring the ongoing safety checks of the burned structure.

He wiped sweat from his brow as he secured a roof timber on the temporary structure. The physical labor felt good—practical, tangible progress. His gaze drifted toward the schoolhouse, where Rose had established a medical station to check on those with lingering smoke exposure.

Even from a distance, he could see her efficient movements as she examined Jed's healing leg. Her hair had come slightly loose from its braid during her work, golden strands catching the light as she bent over her patient.

Simon approached, interrupting Boone's observations. "The Roof's secure," he reported. "Ethel's already declared it suitable for cooking. She's a woman who adapts quickly."

"We all have to," Boone replied, turning his attention back to his foreman. "How's the salvage operation progressing?"

"William's pulled most of the usable metal from the eastern side. The kitchen area is still too hot to safely search."

Boone nodded. "Keep a rotation of men on it, but ensure they work in pairs for safety."

"Already arranged," Simon confirmed. He hesitated, then added with attempted casualness, "So, you and Miss Bellamy..."

Boone shot him a quelling look. "Is there a question there, Simon?"

"Just noting that life takes unexpected turns," Simon replied, undeterred.

"That it does, Simon," he said simply.

Simon nodded, accepting that was all the confirmation he would receive, and moved off to check on the salvage team.

Across the clearing, Boone noticed Campbell deep in discussion with Reverend Parker and several of the women. Their gazes kept shifting toward Rose, and Campbell was gesturing toward an area beyond the schoolhouse.

Boone made his way toward them, catching the tail end of Campbell's enthusiastic proposal.

"—could be finished within two weeks if we prioritize it! A small but proper home, nothing elaborate, but suitable for a lady of Miss Bellamy's standing. Located adjacent to where the new schoolhouse will eventually stand."

"That's very generous," Clara was saying, "but in the meantime—"

"In the meantime," Campbell continued, "perhaps arrangements with one of the families? I understand space is limited in all the cabins, but surely—"

"Miss Bellamy is welcome to stay with us," Clara offered. "It will be tight, but we can manage. Andy can sleep on a floor pallet."

"That's very kind," Rose's voice came from behind Boone. She had approached without his noticing. "I wouldn't want to impose more than a night or two while a more permanent solution is arranged."

"No imposition," Clara assured her. "Simon already agreed."

Campbell rubbed his hands together. "Well then! I'll start drawing up plans for Miss Bellamy's home immediately. Nothing too elaborate, but properly appointed for a lady teacher."

"Mr. Campbell," Rose interjected gently, "while I appreciate the consideration, the new dining hall should take priority over accommodations for me."

"Nonsense!" Campbell exclaimed. "We can manage multiple projects simultaneously. The company is committing significant resources to Trinity Station's development. Besides, a proper homestead for our teacher is an investment in the community's future!"

Reverend Parker studied Rose thoughtfully. "Miss Bellamy's correct about priorities, Joshua. However, establishing proper accommodations for her does serve the community's long-term interests. Perhaps a balanced approach?"

Boone stepped forward. "The reverend's right." All eyes turned to him. "We need permanent housing for Rose, but it doesn't need to be elaborate or immediate. Clara's offer solves the immediate need," Boone continued. "Campbell can draft simple plans for review. Construction can begin once the cookhouse is underway."

"Very sensible," Reverend Parker agreed, nodding approvingly. "Miss Bellamy, does this arrangement meet with your approval?"

"It does," Rose confirmed. "Thank you all for your consideration."

As the group dispersed, Boone found himself momentarily alone with Rose at the edge of the clearing.

"Are you truly comfortable staying with the Blackwoods?" he asked quietly. "Clara means well, but their cabin is crowded."

"It's only temporary. I can manage."

"You've had no time to rest," Boone observed, noting the shadows beneath her eyes despite her energy. "Your arms need tending."

"I'm fine," she started automatically, then caught herself with a small smile. "There are others with greater needs."

Boone frowned. "You can't care for others if you don't care for yourself, Rose."

"Says the man who hasn't stopped working since dawn, I imagine," she countered gently.

Boone glanced at the position of the sun, realizing how much of the day had passed. "Would you—" he began, then paused, conscious of his words in this new territory between them. "I thought we might take a brief respite later. Perhaps visit Eagle's Rest again? There are matters we should discuss."

Rose's expression softened. "I'd like that. Give me an hour."

"I'll meet you by the north trail, then."

Chapter 29

The trail to Eagle's Rest seemed steeper than Rose remembered as she climbed beside Boone later that afternoon. Her muscles ached from yesterday's exertions and today's constant activity, but she welcomed the chance to escape the camp's bustle.

"Campbell's enthusiasm is admirable, if exhausting," Rose remarked as they navigated a particularly rocky section. "He's already named the new dining hall 'Trinity Station Community Center' and added a larger living space for Ethel."

"By the time construction actually begins, he'll have designed a three-story building with a clock tower." Boone said, offering his hand as they approached a steep incline.

Rose placed her hand in his. Boone's grip was solid and warm, his calloused palm a reminder of the hard work that shaped his days. He didn't release her hand immediately when they reached level ground, and Rose didn't pull away.

"The community's response has been remarkable," she observed as they continued walking. "Everyone contributing what they can."

"Frontier towns survive through cooperation," Boone replied. "Though Trinity Station has shown unusual cohesion. I believe you've influenced that."

"Me?"

"Your approach to teaching extends beyond the schoolhouse. You've shown people the value of sharing knowledge and resources." He glanced at her. "It's changed how they interact, even the men at the cutting sites."

Rose considered this. "I hadn't noticed. I thought it was your leadership becoming more community-focused."

"Perhaps we've influenced each other," Boone suggested.

They emerged into the clearing at Eagle's Rest, the vista opening before them. From this elevation, Trinity Station looked both vulnerable and resilient. The blackened remains of the cookhouse stood stark against the surrounding buildings, but the bustle of activity visible even from a distance spoke of determination rather than defeat.

"It puts things in perspective," Rose said softly, moving to stand near the edge of the clearing. "The fire could have been so much worse."

"It very nearly was," Boone replied, his voice tightening at the memory. He joined her, close enough that their shoulders almost touched.

For a few moments, they stood in contemplative silence, watching distant figures move about the camp like industrious ants, rebuilding what had been damaged, adapting to changed circumstances.

"The children created quite a commotion this morning," Rose said finally, a hint of amusement coloring her voice.

"Children lack the filter adults develop," Boone observed dryly. "Though in this case, they merely accelerated the inevitable."

"The inevitable?"

"Community awareness of our... situation."

Rose turned slightly toward him. "And what exactly is our situation, Boone?"

The direct question was characteristic of her, and Boone appreciated it. No games, no coy evasions—just honest inquiry seeking clear understanding.

"Last night, I asked to court you properly," he said, meeting her gaze. "If your answer remains yes, then we are in a courtship, by my understanding."

"It does remain, yes," Rose confirmed, her voice soft but certain. "Though I admit I'm not entirely sure what courtship looks like in a frontier logging camp."

A slight smile touched Boone's lips. "Nor am I. My courtship with Mary occurred in Salem, with proper parlor visits and chaperoned walks."

"Considerably more formal than our circumstances allow," Rose agreed.

"Though no less serious in intention," Boone added, his expression growing solemn. "Rose, I want you to understand something. When I speak of courtship, I do so with clear purpose. I'm not seeking casual companionship."

"I understand," Rose said. "And I share that perspective. Courtship has a purpose, to determine compatibility for marriage."

The word hung between them, both acknowledging the ultimate direction of their path while recognizing the journey still required.

"I've been thinking about Mary's Bible," Boone said after a moment, the apparent change of subject startling Rose. "I kept it in a drawer after she died. Couldn't bear to see it, couldn't bear to part with it."

Rose remained quiet, sensing the importance of letting him navigate this territory at his own pace.

"Sunday, I almost took it with me to the service, then decided against it." He gazed out over the camp, his profile strong against the backdrop of the forest. "I thought I needed a completely fresh start. But when I returned to my cabin last night to prepare the spare room for you, I realized Mary's faith journey is part of mine, not separate from it."

"That sounds like wisdom," Rose said.

"This morning, I read from it for the first time since her death." Boone turned to face Rose directly. "The pages were marked at Ecclesiastes. 'To everything there is a season, and a time, to every purpose under heaven.'"

Rose nodded, recognizing the passage. "A time to weep, and a time to laugh; a time to mourn, and a time to dance."

"Mary believed that," Boone continued. "Even in difficult times, she looked for purpose and meaning. I lost sight of that after her death."

"Grief can do that. It narrows our vision until all we can see is what we've lost."

"Yes." Boone's gaze held hers steadily. "But you've helped me widen that vision again, Rose. To see beyond immediate pain to possible futures."

The simple acknowledgment touched Rose deeply. "I believe God brings people into our lives for purposes we may not immediately understand. Sometimes those purposes become clear only in retrospect."

"Like your arrival at Trinity Station," Boone suggested.

"Yes. I came believing I was called to teach and heal, but the purpose seems to have been broader than I imagined."

Boone nodded thoughtfully. "If we proceed with this courtship, we should establish some guidelines. Practical ones, given our unusual circumstances."

"Such as?"

"Time together should be balanced with our responsibilities to the camp," Boone began. "Neither of us would be comfortable prioritizing personal matters over community needs, especially now."

"Agreed," Rose said. "And our conduct should reflect our Christian values, particularly as the children look to us as examples."

"Propriety matters," Boone agreed. "Though frontier propriety differs somewhat from Eastern standards."

"Indeed. I think what matters most is honor and transparency. No secret meetings or behaviors we wouldn't want witnessed."

"Sensible." Boone's expression remained serious, but his eyes held warmth. "I'd like to escort you to Sunday services regularly. And perhaps share evening meals."

"I'd like that," Rose said. "And walks and outings like this, when the weather permits. I've found conversation flows more naturally during walks."

"Like now," Boone observed.

"Exactly like now."

A comfortable quiet settled between them as they each considered the path ahead. The afternoon light had begun to soften, indicating it would soon be time to return to camp and their respective duties.

"There's something else," Boone said finally. "Something I'd like to do, if you're willing."

"What is it?"

Boone hesitated, an uncharacteristic uncertainty crossing his features. "I think we should pray together. About the camp's recovery, about our courtship... everything."

The request took Rose by surprise. Not because it was unwelcome, quite the opposite, but because it represented such a significant step in Boone's spiritual journey.

"I'd be honored," she said. "Would you like to lead, or shall I?"

"Would you begin?" Boone asked. "I'm... out of practice."

Rose nodded and held out her hand, which he took without hesitation. His larger hand enfolded hers completely, warm and strong.

"Dear Heavenly Father," Rose began, her voice clear in the quiet clearing. "We thank You for Your protection during yesterday's fire, for sparing lives and providing the strength needed to face this challenge. We ask for wisdom as Trinity Station rebuilds and that priorities be clear and resources sufficient."

She paused, giving Boone space to add his voice if he chose. After a moment of silence, he continued, his deeper voice joining hers.

"Lord, guide the men working to salvage what remains and build what's needed. Keep them safe from injury and frustration. Help us all remain mindful of each other's needs during this time."

The simple words, spoken without flourish, moved Rose deeply. His prayer was practical and direct, much like the man himself, yet the fact that he prayed at all represented profound growth.

"And Father," Rose added softly, "we ask Your blessing on this courtship, that it be guided by Your wisdom and filled with Your grace. Help us to honor You and each other as we move forward together. Amen."

"Amen," Boone echoed, his voice low and steady.

As their prayer concluded, Boone didn't immediately release her hand. Instead, he raised it slowly to his lips and pressed a gentle kiss to her knuckles, his eyes never leaving hers.

The gesture, simple yet profoundly intimate, sent warmth cascading through Rose's entire body.

"We should return," Boone said, lowering her hand but still holding it within his own. "Ethel will have the evening meal ready soon."

"Yes," Rose agreed, though part of her wished they could remain in this peaceful moment indefinitely.

As they prepared to leave their sanctuary, Boone glanced once more over the camp spread below. "From up here, you can see how the buildings form a rough heart shape around the central clearing."

Rose followed his gaze, seeing the pattern he indicated. "I never noticed that before."

"Mary did," Boone said, the memory no longer carrying the sharp pain it once would have. "She said the way the camp is shaped around the clearing looked like a heart—and that felt like more than a coincidence. She told Campbell a place built with love and meant to last needed a name that reflected that. Trinity Station... a place grounded in faith, family, and purpose."

"It's a good name," she said. "It reminds us what we're building isn't just for today—it's for generations to come."

Boone nodded, his expression thoughtful. "What we're doing here matters, Rose. Not just the timber or the buildings, but the community. I lost sight of that for a while."

"It's easier to focus on survival than on purpose when you're grieving," Rose observed gently.

"Yes. But purpose makes survival meaningful." Boone's gaze returned to her. "Thank you for reminding me of that."

"You were finding your way back long before I arrived. I merely walked alongside you for part of the journey."

"You undersell your influence. But your modesty is one of many qualities I admire."

The simple compliment brought color to Rose's cheeks. This exchange of honest appreciation still felt new and somewhat vulnerable between them, yet increasingly natural with each conversation.

They began their descent toward camp, hands still joined where the trail permitted. Neither rushed the journey, savoring this interlude of privacy before returning to the community's needs and watchful eyes.

"Clara mentioned that some of the women plan to help you settle in this evening," Boone said as they neared the camp's edge. "They've gathered additional clothing and necessities."

"Their kindness has been overwhelming."

"The community values you," Boone said simply. "As do I."

They paused at the final bend in the trail, just before it opened into camp. Soon they would step back into their public roles, the foreman directing recovery efforts, the teacher tending to medical and educational needs. Their time alone would end, but something precious had been established between them.

"Will you be joining us for the evening meal?" Rose asked.

"Yes. I'll need to check on the night watch arrangements first, but I'll be there."

Rose nodded, glad for even this simple opportunity to see him later. "Until then."

Boone's hand tightened briefly around hers before releasing it. "Until then."

Chapter 30

Rose wiped sawdust from her skirts as she hurried across Trinity Station's central clearing. The camp buzzed with activity despite the early hour. Everyone focused on preparations for the foundation ceremony. Men hauled large stones into place around the excavated foundation, while women arranged tables with food and drink for the celebration.

"Rose! We need your opinion." Martha waved urgently from near the foundation site. "Should we place the tables under the pines or closer to the platform?"

"Under the pines," Rose called back, adjusting course to join Martha. "The shade will be welcome once the ceremony begins."

The past three weeks had transformed Trinity Station. From the ashes of the cookhouse fire had risen not just plans but actual progress. A proper foundation excavated and stone-lined, lumber neatly stacked for walls and roof beams, and a sense of renewed purpose that infused the entire community.

"The children are practicing their song for the ceremony," Martha said as Rose reached her. "They're so excited they can hardly focus."

"I'll check on them shortly," Rose promised, surveying the foundation area where Boone directed several men to position the cornerstone, a massive block of granite that William and Simon had hauled from the river three days ago.

Even from this distance, Boone's authoritative presence commanded attention. He pointed to the northeastern corner, instructing the men with the practiced efficiency of someone accustomed to moving enormous logs through dangerous terrain. Rose noticed how the other men responded to his direction without question, their respect evident in their quick compliance.

"Would you look at that," Martha murmured beside her. "Three weeks ago we were watching our cookhouse burn, and now..."

"Now we're building something bigger and better," Rose finished for her.

"Not just the building," Martha replied with a meaningful glance between Rose and Boone.

Rose felt warmth creep into her cheeks. The past three weeks had indeed transformed more than just the campsite. Her courtship with Boone had progressed steadily, though their moments alone remained precious and somewhat limited amid the constant demands of school teaching, logging operations, and rebuilding.

Rose walked toward the foundation site, pausing briefly to observe the children practicing their song near the schoolhouse steps, tiny voices rising with enthusiasm. Eliza caught sight of her and waved excitedly before Beth redirected her attention back to the rehearsal.

Rose approached the foundation area just as Boone finished instructing the men. He turned, spotting her, and his expression shifted, the stern concentration softening into something warmer.

"Good morning," he greeted her, closing the distance between them. "You're up early."

"Says the man who's probably been working since dawn," Rose replied with a smile.

"Since before dawn, actually," Boone admitted. "Getting that cornerstone in place has been a challenge."

Rose glanced at the massive stone now positioned in the foundation's corner. "It's perfect. Solid beginning for a solid structure."

"That was my thinking." Boone's gaze held hers for a moment longer than necessary, conveying affection that required no words. "Campbell has been hovering all morning, changing his mind about the positioning at least three times."

"Where is he now?"

"With Reverend Parker, working on his speech for the ceremony. God help us all if he's not limited to ten minutes."

Rose laughed, the sound drawing glances from nearby workers, who smiled at the evidence of their foreman's good humor. Still a noteworthy occurrence despite becoming more frequent.

"I made something for you," Boone said, reaching into his pocket. He withdrew a small cloth-wrapped bundle and handed it to her.

Rose carefully unwrapped the cloth to reveal a small, perfectly carved wooden trillium flower, detailed down to the delicate veining in each petal.

"It's beautiful," she breathed, running her finger along the smooth wood. "When did you have time to make this?"

"I worked on it a little each evening," Boone replied. "It kept my hands busy while my mind settled."

The admission touched Rose deeply. She could picture him sitting by lamplight in his cabin, the day's demands gradually easing as he focused on creating this gift for her.

"I'll treasure it always," she said.

Their eyes met, and Boone reached out, briefly touching her arm.

"I should check the children's preparations," Rose said. "They've been working hard on their contribution to the ceremony. We'll talk later?"

"Count on it."

As Rose turned toward the schoolhouse, a flutter of anticipation stirred within her.

"Miss Bellamy!" Samuel's excited voice pulled her from her thoughts as she approached the children. "We practiced the whole song without making any mistakes!"

"That's wonderful," Rose praised. "Are your drawings ready for the ceremony?"

"Yes!" Eliza joined them, proudly displaying a carefully folded paper. "I drew our new school with the bell tower, Mr. Campbell promised."

"And I drew the blacksmith shop my pa runs," Timmy added. "With me helping him when I'm grown."

Rose knelt to examine each drawing the children eagerly presented. Each one depicted some aspect of Trinity Station's future: buildings not yet constructed, gardens not yet planted, and hopes not yet realized but vividly imagined.

"These are perfect," she assured them. "The very best foundation we could ask for is your hopes and dreams for this community."

"Will they really stay in the building forever?" Hannah asked, eyes wide.

"They'll be sealed inside the cornerstone," Rose explained. "So they'll always be a part of Trinity Station, just like each of you."

The children's excited chatter surrounded her as they discussed what it meant to be part of something permanent. Rose watched them with quiet joy, remembering her first days at Trinity Station when the future had seemed so uncertain. Now, amid the sounds of hammering and sawing that filled the air, permanence no longer felt like a distant dream but an unfolding reality.

Chapter 31

By mid-morning, the entire population of Trinity Station had gathered around the foundation site. Women wore their best dresses, men had donned clean shirts, and even the children had been scrubbed to unusual shininess for the occasion. A wooden platform had been constructed beside the foundation, draped with the American flag and adorned with pine boughs.

Rose took her place among the gathered community. She spotted Boone near the platform, conversing with Reverend Parker. He wore his good coat, the same one he'd worn to his first church service, his hair neatly combed, and his usual stern expression replaced by one of solemn dignity appropriate to the occasion.

Joshua Campbell stepped onto the platform, raising his hands for silence. The buzz of conversation gradually faded as everyone turned their attention to him.

"Friends and neighbors of Trinity Station," he began, his voice carrying clearly across the gathering. "Today marks not merely the beginning of a building, but the continuation of a dream that has grown stronger through adversity!"

Campbell's natural enthusiasm seemed magnified by the occasion as he launched into a history of Trinity Station, from its inception as a simple logging camp to its current evolution toward a permanent settlement. Rose noted how he carefully credited both the company's vision and the community's resilience, a diplomatic balance that showed his growing understanding of frontier sensibilities.

"When fire struck three weeks ago," Campbell continued, gesturing toward the blackened remnants of the cookhouse still visible beyond the new foundation, "it could have meant defeat. Instead, it became an opportunity! The structure we commence today will be more than a replacement... it will be the heart of Trinity Station's future."

Murmurs of approval rippled through the crowd. Rose glanced at Ethel, who stood with arms crossed, nodding decisively. The cook had been instrumental in modifying Campbell's grandiose initial designs into something practical that still honored his vision for growth.

"Reverend Parker will offer a blessing, after which we'll observe a frontier tradition I believe particularly fitting for Trinity Station," Joshua said.

He stepped back, yielding the platform to Noah. The reverend moved forward with quiet dignity, his Bible in hand.

"Let us pray," he began, and heads bowed throughout the gathering. "Almighty God, we stand before You today on ground that has known both prosperity and loss. We ask Your blessing upon the foundation we lay, that the structure rising from it may shelter and nourish this community for generations to come. May the work of our hands honor You, and may all who gather within these future walls know Your presence."

Noah continued his prayer simple yet profound, acknowledging both the practical and spiritual dimensions of the occasion. As he concluded, Rose noticed Boone's posture, head bowed respectfully, no longer the reluctant participant but a man genuinely engaged in the spiritual life of the community.

"Amen," the gathering responded in unison.

Campbell returned to the center of the platform, his expression bright with excitement. "Frontier settlements have long observed a tradition of placing meaningful items within their foundational structures," he explained. "Items representing hopes, memories, and commitments to the future. Today, we continue this tradition with our cornerstone box."

William stepped forward, carrying a metal box he had crafted specifically for the occasion. He placed it on a small table beside the platform.

"This box will be sealed within our cornerstone," Campbell continued. "Each family or individual may place something inside, a token of your commitment to Trinity Station's future."

Rose watched as families exchanged glances, many holding small items they had prepared. The ceremony had been announced days ago, giving everyone time to consider their contributions.

"Children first," Campbell declared, gesturing to where the youngsters waited with barely contained excitement.

The children came forward one by one, carefully placing their drawings into the box. Each paused to explain their contribution from Eliza's schoolhouse with its magnificent bell tower to James Riley's ambitious rendering of a proper church with stained-glass windows.

"These drawings show what Trinity Station will become," Campbell said approvingly. "The vision of our youngest citizens!"

Next came the adults. Martha and John placed a small cloth pouch in the metal box. "Seeds from back East," Martha explained. "Fore rebirth and hope of abundance."

William contributed a small iron nail. "The first one I forged here at Trinity Station," he said simply.

Clara and Simon added a small carved wooden figure. "For all the children yet to come to Trinity Station," Clara said, her hand resting protectively on her stomach in a gesture Rose recognized with quiet joy. The Blackwoods hadn't announced their expectation publicly yet, but Rose had suspected for several days.

The procession continued, each contribution representing some aspect of Trinity Station's life and future. Ethel approached with particular solemnity, holding a folded piece of paper.

"My biscuit recipe," she announced. "It's been feeding folks for years. I figure it ought to keep doing so even after I'm gone."

A ripple of appreciative laughter moved through the crowd, followed by nods of understanding. Ethel's cooking was as much a foundation of camp life as the lumber industry itself.

As the last of the families made their contributions, Campbell gestured to the platform. "Reverend Parker, perhaps you would like to add something on behalf of Trinity Station's spiritual community?"

Noah stepped forward, holding a small leather-bound volume. "A hymnal," he explained. "Music draws us together in worship and celebration. May it represent the harmony we seek in all aspects of community life."

He placed it carefully in the box, now nearly filled with the community's tokens, hopes, and memories.

Campbell turned expectantly toward Boone, who had remained near the platform throughout the proceedings. "Mr. McAlister, as

Trinity Station's foreman and leader, would you like to contribute something to our cornerstone?"

A hush fell over the gathering as Boone stepped onto the platform. Rose noticed that he carried something wrapped in cloth. His expression was solemn but composed as he faced the community.

"Most of you know I'm not one for speeches," Boone began, his deep voice carrying easily without being raised. "But some occasions warrant words as well as actions."

He unwrapped the cloth, revealing Mary's Bible. A ripple of recognition moved through the crowd, and they all understood the significance of this particular book.

"Foundations matter," Boone continued. "Not just for buildings, but for communities and lives. Trinity Station began as a temporary logging operation, but it's becoming something permanent. Something with roots and purpose beyond timber."

He opened the Bible carefully, removing a folded piece of paper from between its pages.

"My late wife Mary had a vision for what this place could become," he said, his voice steady. "Before her death, she wrote this verse from Psalm 127 and placed it in her Bible: 'Unless the Lord builds the house, the builders labor in vain.'"

Boone held up the paper, Mary's handwriting visible to those nearest the platform. "This represents honoring the foundations of our past while building toward our future. Trinity Station was built on faith and love from its beginning. It will continue to grow the same way, with the wisdom of those who came before guiding us forward."

His gaze moved through the crowd until it found Rose standing quietly with the women. Their eyes met across the distance, and Boone's voice took on a different quality, more personal despite the public setting.

"And if Rose is willing, I hope to build not just this community, but a life together, founded on the same principles."

The simple declaration hung in the air, direct and unambiguous. Rose felt every eye turn toward her, but her focus remained on Boone, whose steady gaze conveyed both certainty and question.

Without conscious decision, Rose moved forward through the crowd, which parted naturally before her. She approached the platform, aware of the significance of this moment, not just for her and Boone, but for the entire community witnessing it.

Boone extended his hand, which she took as she joined him on the platform. From her medical bag, Rose withdrew a small, worn leather-bound book—her grandmother's herbal medicine journal, filled with handwritten remedies, observations, and wisdom accumulated over generations.

"My grandmother taught me that true healing addresses body, mind, and spirit," Rose said, her voice clear despite the emotion tightening her throat. "This book represents that knowledge, passed down through generations of women in my family. I have copied several of her remedies on paper to place in the cornerstone box."

She turned slightly toward Boone, aware but unconcerned about their audience. "I would be honored to build a life with you, Boone McAlister, here at Trinity Station. To continue both our families' legacies of faith, healing, and community."

Together, they placed Mary's scripture verse and Rose's grandmother's remedies into the cornerstone box. Their hands touched as they arranged the items, fingers briefly intertwining in a gesture of unity that spoke volumes to the watching community.

Campbell stepped forward, visibly moved, despite his typical exuberance. "I can think of no finer foundation for our cornerstone than this commitment to both shared pasts and futures," he declared. "William, if you would secure the box?"

William came forward with the lid he had crafted, fitting it carefully over the box and securing it with small bolts that would protect the contents from moisture and time. Boone, Simon, Reverend Noah, and William then lifted the sealed box together and placed it in the hollow carved into the massive cornerstone.

"With this cornerstone," Campbell announced, "we officially commence construction of the Trinity Station Community Center! May it stand for generations as testimony to what can be built when vision, faith, and hard work unite!"

A cheer rose from the gathered community. Mortar was applied with a ceremonial flourish, Campbell insisted on placing a trowelful himself, followed by Reverend Parker, Boone, and finally Rose, whose inexpert attempt brought good-natured laughter from the crowd.

The celebration shifted to the tables arranged beneath the pines. Ethel had somehow produced a feast from her makeshift kitchen, proving that her culinary skills transcended physical limitations. Children ran, playing between the tables, their earlier formality forgotten in the excitement of the day.

Rose found herself surrounded by women offering congratulations, their approval of her relationship with Boone openly expressed. Clara hugged her tightly, whispering, "I told Simon weeks ago you two would make it official before winter."

Across the clearing, Rose could see Boone similarly surrounded by men offering congratulatory handshakes and backslaps. Despite the unwanted attention, he bore it with better grace than she might have expected, accepting the community's approval of their relationship with dignified acknowledgment.

The celebration continued through midday, gradually transitioning back to work as men returned to construction tasks and women to their various responsibilities. Rose supervised the children's return to abbreviated lessons, modified to accommodate the special day while still maintaining educational routine.

Late in the afternoon, as Rose dismissed the children, she noticed Boone approaching the schoolhouse. He had changed from his formal attire back to his usual work clothes, but his expression carried a determination that quickened her pulse.

"Do you have time for a walk before sunset?" he asked without preamble.

Rose glanced at the schoolhouse, mentally cataloging her remaining tasks. "Let me gather my things," she replied. "I'll only be a moment."

Inside, she quickly organized the children's slates and collected her shawl, aware of an anticipation that made her fingers less steady than usual. When she emerged, Boone waited patiently, his expression revealing nothing of his thoughts.

"Shall we?" he asked, offering his arm.

Rose placed her hand on his forearm, feeling the solid strength beneath the fabric of his shirt. They walked in a companionable rhythm, nodding to the camp members they passed.

"The ceremony went well," Rose observed as they approached the north trail leading to Eagle's Rest.

"Better than expected," Boone agreed. "Campbell kept his speech under fifteen minutes, which might be a personal record."

Rose laughed. "The children were so proud of their contributions. Eliza asked if people would dig up the cornerstone in a hundred years to see her drawing."

"They might," Boone replied thoughtfully. "Though I hope the building lasts longer than that."

They continued up the familiar trail, their conversation flowing naturally between observations about the ceremony and plans for continued construction. Rose noted that Boone seemed simultaneously relaxed and alert, his attention fully present while clearly anticipating something ahead.

As they neared Eagle's Rest, Boone slowed their pace. "I meant what I said during the ceremony," he said, his voice quieter than before. "About building a life together."

"I know," Rose replied simply. "I meant my answer."

He nodded, seeming pleased but not surprised by her confirmation. "We're nearly there."

When they emerged into the clearing at Eagle's Rest, Rose gasped softly. Someone Boone himself, she suspected, had prepared the space with thoughtful care. A woolen blanket lay spread on the ground near the best viewpoint, with a small basket beside it. Several lanterns stood ready for lighting when darkness fell.

"When did you arrange this?" she asked, surveying the simple but meaningful preparation.

"This morning, before dawn," Boone admitted. "Simon helped carry the items up."

"So that's why you were working before dawn," Rose said with a smile. "I assumed you meant with the cornerstone."

"That too," Boone said. "I can manage multiple tasks when properly motivated."

He led her to the blanket, where they sat facing the spectacular view of Trinity Station below. The camp looked different now, the foundation of the new community center clearly visible, the orderly stacks of building materials suggesting the structure soon to rise. Beyond that, the tidy cabins and work buildings spread in the heart-shaped pattern Mary had once observed.

"It's changing so quickly," Rose observed. "When I first arrived, I never imagined how different it would look in just a few months."

"Or how different we would be," Boone added.

Rose turned to him, struck by the openness of his expression. The guarded man who had greeted her so coldly that first day had transformed almost beyond recognition, though his core strength and integrity remained unchanged.

"I was thinking about our first meeting earlier today," Rose admitted. "How reluctant you were to accept even the idea of a school-teacher in Trinity Station."

"I was wrong. About many things."

"We both had adjustments to make," Rose replied. "I arrived with rather idealistic expectations that needed tempering with reality."

Boone reached for her hand, his larger one enveloping hers with gentle strength. "That balance between idealism and practicality seems to work for us. You've helped me see possibilities beyond immediate concerns, and perhaps I've helped ground your vision in practical application."

"You have," Rose agreed, squeezing his hand. "We complement each other well."

Boone's expression grew more serious. "Rose, I asked you here because there's something specific I want to discuss." He paused, seeming to gather his thoughts carefully. "The past few months have taught me that life offers no guarantees of time. We can plan for years ahead and have only days, or face catastrophe and rebuild stronger than before."

Rose nodded, sensing the significance of whatever he was working toward.

"When Mary died, I thought certain parts of me died with her," Boone continued. "The capacity for joy, for trust, for faith... for love. I convinced myself that closing off those vulnerabilities was strength."

He gazed out over the camp below, the embodiment of his daily responsibilities and leadership. "You showed me that real strength comes from opening ourselves to possibilities despite knowing the risks. That faith isn't a shield against hardship, but a foundation that helps us endure it."

Boone turned back to her, his expression more vulnerable than she had ever seen it. "I love you, Rose. Not as a replacement for what was lost, but as the unexpected gift you are. I want to spend my life with you, building this community, raising a family together, using the talents God gave each of us to serve others and each other."

He reached into his pocket and withdrew something small, holding it carefully in his palm. "Mary once told me that love isn't diminished by sharing it. It only grows. I've come to understand what she meant."

He opened his hand to reveal a simple gold band. "This was Mary's ring. I've kept it all this time, unable to part with it, but not knowing what its purpose might be."

Rose looked at the ring, understanding its profound significance, not just as a symbol of commitment to her, but as evidence of Boone's complete reconciliation with his past.

"Some might think it strange to offer a new bride a ring from a previous marriage," Boone acknowledged. "But to me, it represents continuity of purpose and faith. Mary helped lay Trinity Station's first foundations. You and I will build upon them. This ring connects those chapters in a way that honors both."

He took Rose's hand, his expression now one of absolute certainty. "Rose Bellamy, will you build a life with me here, bringing education and faith to this community, creating a family together beneath these Oregon pines?"

Rose felt tears gathering in her eyes, not from sorrow but from the fullness of her heart. "Yes, Boone. With all my heart, yes."

Boone slipped the ring onto her finger. It fit almost perfectly, the simple gold band catching the late afternoon light. Rose stared at it for a moment, then up at Boone, whose face reflected joy mingled with profound reverence for the commitment they were making.

"May I kiss you?" he asked, the formal request reflecting his deep respect for her.

Rose nodded, her breath catching as Boone leaned forward. Their lips met in a kiss that began gently but deepened with the honest emotion flowing between them. His hand cradled her cheek with infinite tenderness, while hers rested against his chest, feeling the strong, steady beat of his heart.

When they parted, Boone kept his forehead touching hers for a moment longer, both of them absorbing the magnitude of what had just transpired between them.

"When would you like to be married?" Boone asked, his voice husky with emotion.

"Soon," Rose replied without hesitation. "Before winter sets in. I've never been particularly interested in elaborate weddings."

"Pastor Parker could officiate whenever we're ready," Boone agreed. "Though we should give Campbell time to organize a community celebration. He'd be devastated to miss the opportunity."

Rose laughed, picturing Campbell's enthusiastic planning. "True. Perhaps when the community center walls are raised? That seems a fitting milestone."

"Four weeks, then," Boone calculated.

"Four weeks," Rose agreed. She glanced again at the ring on her finger. "I understand the significance of Mary's ring, and I'm honored to wear it. But I want you to know I never felt I was competing with her memory."

"I know," Boone said. "That's one of the countless things I love about you. Your confidence in who you are and your place in God's plan allowed me space to reconcile my past with my present."

He reached into the basket beside them, removing a carefully wrapped package. "I have something else for you."

Rose unwrapped the package to find a beautifully bound leather Bible. Opening the cover, she found an inscription: "To Rose, whose faith illuminated the path when mine had grown dark. May we walk together in God's light for all our days. With love, Boone."

"It's perfect," she whispered, running her fingers over the inscription. "Our first family Bible."

"The first of many books, I hope," Boone replied. "I imagine our future home with shelves of books—your medical texts alongside teaching materials, children's stories, and family Bibles recording births, marriages, and all that comes with a life fully lived."

The vision he painted stirred Rose deeply, not just the physical home he described, but the richness of life it represented. A life of purpose and service, of family and community, of faith actively expressed through daily choices.

"I've been thinking about that," she said. "A home, I mean. Campbell's been so focused on the community center construction that he seems to have forgotten his plans for my cabin."

"He hasn't forgotten," Boone corrected her with a slight smile. "I asked him to modify those plans into something more suitable for a family rather than a single teacher. The location I selected isn't far from here, higher ground with a view of both the camp and the river. If you'd like to see it tomorrow and approve of it, I could show you."

"I would like that very much," Rose replied, touched by his thoughtful planning. "Though I suspect you already know my preferences better than I might imagine."

"I pay attention," Boone acknowledged. "I've noticed you prefer morning light for reading, that you need space for your herbs to dry properly, that you value a certain amount of privacy while still remaining connected to the community."

The detailed observations revealed how closely he had attended to her habits and needs, even during times when they were ostensibly at odds. It demonstrated a depth of consideration that moved her deeply.

"What about you?" she asked. "What do you need in a home?"

Boone considered this seriously. "Space for woodworking in the evenings. A porch facing west to watch storms roll in. Room for children to grow and play safely." He paused, then added more quietly, "And you, Rose. That's what would make any structure truly home."

The simple declaration settled in Rose's heart like a promise. She leaned against Boone's shoulder, feeling his arm slip naturally around her as they watched the activity continuing in Trinity Station below. The September air carried a hint of autumn crispness, suggesting the changing season ahead.

"We should light the lanterns soon," Boone observed as shadows lengthened across the clearing. "Unless you'd prefer to return to camp before dark."

"Not yet," Rose replied. "I'd like to stay a while longer."

Boone nodded, reaching for the matches to light the lanterns he had positioned around the clearing. As warm golden light bloomed against the gathering dusk, Rose watched him move with careful efficiency, the same attention to detail evident in this romantic gesture as in his daily work leading the camp.

"I love you," he said simply as he joined her on the blanket.

"And I love you," Rose replied, her heart full.

Epilogue

Rose adjusted her simple lace veil one final time, her fingers trembling with anticipation rather than nervousness. Through the sheer fabric, she could see the gathered community of Trinity Station, arranged in neat rows of benches facing the river. Flower garlands adorned each row end, wildflowers and greenery carefully gathered by the children.

"Are you ready?" Ethel asked, smoothing a wrinkle from Rose's white dress. "Everyone's waiting, and Boone looks like he might wear a path on the riverbank if you don't appear soon."

Rose laughed, picturing Boone's restless energy. "I'm ready," she said, taking a deep breath. "More than ready."

Ethel nodded approvingly, giving Rose's hand a squeeze. "You look beautiful. Now, let's not keep that man waiting any longer. He's been patient enough these past weeks."

Together, they stepped from behind the screen of pine branches that had served as an impromptu bridal preparation area. The assembled community turned as one, faces lighting with smiles and murmurs of appreciation as Rose walked toward the flower-adorned arch that Boone and Simon had constructed.

Rose barely noticed the modest decorations or the assembled guests. Her attention fixed immediately on Boone, standing tall and straight beside Reverend Parker beneath the arch. He wore a new suit ordered specially from Portland, his usually windswept hair neatly combed, his face freshly shaven. But it was his expression that captured her heart. The unmistakable look of a man watching his deepest wish materialize before him.

William Wilson rose from a bench, stepping forward to offer his arm. When they'd planned the ceremony, Rose had quietly mentioned her father's absence, and William had immediately volunteered to escort her. The kind blacksmith had lost his wife years ago, and his emotional understanding of both loss and new beginnings made him the perfect choice.

"Miss Bellamy," he said formally, offering his arm. "It would be my honor."

"Thank you, William," Rose replied, taking his arm.

The reverend nodded to Simon, who began playing a simple melody on his fiddle. The sweet, plaintive notes carried across the clearing as Rose and William began their procession.

Rose felt a momentary flash of memory, her arrival at Trinity Station months ago, the dusty trail, the uncertain welcome, and her determination despite Boone's initial resistance. Now that same man waited for her with love evident in every line of his body.

As they reached the front of the assembly, William placed Rose's hand in Boone's, his voice gruff with emotion as he said, "I give this woman into your keeping, Boone McAlister."

"I will treasure her always," Boone replied, his eyes never leaving Rose's face.

Reverend Parker stepped forward, his Bible open in his hands. "Dearly beloved," he began, his voice carrying easily across the hushed gathering, "we are assembled here in the sight of God and these witnesses to join this man and this woman in holy matrimony."

Rose barely heard the familiar words that followed, her attention caught by the warmth of Boone's hand holding hers, and the intensity of his gaze. The slight tremor she felt in his fingers revealed his emotions ran as deep as her own.

"Marriage," Noah continued, "is not to be entered into lightly, but reverently and deliberately. It represents the covenant relationship that Christ has with His church—faithful, enduring, and transformative."

A ripple of agreement moved through the gathering. Rose noticed Campbell dabbing suspiciously at his eyes in the front row, while Ethel sat beside him with uncharacteristic stillness, her usual practical energy subdued by the solemnity of the occasion.

"Boone and Rose have chosen to write their vows," Noah announced, stepping back slightly.

Boone turned to face Rose fully, taking both her hands in his. He cleared his throat, and when he spoke, his voice carried the steady authority that had first impressed her, now tempered with tenderness.

"Rose Bellamy, when you first arrived at Trinity Station, I saw only an impractical dreamer whose ideas seemed disconnected from the harsh realities of frontier life." A ripple of knowing laughter moved through the crowd, earning a brief smile from Boone before he continued. "I was wrong. Your vision wasn't impractical, it was essential. You saw possibilities where I saw only obstacles, community where I saw only workers, and hope where I saw only struggle."

He squeezed her hands gently. "You brought light back into my life when I thought darkness was all that remained for me. You respected my grief without allowing it to define me. You challenged my cynicism with steady faith. You offered friendship when I deserved little more than professional courtesy."

Boone's voice deepened with emotion. "Today, I promise to honor the gift of your love with faithfulness and devotion all the days of my life. I promise to protect and provide for you, to share both burdens and joys, to build our home and family with God at the center. I promise to cherish you as the extraordinary blessing you are, and to walk beside you through whatever paths God sets before us."

Rose blinked back tears, overwhelmed by the open declaration from a man once so guarded by his emotions. When it was her turn to speak, she took a steadying breath.

"Boone McAlister, I came to Trinity Station believing God had called me here to teach. I never imagined He had also led me to the person who would become the other half of my heart." She smiled, remembering their early encounters. "Behind your rugged exterior, I discovered a man of profound integrity, quiet compassion, and re-markable strength, not just physical strength, but the harder kind that continues when the path grows difficult."

She tightened her grip on his hands. "You've shown me that faith isn't just about belief, but about walking steadily forward even when the way is unclear. You've taught me that protecting a community means more than physical safety. It means creating space for others to grow and thrive."

Rose's voice grew stronger as she continued. "Today, I promise to stand beside you through every season of our life together. I promise to support your leadership while offering honest counsel. I promise to build our home and family in faith, to teach our children about both spiritual wisdom and practical knowledge. I promise to love you, not with blind devotion, but with eyes wide open, seeing all that you are and cherishing every part."

A murmur of approval rippled through the gathering at their heartfelt words. Reverend Parker stepped forward again, his expression reflecting the sacred gravity of the moment.

"Do you have tokens to exchange as symbols of these vows?" he asked.

Boone nodded, turning to Simon, who stepped forward with two rings. The first was Mary's ring, now properly sized for Rose. The second was a wider gold band that William had crafted, melting down a gold coin Boone had kept from his earlier days.

"These rings," Noah said, "are symbols of the unbroken circle of love. With no beginning and no end, they represent the commitment you make today... eternal, enduring, and complete."

Boone took Rose's ring, holding it poised at her finger. "With this ring, I thee wed," he said, sliding it into place beside her engagement ring. "With my body I thee worship, and with all my worldly goods I thee endow."

Rose then took Boone's ring, her fingers steadier now. "With this ring, I thee wed," she repeated, sliding the band onto his finger. "With my body I thee worship, and with all my worldly goods I thee endow."

Reverend Parker closed his Bible, placing one hand over their joined hands. "By the authority vested in me as a minister of the Gospel, and in accordance with the laws of the Oregon Territory, I now pronounce you husband and wife." He smiled at Boone. "You may kiss your bride."

A tremor passed through Boone's hands as he gently lifted Rose's veil. For a heartbeat, they simply gazed at each other, the significance of the moment etched in both their expressions. Then Boone leaned down, kissing her with a reverent tenderness that gradually deepened into something more profound as the assembled community broke into applause.

When they parted, Reverend Parker turned them to face the gathering. "May I present to you, Mr. and Mrs. Boone McAlister!"

Cheers erupted from the assembly, led by Campbell's enthusiastic whooping and punctuated by Simon's piercing whistle. Children darted forward, scattering flower petals along the path as Boone and Rose walked back down the makeshift aisle, now husband and wife.

As they reached the end of the aisle, Rose caught sight of the newly completed walls of the community center rising beyond the gathering. The foundation ceremony four weeks ago had launched not just the construction of the building but the final preparations for their wedding. The community's two most significant builds—physical and relational—had progressed together, each milestone in one marking progress in the other.

Boone followed her gaze. "Beautiful, isn't it?" he said quietly. "Walls rising strong and true."

"Just like us," Rose replied, squeezing his hand.

Leave A Review

If you enjoyed this book, please consider leaving an honest review on Amazon

Visit Our Website:

www.vivianbelle.com

Visit Our Amazon Author Page HERE

Find Us On Social Media:

Facebook

Facebook Author Page

Instagram